THE ROAD OF AZRAEL

As a child my hair used to stand straight up when I heard of the wagon that moved down the Wilderness roads in the dark of the night, with never a horse drawing it—the wagon that was full of severed heads and dismembered limbs; and the yellow horse, the ghastly dream horse that raced up and down the stairs of the grand old plantation house where a wicked woman lay dying; and the ghost-switches that swished against doors when none dared open those doors lest reason be blasted by what was seen . . .

ROBERT E. HOWARD

THE ROAD OF AZRAEL

ROBERT E. HOWARD

THE ROAD OF AZRAEL
A Bantam Book / July 1980

PRINTING HISTORY

ACKNOWLEDGMENTS

Gates of Empire, copyright 1938 by Sun Publications
for *Golden Fleece*, January 1939.
The Road of Azrael, copyright 1976 by the
Nemedian Chronicles for *Chacal #1*.

ISBN 0-553-13326-8

Published simultaneously in the United States and Canada

PRINTED IN THE UNITED STATES OF AMERICA

0 9 8 7 6 5 4 3 2 1

CONTENTS

THE ROAD OF AZRAEL

INTRODUCTION

Like all great storytellers, Robert E. Howard was unique, and the stories that he gave us, therefore, are born of, and nourished in, that uniqueness. This is characteristic of great storytellers, for, in the final essential, story-telling is the highest art of literature, even if it is often unrecognized as such by reviewers and critics caught up by whatever in current literature is considered admirable according to the standards of the immediate moment. Great storytellers make their art look easy, as if anyone could do it. In fact, it is not something anyone else can do; it is something no one else can do.

Just so, in such reviews and criticism we most frequently find a misuse of the word "classic." We will find it put to work there to describe some novel or short story that has just appeared upon the horizon, and which the critic or reviewer admires and measures by his and the moment's standards. As a result there is a certain amount of confusion about what the word actually means.

But there should not be. There can be only one worthwhile definition for "classic," and that is a definition which applies it only to those literary works that have proved themselves at the hands of countless readers. These are the true classics, and they are by no means difficult to find. All that is required of any seeker is to go to the fiction shelves of the nearest library and look for what is still there of what was written a century or more ago—such as the novels by Robert Louis Stevenson, Charles Dickens, Alexandre Dumas, Leo Tolstoy and others.

These works are all unique. That is one of the requirements of a classic story, and one of the requirements of an author of classic stories. Such authors have one element in common. They are, first and foremost, storytellers and the result has been, in the cases of the authors mentioned here, that the stories they produced have become stories that are enjoyable reading in the context of a larger time period than the century of their conception.

When the author is a true storyteller and the stories he writes are lasting stories, they may not have been recognized as such immediately on publication, but, as the years go by and they continue to be read, and reread, and gather new readers, they will begin to emerge from the mass of other fiction published about the same time. They will then be in the process of that same accomplishment that has brought other works before them to the true rank of classics—they will be proving themselves at the hands of the readers.

Such work only proves itself if it has something to give us that we can find nowhere else, an unforgettable literary experience that cannot be duplicated for us by any other writer. That sort of experience comes only from an author who has something to give which did not exist in the world before he came into it, and which disappeared forever when he went out of it. It is the golden bell-sound that only his voice can offer.

Each of the writers of the true, established classics has such a special sound in the works he or she has given us. Each has something not to be matched by anyone else, even his peers. Howard has such a uniqueness. In his case, it is the extreme intensity of his vision. Like all classic storytellers, his fiction is without obvious adornment. The reader, in reading him, does not read *words*, but falls through the words into the actual experience of the story.

So it is with Robert Howard's fiction. He makes his writing look easy, as if anyone could do it. But at the same time the scenes and actions in which he involves us are so unforgettably brilliant and sharply etched that they seem printed on the mind's eye in the very instant of seeing them on the page, like a scene suddenly revealed out of utter darkness by an unexpected flash of lightning.

Just so, in the stories of this collection, we are suddenly with Giles Hobson and Giscard de Chastillon in the story "Gates," the two of them who have been opposed all through the story, riding together shoulder to shoulder into the melee at the battle of el Baban. The road of the eagles prints itself forever upon our eyes in "The Way of the Words." The bedouin attack swirls around us in "The Road of Azrael." We are the naked Roger De Bracey fighting for his life against an armed and armored horseman in "The Track of Bohemund" and we are De Guzman within the forbidden confines of el Khiral in "Hawks over Egypt."

This is the classic genius of Robert Howard, to give our imaginations these characters and these events in three dimensions, and with an intensity and fierceness that has never been matched by any other author. It is a genius that sprang naturally in him from his own larger-than-human ability to live such stories in his own head before he even began to put them down on paper.

This was his gift, and, in a way, his curse. Because it marked off his difference from other people. What we can learn of him—the great majority of us who were not privileged to know him in person—tells us of a tall, powerful Texan, who, before his death at the age of thirty, gave us no small amount of memorable literature. We picture a man who seems to have been designed by nature to handle life easily. A second look gives us the deeper picture, the intensity of the inner man—and the roots of his matchless quality of the imagination.

But E. Hoffman Price, in *A Memory of Robert E. Howard*, speaks of Howard's "deeply ingrained sense of being different . . .", and Glenn Lord, in "Lone Star Fictioneer," a biography reprinted recently in *The Last Celt*, a bio-bibliography of Howard edited and compiled in 1976 by Lord, quotes Howard on the subject of his own imagination and its early nurture.

No Negro ghost story ever gave me the horrors as did the tales told by my grandmother. All the gloominess and dark mysticism of the Gaelic nature was hers, and there was no light and mirth in her. Her tales showed what a strange legion of folklore grew up in the Scotch-Irish settlements of the Southwest, where transplanted Celtic myths and fairy tales met and mingled with a substratum of slave legends. My grandmother was but one generation removed from South Ireland, and she knew by heart all the tales and superstitions of the folks, black and white, about her. As a child, my hair used to stand straight up when she would tell of the wagon that moved down the Wilderness roads in the dark of the night, with never a horse drawing it—the wagon that was full of severed heads and dismembered limbs; and the yellow horse, the ghastly dream horse that raced up and down the stairs of the grand old plantation house where a wicked woman lay dying; and the ghost-switches that swished against doors when none dared open those doors lest reason be blasted at what was seen. And in many of her tales, also, appeared the old, deserted plantation mansion, with the weeds growing rank about it, and the ghostly pigeons flying up from the rails of the verandah.

. . . Long narrative dreams are fairly common with me, and sometimes my dream personality is in no way connected with my actual personality. I have been a sixteenth century Englishman, a prehistoric man, a blue-coated United States cavalryman campaigning against the Sioux in the years following the Civil War, a yellow-haired Italian of the Renaissance, a Norman nobleman of the eleventh century, a weird-eyed, flowing-bearded Gothic fighting man, a barefooted Irish kern of the seventeenth century, an Indian, a Serb in baggy trousers fighting Turks with a curved saber, a prize-fighter, and I've wandered all up and down the nineteenth century as a trapper, a westward-bound emigrant, a bartender, a hunter, an Indian fighter, a traildriver, cowboy—once I was John Wesley Hardin!

Note that Howard speaks of *being* these men, not merely of imagining that he is them, or picturing himself as being them. In my own experience, and talking to writers whose work has been powerfully effective upon readers, the supranormal, almost trance state of full creation can be evidence that what is being brought to life in words at the moment of writing is something more than ordinary narration. It is, apparently, like a signal that the story-telling mechanism is in overdrive.

Robert E. Howard, clearly, had in him a deeper and more ready access to this state than others enjoy; from that has come the magic of reality that infuses his stories and makes of them the sort to be found on library shelves a hundred years from now, when most of his contemporaries will be forgotten. It is, in a way, a pity that he will not be there, a hundred years from this moment, to take one of his own books from a library shelf and read it as others will read it then.

But then we, and readers to come, have only the words he has left us, the powerful words that evoked his images. What would it be like for any of us to have actually inhabited his fictional characters, to have *lived*, as Robert Howard himself did, in the very actions and people about which the stories are written? We might then ourselves have touched the raw and living energy that was at the core of Robert E. Howard's unique genius, and with which he fired his stories to a brilliance that will last as long as story-telling itself.

—GORDON R. DICKSON

Hawks Over Egypt

HAWKS OVER EGYPT

I

The tall figure in the white *khalat* wheeled, cursing softly, hand at scimitar hilt. Not lightly men walked the nighted streets of Cairo in the troublous days of the year 1021 A.D. In this dark, winding alley of the unsavory river quarter of el Maks, anything might happen.

"Why do you follow me, dog?" The voice was harsh, edged with a Turkish accent.

Another tall figure emerged from the shadows, clad, like the first, in a *khalat* of white silk, but lacking the other's spired helmet.

"I do not follow you!" The voice was not so guttural as the Turk's, and the accent was different. "Can not a stranger walk the streets without being subjected to insult by every reeling drunkard of the gutter?"

The stormy anger in his voice was not feigned, any more than was the suspicion in the voice of the other. They glared at each other, each gripping his hilt with a hand tense with passion.

"I have been followed since nightfall," accused the Turk. "I have heard stealthy footsteps along the dark alleys. Now you come unexpectedly into view, in a place most suited for murder!"

"Allah confound you!" swore the other wrathfully. "Why should I follow you? I have lost my way in the streets. I never saw you before, as I hope never to see you again. I am Yusuf ibn Suleyman of Cordova, but recently come to Egypt—you Turkish dog!" he added, as if impelled by overflowing spleen.

"I thought your accent betokened the Moor," quoth the Turk. "No matter. An Andalusian sword can be bought as easily as a Cairene's, and—"

"By the beard of Ali!" exclaimed the Moor in a gust of ungovernable passion, tearing out his saber; then a stealthy pad of feet brought him round, springing back and wheeling to keep both the Turk and the newcomers before him.

3

But the Turk had drawn his own scimitar, and was glaring past him.

Three huge figures loomed menacingly in the shadows, the dim starlight glinting on broad curved blades. There was a glimmer, too, of white teeth, and rolling white eyeballs.

For an instant there was tense stillness; then one muttered in the thick gutturals of the Sudan. "Which is the dog? Here be two clad alike, and the darkness makes them twins."

"Cut them both down," replied another, who towered half a head above his tall companions. "We must make no mistake, nor leave any witness."

And so saying, the three Negroes came on in deadly silence, the giant advancing on the Moor, the other two on the Turk.

Yusuf ibn Suleyman did not await the attack. With a snarling oath, he ran at the approaching colossus and slashed furiously at his head. The black man caught the stroke on his uplifted blade, and grunted beneath the impact. But the next instant, with a crafty twist and wrench, he had locked the Moor's blade under his guard and torn the weapon from his opponent's hand, to fall ringing on the stones. A searing curse ripped from Yusuf's lips. He had not expected to encounter such a combination of skill and brute strength.

But, fired to fighting madness, he did not hesitate. Even as the giant swept the broad scimitar aloft, the Moor sprang in under his lifted arm, shouting a wild war-cry, and drove his poniard to the hilt in the Negro's broad breast. Blood spurted along Yusuf's wrist, and the scimitar fell waveringly, to cut through his silk *kafiyeh* and glance from the steel cap beneath. The giant sank, dying, to the ground.

Yusuf ibn Suleyman caught up his saber and looked about to locate his late antagonist.

The Turk had met the attack of the two Negroes coolly, retreating slowly to keep them in front of him, and suddenly slashed one across the breast and shoulder, so that he dropped his sword and fell to his knees with a moan. But even as he fell, he gripped his slayer's knees and hung on like a brainless leech, without mind or reason. The Turk kicked and struggled in vain, those black arms, bulging with iron muscles, held him motionless, while the remaining black redoubled the fury of his strokes. The Turk could neither advance nor retreat, nor could he spare the single lightning flicker of his blade that would have rid him of his incubus.

Even as the black swordsman drew breath for a stroke that the cumbered Turk could not have parried, he heard the swift rush of feet behind him, cast a wild glance over his shoulder, and saw the Moor close upon him, eyes blazing, lips asnarl in the starlight. Before the Negro could turn, the Moorish saber drove through him with such fury that the blade sprang its full length out of his breast, while the hilt smote him fiercely between the shoulders; life went out of him with an inarticulate cry.

The Turk caved in the shaven skull of the other Negro with his scimitar hilt, and, shaking himself free of the corpse, turned to the Moor, who was twisting his saber out of the twitching body it transfixed.

"Why did you come to my aid?" inquired the Turk. Yusuf ibn Suleyman shrugged his broad shoulders at the unnecessary quality of the question.

"We were two men beset by rogues," quoth he. "Fate made us allies. Now if you wish, we will take up anew our quarrel. You said I spied upon you."

"And I see my mistake and crave your pardon," answered the other promptly. "I know now who has been skulking after me down the dark alleys."

Sheathing his scimitar, he bent over each corpse in turn, peering intently at the bloody features. When he reached the body of the giant slain by the Moor's poniard, he paused longer, and presently murmured softly, as if to himself "Soho! Zaman the Sworder! Of high rank, the archer whose shaft is panelled with pearls!" And, wrenching from the limp black finger a heavy, curiously bezelled ring, he slipped it into his girdle, and then laid hold on the garments of the dead man.

"Aid me, brother," said he. "Let us dispose of this carrion, so that no questions will be asked."

Without question, Yusuf ibn Suleyman grasped a blood-stained jacket in each hand, and dragged the bodies after the Turk, down a reeking black alley, in the midst of which rose the broken curb of a ruined and forgotten well. The corpses plunged headfirst into the abyss, and struck far below with a sullen splash; with a light laugh, the Turk turned to the Moor.

"Allah hath made us allies," he repeated. "I owe you a debt."

"You owe me naught," answered the Moor in a rather surly tone.

"Words can not level a mountain," returned the Turk imperturbably. "I am al Afdhal, a Memluk. Come with me out of these rat dens, and we will converse."

Yusuf ibn Suleyman sheathed his saber somewhat grudgingly, as if he rather regretted the decision of the Turk toward peace, but he followed the latter without comment. Their way led through the rat-haunted gloom of reeking alleys, and across narrow winding streets, noisome with refuse. Cairo was then, as later, a fantastic contrast of splendor and decay, where exotic palaces rose among the smoke-stained ruins of forgotten cities; a swarm of motley suburbs clustering about the walls of el Kahira, the forbidden inner city where dwelt the caliph and his nobles.

Presently the companions came to a newer and more respectable quarter, where the overhanging balconies, with their richly latticed windows of cedar and nacre inlay, almost touched one another across the narrow street.

"All the shops are dark," grunted the Moor. "A few days ago the city was lighted like day, from dusk to sunrise."

"That was one of al Hakim's whims," said the Turk. "Now he has another whim, and no lights burn in the streets of *al medina*. What his mood will be tomorrow, only Allah knows."

"There is no knowledge, save in Allah," agreed the Moor piously, and scowled. The Turk had tugged at his thin drooping moustache as if to hide a grin.

They halted before an iron-bound door in a heavy stone arch, and the Turk rapped cautiously. A voice challenged from within, and was answered in the gutturals of Turan, unintelligible to Yusuf ibn Suleyman. The door was opened, and al Afdhal pushed into thick darkness, drawing the Moor with him. They heard the door close behind them, then a heavy leather curtain was pulled back, revealing a lamplit corridor, and a scarred ancient whose fierce mustachios proclaimed the Turk.

"An old Memluk turned to wine-selling," said al Afdhal to the Moor. "Lead us to a chamber where we can be alone, Ahmed."

"All the chambers are empty," grumbled old Ahmed, limping before them. "I am a ruined man. Men fear to touch the cup, since the caliph banned wine. Allah smite him with the gout!"

Bowing them into a small chamber, he spread mats for them, set before them a great dish of pistachio kernels, Tihamah raisins, and citrons, poured wine from a bulging skin, and limped away, muttering under his breath.

"Egypt has come upon evil days," drawled the Turk lazily, quaffing deep of the Shiraz liquor. He was a tall man, leanly but strongly built, with keen black eyes that danced restlessly and were never still. His *khalat* was plain, but of costly fabric; his spired helmet was chased with silver, and jewels glinted in the hilt of his scimitar.

Over against him, Yusuf ibn Suleyman presented something of the same hawk-like appearance, which is characteristic of all men who live by war. The Moor was fully as tall as the Turk, but with thicker limbs and a greater depth of chest. His was the build of the mountaineer—strength combined with endurance. Under his white *kafiyeh* his brown face showed smooth-shaven, and he was lighter in complexion than the Turk, the darkness of his features being more of the sun than of nature. His gray eyes, in repose, were cold as chilled steel, but even so there smoldered in them a hint of stormy fires.

He gulped his wine and smacked his lips in appreciation, and the Turk grinned and refilled his goblet.

"How fare the Faithful in Spain, brother?"

"Badly enough, since the Vizir Mozaffar ibn al Mansur died," answered the Moor. "The Caliph Hischam is a weakling. He can not curb his nobles, each of whom would set up an independent state. The land groans under civil war, and yearly the Christian kingdoms wax mightier. A strong hand could yet save Andalusia but in all Spain there is no such strong hand."

"In Egypt such a hand might be found," remarked the Turk. "Here are many powerful emirs who love brave men. In the ranks of the Memluks there is always a place for a saber like yours."

"I am neither Turk nor slave," grunted Yusuf.

"No!" Al Afdhal's voice was soft; the hint of a smile touched his thin lips. "Do not fear; I am in your debt, and I can keep a secret."

"What do you mean?" The Moor's hawk-like head came up with a jerk. His grey eyes began to smolder. His sinewy hand sought his hilt.

"I heard you cry out in the stress of the fight as you smote the black sworder," said al Afdhal. "You roared 'Santiago!' So shout the Caphars of Spain in battle. You are no Moor; you are a Christian!"

The other was on his feet in an instant, saber drawn. But al Afdhal had not stirred; he reclined at ease on the cushions, sipping his wine.

"Fear not," he repeated. "I have said that I would keep your secret. I owe you my life. A man like you could never be a spy; you are too quick to anger, too open in your wrath. There can be but one reason why you come among the Moslems—to avenge yourself upon a private enemy."

The Christian stood motionless for a moment, feet braced as if for an attack, the sleeve of his *khalat* falling back to reveal the ridged muscles of his thick brown arm. He scowled uncertainly, and, standing thus, looked much less like a Moslem than he had previously looked.

There was an instant of breathless tension, then, with a shrug of his brawny shoulders, the false Moor reseated himself, though with his saber across his knees.

"Very well," he said candidly, tearing off a great bunch of grapes with a bronzed hand and cramming them into his mouth. He spoke through mastication. "I am Diego de Guzman, of Castile. I seek an enemy in Egypt."

"Whom?" inquired al Afdhal with interest.

"A Berber named Zahir el Ghazi, may the dogs gnaw his bones!"

The Turk started.

"By Allah, you aim at a lofty target! Know you that this man is now an emir of Egypt, and general of all the Berber troops of the Fatimid caliphs?"

"By San Pedro," answered the Spaniard, "it matters as little as if he were a street-sweeper."

"Your blood feud has led you far," commented al Afdhal.

"The Berbers of Malaga revolted against their Arab governor," said Guzman abruptly. "They asked aid of Castile. Five hundred knights marched to their assistance. Before we could reach Malaga, this accursed Zahir el Ghazi had betrayed his companions into the hands of the caliph. Then he betrayed us, who were marching to their aid. Ignorant of all that had passed, we fell into a trap laid by the Moors. Only I escaped with my life. Three brothers and an uncle fell beside me on that day. I was cast into a Moorish prison, and a year passed before my people were able to raise enough gold to ransom me.

"When I was free again, I learned that Zahir had fled from Spain, from fear of his own people. But my sword was needed in Castile. It was another year before I could take the road of vengeance. And for a year I have sought through the Moslem countries, in the guise of a Moor, whose speech and customs I have learned through a lifetime of battle against them, and by reason of my captivity among them. Only recently, I learned that the man I sought was in Egypt."

Al Afdhal did not at once reply, but sat scanning the rugged features of the man before him, seeing reflected in them the untamable nature of the wild uplands where a handful of Christian warriors had defied the swords of Islam for three hundred years.

"How long have you been in *al medina*?" he demanded abruptly.

"Only a few days," grunted Guzman. "Long enough to learn that the caliph is mad."

"There is more to learn," returned al Afdhal. "Al Hakim is, indeed, mad. I say to a *Feringhi* what I dare not say to a Moslem—yet all men know it. The people, who are Sunnites, murmur under his heel. Three bodies of troops uphold his power. First, the Berbers from Kairouan, where this Shiah dynasty of the Fatimids first took root; secondly, the black Sudani, who under their general Othman yearly gain more power; and thirdly, the Memluks, or Baharites, the White Slaves of the River—Turks and Sunnites, like myself. Their emir is es Salih Muhammad, and between him, and el Ghazi, and the black Othman, there is enough hate and jealousy to start a dozen wars.

"Zahir el Ghazi came to Egypt three years ago as a penniless adventurer. He has risen to emir, partly by virtue of a Venetian slave woman named Zaida. There is a woman behind the curtain of the caliph, too: the Arab, Zulaikha. But no woman can play with al Hakim."

Diego set down his empty goblet and looked straight at al Afdhal. Spaniards had not yet acquired the polished formality which men later came to consider their dominant characteristic. The Castilian was still more Nordic than Latin. Diego de Guzman possessed the open bluntness of the Goths who were his ancestors.

"Well, what now?" he demanded. "Are you going to betray me to the Moslems, or did you speak truth when you said you would keep my secret?"

"I have no love for Zahir el Ghazi," mused al Afdhal, as if to himself, turning in his fingers the ring he had taken from the black giant. "Zaman was Othman's dog; but Berber gold can buy a Sudani sword." Lifting his head, he returned Guzman's direct and challenging stare.

"I, too, owe Zahir a debt," he said. "I will do more than keep your secret. I will aid you in your vengeance!"

Guzman started forward and his iron fingers gripped the Turk's silk-clad shoulder like a vise.

"Do you speak truth?"

"Let Allah smite me if I lie!" swore the Turk. "Listen, while I unfold my plan . . ."

2

And while in the hidden wineshop of Ahmed the Crippled a Turk and a Spaniard bent their heads together over a darksome plot, within the massive walls of el Kahira a stupendous event was coming to pass. Under the shadows of the *meshrebiyas* stole a veiled and hooded figure. For the first time in seven years, a woman was walking the streets of Cairo.

Realizing her enormity, she trembled with fear that was not inspired wholly by the lurking shadows, which might mask skulking thieves. The stones hurt her feet in her tattered velvet slippers; for seven years the cobblers of Cairo had been forbidden to make street shoes for women. Al Hakim had decreed that the women of Egypt be shut up, not, indeed, like jewels in vaults, but like reptiles in cages.

Though clad in castoff rags, it was no common woman who stole shuddering through the night. On the morrow the word would run through the mysterious channels of communication from *harim* to *harim*, and spiteful women lolling on satin cushions would laugh gleefully at the shame of an envied and hated sister.

Zaida, the red-haired Venetian, favorite of Zahir el Ghazi, had wielded more power than any other woman in Egypt. And now, as she stole through the night, an outcast, the thought that burned her like a white-hot brand was the realization that she had aided her faithless lover and master in his climb to the high places of the world, only for another woman to enjoy the fruits of that toil.

Zaida came of a race of women accustomed to swaying thrones with their beauty and wit. She scarcely remembered the Venice from which she had been stolen as a child by Barbary pirates. The corsair who had taken her and raised her for his *harim* had fallen in battle with the Byzantines, and, as a supple girl of fourteen, Zaida had passed into the hands of a prince of Crete, a languorous, effeminate youth, whom she came to twist about her pink fingers. Then, after some years, had come the raid of the Egyptian fleet on the islands of the Greeks, plunder, slaughter, fire, crashing walls, and shrieks of death, a red-haired girl screaming in the iron arms of a laughing Berber giant.

Because she came of a race whose women were rulers of men, Zaida neither perished nor became a whimpering toy. Her nature was supple, as the sapling which bends to the wind and is not uprooted. The time was not long when, if she never mastered Zahir el Ghazi in turn, she at least stood on equal footing with him, and because she came of a race of kingmakers, she set forth to make a king of Zahir el Ghazi. The man had intelligence, super vitality, and strength of mind and body; he needed but one stimulant to his ambition. Zaida was that incentive.

And now Zahir, considering himself fully able to climb the shining rungs of the ladder without her, had cast her aside. Because Allah gave him a lust no one woman, however desirable, could wholly satisfy, and because Zaida would endure no rival, a supple Arab had smiled at the Berber, and the red-haired Venetian's world had crashed. Zahir had stripped her and driven her into the street like a common slut, only the compassion of a slave covering her nakedness.

Engrossed in her searing thoughts, she looked up with a start as a tall hooded figure stepped from the shadows of an overhanging balcony and confronted her. A wide cloak was drawn close around him, his coif concealed the lower parts of his features. Only his eyes burned at her, almost luminous in the starlight. She cowered back with a low cry.

"A woman on the streets of *al medina*!" The voice was strange, hollow, almost ghostly. "Is this not in defiance of the command of the caliph, on whom be peace?"

"I walk not the streets by choice, *ya khawand*," she answered. "My master has cast me forth, and I have not where to lay my head."

The stranger bent his hooded head and stood statue-like for a space, like a brooding image of night and silence. Zaida watched him nervously. There was something gloomy and portentous about him; he seemed less like a man pondering over the tale of a chance-met slave-girl than a sombre prophet weighing the doom of a sinful people.

At last he lifted his head.

"Come!" said he, in a voice of command rather than invitation. "I will find a place for you." And without pausing to see if she obeyed, he stalked away up the street. She hurried after him, clutching her draggled robe about her. She could not walk the streets all night; any officer of the caliph would strike off her head for violating the edict of al Hakim. This stranger might be leading her into slavery, but she had no choice.

The silence of her companion made her nervous. Several times she essayed speech, but his grim unresponsiveness struck her silent in turn. Her curiosity was piqued, her vanity touched. Never before had she failed so signally to interest a man. Faintly, she sensed an imponderable something she could not overcome—an unnatural and frightening aloofness she could not touch. Fear began to grow on her, but she followed, because she knew not what else to do. Only once he spoke, when, looking back, she was startled to see several furtive and shadowy forms stealing after them.

"Men follow us!" she exclaimed.

"Heed them not," he answered in his weird voice. "They are but servants of Allah that serve Him in their way."

This cryptic answer set her shuddering, and nothing further was said until they reached a small arched gate set in a lofty wall. There the stranger halted and called aloud. He was answered from within, and the gate opened, revealing a black mute holding a torch on high. In its lurid gleam the height of the robed stranger was inhumanly exaggerated.

"But this—this is a gate of the Great Palace!" stammered Zaida.

For answer the man threw back his hood, revealing a long pale oval of a face, in which burned those strange luminous eyes.

Zaida screamed and fell to her knees. "*Al Hakim!*"

"Aye, al Hakim, oh faithless and sinful one!" The hollow voice was like a knell. Sonorous and inexorable as the brazen trumpets of doom, it rolled out in the night. "Oh, vain and foolish woman, who dare ignore the command of al Hakim, which is the word of God! Who treads the street in sin, and sets aside the mandates of the Beneficent King! There is no majesty, and there is no might, save in Allah, the glorious, the great! Oh, Lord of the Three Worlds, why withhold Thy levin fire to burn her into a charred and blackened brand for all men to behold and shudder thereat!"

Then, changing his tone suddenly, he cried sharply, "Seize her!" and the dogging shadows closed in, revealing themselves as black men with the wizened features of mutes. As their fingers closed on her flesh, Zaida fainted for the first and last time in her life.

She did not feel herself being lifted and carried through the gate, across gardens waving with blossoms and reeking with spice, through corridors lined with spiral columns of alabaster and gold, and into a chamber without windows, the arched doors of which were bolted with bars of gold, gemmed with amethysts.

It was upon the carpeted, cushion-strewn floor of this chamber that the Venetian regained consciousness. She looked dazedly about her, then the memory of her adventure came back with a rush, and with a low cry she stared wildly about for her captor. She shrank down again to see him standing above her, arms folded, head bent gloomily while his terrible eyes burned into her soul.

"Oh, Lion of the Faithful!" she gasped, struggling to her knees. "Mercy! Mercy!"

Even as she spoke she was sickeningly aware of the futility of pleading for mercy where mercy was unknown. She was crouching before the most feared monarch in the world. The man whose name was a curse in the mouths of Christians, Jews, and orthodox Moslems alike; the man who, claiming descent from Ali, the nephew of the Prophet, was the head of the Shiah world, the Incarnation of Divine Reason to all Shiites; the man who had ordered all dogs killed, all vines cut down, all grapes and honey dumped into the Nile; who had banned all games of chance, confiscated the property of the Coptic Christians, and given the people themselves over to abominable tortures; who believed that to disobey one of his commands, however trivial, was the blackest sin conceivable. He roamed the streets at night in disguise, as Haroun or Raschid had done before him, and as Baibars did after him, to see that his commands were obeyed.

So al Hakim stared at her with wide unblinking eyes, and Zaida felt her flesh shrivel and crawl in horror.

"Blasphemer!" he whispered. "Tool of Shaitan! Daughter of all evil! Oh, Allah!" he cried suddenly, flinging aloft his wide-sleeved arms. "What punishment shall be devised for this demon? What agony terrible enough, what degradation vile enough to render justice? Allah, grant me wisdom!"

Zaida rose upon her knees, snatching off her torn veil. She stretched out her arm, pointing at his face.

"Why do you call on Allah?" she shrieked hysterically. "Call on al Hakim! *You* are Allah! *Al Hakim is God!*"

He stopped short at her cry; he reeled, catching at his head, crying out incoherently. Then he straightened himself and looked down at her dazedly. Her face was chalk white, her wide eyes staring. To her natural acting ability was added the real and desperate horror of her position. To al Hakim it seemed that she was dazed and dazzled by a vision of celestial splendor.

"What do you see, woman?" he gasped.

"Allah has revealed Himself to me!" she whispered. "In your face, shining like the morning sun! Nay, I burn, I die in the blaze of thy glory!"

She sank her face in her hands and crouched trembling. Al Hakim passed a trembling hand over his brow and temples.

"*God!*" he whispered, "Aye, I *am* God! I have guessed it—I have dreamed it—I, and I alone, possess the wisdom of the Infinite. Now a mortal has seen it, has recognized the god in the form of man. Aye, it is the truth taught by the teachers of the Shiah—the Incarnation of the Godhead—I see the Truth behind the truth at last. Not a mere incarnation of divinity—divinity itself! *Allah!* Al Hakim is Allah!"

Bending his gaze upon the woman at his feet, he ordered, "Rise, woman, and look upon thy god!"

Timidly she did so, and stood shrinking before his unwinking gaze. Zaida the Venetian was not extremely beautiful according to certain arbitrary standards which demand the perfectly chiseled features, the delicate frame—but she was good to look at. She was somewhat broadly built, with big breasts and haunches, and shoulders wider than most. Her face was not the classic of the Greeks, and was faintly freckled. But there was about her a vital something transcending mere superficial beauty. Her brown eyes sparkled, reflecting a keen intelligence and the physical vigor promised by her thick limbs and big hips.

As he looked at her a change clouded the wide eyes of al Hakim; he seemed to see her clearly for the first time.

"Thy sin is pardoned," he intoned. "Thou wert first to hail thy God. Henceforth thou shalt serve me in honor and splendor."

She prostrated herself, kissing the carpet before his feet, and he clapped his hands. A eunuch entered, bowing low.

"Go quickly to the house of Zahir el Ghazi," said al Hakim, seeming to look over the head of the servitor, and see him not at all. "Say to him: 'This is the word of al Hakim, who is God; that on the morrow shall be the beginning of happenings, of the building of ships, and the marshaling of hosts, even as thou hast desired; for God is God, and the unbelievers too long have blasphemed against Him!"

"Hearkening and obeying, master," mumbled the eunuch, bowing to the floor.

"I doubted and feared," said al Hakim dreamily, gazing far and beyond the confines of reality into some far realm only he could see. "I knew not—as now I know—that Zahir el Ghazi was the tool of Destiny. When he urged me to the world conquest, I hesitated. But I am God, and to gods all things are possible, yea, all kingdoms and glory!"

3

Glance briefly at the world on that night of portent, 1021 A.D. It was a night in an age of change, an age writhing in the throes of labor in which all that goes to make up the modern world was struggling for birth. It was a world crimson and torn, chaotic and awful, pregnant with imponderable power, yet apparently sinking into stagnation and ruin.

In Egypt a Sunnite population groaned under the heel of a Shiite dynasty—a dynasty shrunken and shrivelled from world empire, but still mighty, reaching from the Euphra-

tes to the Sudan. Between the borders of Egypt and the
western sea stretched a vast expanse inhabited by wild
tribes nominally under the caliph's sceptre, the same tribes
which had in an earlier day crushed the Gothic kingdom
of Spain, and which now stirred restlessly in their mountains, needing only a powerful leader to sweep them again
in an overwhelming wave against Christendom.

In Spain the divided Moorish provinces gave ground before the hosts of Castile, Leon, and Navarre. But these
Christian kingdoms, forged of blood and iron though they
were, were not numerically powerful enough to have with-
stood the combined onslaught of Islam. They formed Christendom's western frontier, while Byzantium formed the
eastern frontier, as in the days of Omar and the conquering
Companions, holding back the horns of the Crescent that
else had met in middle Europe to form an inexorable circle. And the Crescent was never dead; it only slept, and
even in its slumber throbbed the drums of empire.

Europe, in the grip of feudalism, was weaker internally
than on her borders. The nations were already taking shadowy shape, but as yet there was no real national spirit. In
France there was neither Charlemagne nor Martel—only
starving, plague-harried peasantry, warring fiefs, and a land
torn by strife between Capet and Norman duke, overlord
and rebellious vassal. And France was typical of Europe.

There were, it is true, strong men in the West. Canute
the Dane, ruling Saxon England; Henry of Germany, Emperor of the shadowy Holy Roman Empire. But Canute
was almost like the king of another world, in his sea-girt
isolation, and the Emperor had his hands full in seeking to
weld his rival realms of Germany and Italy, and in beating
back the encroaching Slavs.

In Byzantium the glorious reign of Basil Bulgaroktonos
was drawing to a close. Already long shadows were falling
from the east across the Golden Horn. Byzantium was still
Christendom's mightiest bulwark; but westward from Bokhara were moving the horsemen of the steppes destined
swiftly to wrest from the Eastern Empire her last Asiatic
possession. The Seljuks, blocked on the south by the glittering Indo-Iranian empire of Mahmud of Ghazni, were riding toward the setting sun, not to be halted until their
horses' hoofs splashed the waters of the Mediterranean.

In Baghdad the Persian Buides fought in the streets with
the Turkish mercenaries of the weak Abbaside caliph. But

Islam was not crushed, but only broken into many parts, like the shards of a shining blade. Active strength lay in Egypt, in Ghazni, in the marauding Seljuks. Potential strength slumbered in Syria, in Irak, in Arabia, in the restless tribes of the Atlas—strength enough to burst the western barriers of Christendom, were the various separate elements united under a strong hand.

Byzantium was still unassailable; but let the Spanish kingdoms fall before a sudden onrush from Africa, and the hordes would gush into Europe almost without opposition. Such was the picture of the age: both East and West divided and inert; in the West was yet unborn that flaming spirit which, seventy years later, stormed eastward in the Crusades; in the East neither a Saladin nor a Genghis Khan was apparent. Yet, let such a man appear, and the horns of the revived Crescent might yet complete the circle, not in central Europe, but over the crumbling walls of Constantinople, assailed from north as well as south.

Such was the panorama of the world on that night of doom and portents, when two hooded figures halted in a group of palm trees among the ruins of nighted Cairo.

Before them lay the waters of el Khalij, the canal, and beyond it, rising from its very bank, the great bastioned wall of sun dried brick which encircled el Kahira, separating the royal heart of *al medina* from the rest of the city. Built by the conquering Fatimids half a century before, the inner city was in realty a gigantic fortress, sheltering the caliphs and their servants and certain troops of their mercenaries—forbidden to common men without special permit.

"We could climb the wall," muttered Guzman.

"And find ourselves no nearer our enemy," answered al Afdhal, groping in the shadows under the clustering trees. "Here it is!"

Staring over his shoulder, Guzman saw the Turk fumbling at what appeared to be a shapeless heap of marble. This particular locality was occupied entirely by ruins, inhabited only by bats and lizards.

"An ancient pagan shrine," said al Afdhal. "Shunned because of superstition, and long crumbled—but it hides more than a grove of palm-trees shows!"

He lifted away a broad slab, revealing steps leading down into a black gaping aperture; Guzman frowned suspiciously.

"This," said al Afdhal, sensing his doubt," is the mouth of a tunnel which leads under the wall and up into the house of Zahir el Ghazi, which stands just beyond the wall."

"Under the canal?" demanded the Spaniard incredulously.

"Aye; once el Ghazi's house was the pleasure house of the Caliph Khumaraweyh, who slept on an air-cushion which floated on a pool of quick silver, guarded by lions— yet fell before the avenger's dagger, in spite of all. He prepared secret exits from all parts of his palaces and pleasure houses. Before Zahir el Ghazi took the house, it was occupied by his rival, es Salih Muhammad. The Berber knows nothing of this secret way. I could have used it before, but until tonight I was not sure that I wished to slay him. Come!"

Swords drawn, they groped down a flight of stone steps and advanced along a level tunnel in pitch blackness. Guzman's groping fingers told him that the walls, floor, and ceiling were composed of huge blocks of stone, probably looted from edifices reared by the Pharoahs. As they advanced, the stones became slippery underfoot, and the air grew dank and damp. Drops of water fell clammily on Guzman's neck, and he shivered and swore. They were passing under the canal. A little later this dankness abated somewhat, and shortly thereafter al Afdhal hissed a warning, and they began to mount another flight of stone stairs.

At the top the Turk halted and fumbled at some bolt or catch. A panel slid aside, and a soft light streamed in from a vaulted and tapestried corridor. Guzman realized that they had indeed passed under the canal and the great wall, and stood in the forbidden confines of Kahira, the mysterious and fabulous.

Al Afdhal slipped lithely through the opening, and after Guzman had followed, closed it behind them. It became one of the inlaid panels of the wall, differing not from the other sandalwood panels. Then the Turk went swiftly down the corridor, going without hesitation, like a man who knew his way. The Spaniard followed, saber in hand, glancing incessantly to right and left.

They passed through a dark velvet curtain and came full upon an arched doorway of gold-inlaid ebony. A brawny black man, naked but for voluminous silk breeches, who had been dozing on his haunches, started up, swinging a great scimitar. But he did not cry out; his was the bestial face of a mute.

"The clash of steel will rouse the household," snapped al Afdhal, avoiding the sweep of the eunuch's sword. As the black man stumbled from his wasted effort, Guzman tripped him. He fell sprawling, and the Turk passed his blade through the black body.

"That was quick and silent enough!" laughed al Afdhal softly. "Now for the real prey!"

Cautiously he tried the door, while the Spaniard crouched at his shoulder, breathing between his teeth, his eyes beginning to burn like those of a hunting cat. The door gave inward and Guzman sprang past the Turk into the chamber. Al Afdhal followed and, closing the door, set his back to it, laughing at the man who leaped up from his divan with a startled oath.

"We have run the buck to cover, brother!"

But there was no laughter on the lips of Diego de Guzman, as he stood over the half-risen occupant of the chamber, and al Afdhal saw the lifted saber quiver in his muscular hand.

Zahir el Ghazi was a tall, lusty man, his sandy hair close-cropped, his short tawny beard carefully trimmed. Late as the hour was, he was fully clad in bag-trousers of silk, girdle, and velvet vest.

"Lift not your voice, dog," advised the Spaniard. "My sword is at your throat."

"So I see," answered Zahir el Ghazi imperturbably. His blue eyes roved to the Turk, and he laughed with harsh mockery. "So you avoided the spillers of blood? I had thought you dead by this time. But the result will be the same. Fool! You have cut your throat! How you came into my chamber I know not; but one shout will bring my slaves."

"Ancient houses have ancient secrets," laughed the Turk. "One you have learned—that the walls of this chamber are so constructed as to muffle screams. Another you have not learned—the secret by which we came here tonight." He turned to Diego de Guzman. "Well, why do you hesitate?"

Guzman drew back and lowered his saber. "There lies your sword," he said to the Berber, while al Afdhal swore, half in disgust, half in amusement. "Take it up. If you are man enough to slay me, be it so. But I think you will never see the sun rise again."

Zahir peered curiously at him.

"You are no Moor," said the Berber. "I was born in the Atlas mountains, but I was raised in Malaga. You are a Spaniard. Who are you?"

Diego threw aside his tattered *kaftyeh*.

"Diego de Guzman," said Zahir calmly. "I might have guessed. Well, *hidalgo*, you have come a long way to die—"

He swooped up the heavy scimitar, then hesitated.

"You wear armor while I am naked but for silk and velvet."

Diego kicked a helmet toward him, one of several pieces of armor cast carelessly about the chamber.

"I see the glint of mail beneath your vest," he said. "You always wore a steel shirt. We are on equal terms. Stand to it, you dog; my soul thirsts for your blood."

The Berber bent, donned the headpiece—leaped suddenly, hoping to catch his antagonist off guard. But the Moorish saber clanged in midair against the Berber scimitar, and sparks showered as the two long curved blades wheeled, flashed, rose, and fell, flickering in the lamplight.

Both attacked, smiting furiously, each too intent on the life of the other to give much thought for showy swordplay. Each stroke had full weight and murderous will behind it. Such a battle could not long continue; the desperate recklessness of the combat must quickly bring it to a bloody conclusion, one way or another.

Guzman fought in silence, but Zahir el Ghazi laughed and taunted his foe between lightning strokes.

"Dog!" The play of the Berber's arm did not interfere with the play of his tongue. "It irks me to slay you here. Would that you might live to see the destruction of your accursed people. Why did I come to Egypt? Merely for refuge? Ha! I came to forge a sword for mine enemies, Christian and Moslem alike! I have urged the caliph to build a fleet— to lift the standards of *jihad*— to conquer the caliphate of Cordova!

"The Berber tribes are ripe for such a war. We will roar westward from Egypt like an avalanche that gains volume and momentum as it advances. With half a million warriors we will sweep into Spain—stamp Cordova into dust and incorporate its warriors into our ranks! Castile can not stand before us, and over the bodies of the Spanish knights we will sweep out into the plains of Europe!"

Guzman spat a curse.

"Al Hakim has hesitated," laughed Zahir breathing evenly and easily, as he parried the whirring saber. "But tonight he sent me word—I have just come from the palace, where he told me it shall be as I have desired. He has a new whim; he believes himself to be God! No matter. Spain is doomed! If I survive, *I* shall be its caliph some day! And even if you slay me, you can not stop al Hakim now. The *jihad* will be launched. The *harims* of Islam shall be filled with Castilian girls—"

From Guzman's lips burst a harsh savage cry, as if he realized for the first time that the Berber was not merely taunting him with idle words, but was voicing an actual plot of conquest.

Face grey and eyes glaring, he plunged in with a fresh ferocity that made al Afdhal stare. Zahir's bearded lips offered no more taunts. The Berber's whole attention was devoted to parrying the Spanish saber, which beat on his blade like a hammer on an anvil.

The clash of steel rose until al Afdhal chewed his lip in nervousness, knowing that some echo of the noise would surely reverberate beyond the muffling walls.

The sheer strength and berserk fury of the Spaniard were beginning to tell. The Berber was pallid under his bronzed skin. His breath came in gasps, and he continually gave ground. Blood streamed from gashes on arms, thigh, and neck. Guzman was bleeding too, but there was no slackening in the headlong frenzy of his attack.

Zahir was close to the tapestried wall, when suddenly he sprang aside as Guzman lunged. Carried off balance by the wasted thrust, the Spaniard plunged forward, and his saber point clashed against the stone beneath the tapestry. At the same instant Zahir slashed at his enemy's head with all his waning power. But the saber of Toledo steel, instead of snapping, like a lesser blade, bent double, and sprang straight again. The descending scimitar bit through the Moorish helmet into the scalp beneath, but before Zahir could recover his balance, Guzman's saber sheared upward through steel links and hipbone to grate into his spinal column.

The Berber reeled and fell with a choking cry, his entrails spilling on the floor. His fingers clawed briefly at the nap of the heavy carpet, then went limp.

Guzman, blind with blood and sweat, was driving his sword in silent frenzy again and again into the form at his feet, too drunk with fury to know that his foe was dead, until al Afdhal, cursing in something nearly like horror, dragged him away. The Spaniard dazedly raked the blood and sweat from his eyes and peered down groggily at his foe. He was still dizzy from the stroke that had cloven his steel headpiece. He tore off the riven helmet and threw it aside. It was full of blood, and a crimson torrent descended into his face, blinding him.

Cursing earnestly, he began groping for something to wipe it away, when he felt al Afdhal's fingers at work. The Turk swiftly mopped the blood from his companion's features, and made shift to bind up the wound with strips torn from his own clothing.

Then, taking from his girdle something which Guzman recognized as the ring al Afdhal had taken from the finger of the black killer, Zaman, the Turk dropped it on the rug near Zahir's body.

"Why did you do that?" demanded the Spaniard.

"To blind the avengers of blood. Let us go quickly, in the name of Allah. The Berber's slaves must be all deaf or drunk, not to have awakened before now."

Even as they emerged into the corridor, where the dead mute stared sightlessly at the painted ceiling, they heard sounds indicative of wakefulness—a vague murmur of voices, a distant tramp of feet. Hurrying down the hallway to the secret panel, they entered and groped in darkness until they emerged once more in the silent grove.

The paling stars were mirrored in the dark waters of the canal, and the first hint of dawn etched the minarets.

"Do you know a way into the palace of the caliph?" asked Guzman. The bandage on his head was soaked with blood, and a thin trickle stole down his neck.

Al Afdhal turned, and they faced one another under the shadow of the trees.

"I aided you to slay a common enemy," said the Turk. "I did not bargain to betray my sovereign to you! Al Hakim is mad, but his time has not yet come. I aided you in a matter of private vengeance—not in the war of nations. Be content with your vengeance, and remember that to fly too high is to scorch one's wings in the sun."

Guzman mopped blood and made no reply.

"You had better leave Cairo as soon as possible," said al Afdhal, watching him narrowly. "I think it would be safer for all concerned. Sooner or later you will be detected as a

Ferenghi by someone not in your debt. I will furnish you with monies and horses—"

"I have both," grunted Guzman, wiping the blood from his neck.

"And you will depart in peace?" demanded al Afdhal.

"What choice have I?" returned the Spaniard.

"Swear," insisted the Turk.

"By God, you are insistent," grumbled Guzman. "Very well. I swear by Saint James of Compostello, that I will leave the city before the sun reaches its zenith."

"Good!" The Turk breathed a sigh of relief. "It is for your own good as much as anything else that I—"

"I understand your altruistic motives," grunted Guzman. "If there was any debt between us, consider it paid, and let each man act accordingly."

And turning, he strode away with a horseman's swinging stride. Al Afdhal watched his broad shoulder receding through the trees, with a slight frown that betokened doubt.

4

From mosque and minaret went forth the sonorous *adan*. Before the mosque of Talai, outside the Bab Zuweyla, stood Darazai, the mullah, and when he lifted his voice, and when he tolled it out across the tense throngs, men shuddered and fingernails bit into dusky palms.

"—and for that your divinely appointed caliph, al Hakim, is of the seed of Ali, who was of the blood of the Prophet, who was God Incarnate, so is God this day among ye! Yea, the one God moves among ye in mortal shape! And now I command ye, all Believers in al Islam, recognize and bow down and worship the one true God, Lord of the Three Worlds, the Creator of the Universe, Who set up the firmament without pillars in its stead, the Incarnation of Divine Wisdom, who is God, who is al Hakim, the seed of Ali!"

A great shudder rippled across the throng, then a frenzied yell broke the breathless stillness. A wild-haired figure ran forward, a half-naked Arab. With a shriek of "Blasphemer!" he caught up a stone and hurled it. The missile struck the mullah full in the mouth, breaking his teeth. He staggered, blood streaming down his beard. And with an awesome roar, the mob heaved and billowed and surged forward. Taxation, starvation, rapine, massacre—all these the Egyptians could endure, but this stroke at the roots of their religion was the last straw. Staid merchants became madman, cringing beggars turned into rabid-eyed devils.

Stones flew like hail, and louder and louder rose the roar, the bedlam of wild beasts, or men gone mad. Hands were clutching at the stunned Darazai's garments, when men of the Turkish guard in chain mail and spired helmets beat the mob back with their scimitars, and carried the terrified mullah into the mosque, which they barricaded against the surging multitude.

With a clanking of weapons and a jingling of bridle-chains, a troop of Sudani horse, resplendent in gold-chased corselets and silk breeches, galloped out of the Zuweyla gate. The white teeth of the black riders shone in wide grins of glee, their eyes rolled, they licked their thick lips in anticipation. The stones of the mob rattled harmlessly on their cuirasses and hippo-hide bucklers. They urged their horses into the press, slashing with their curved blades. Men rolled, howling, under the stamping hoofs. The rioters gave way, fleeing wildly into shops and down alleys, leaving the square littered with writhing bodies.

The black riders leaped from their saddles and began crashing in doors of shops and dwellings, heaping their arms with plunder. Screams of women resounded from within the houses. A shriek, a crash of glass and lattice-work, and a white-clad body struck the street with a bone-crushing impact. A black face looked down through the ruined casement, split in an empty belly-shaking laugh. A black horseman spurred forward, bent from his saddle, and thrust his lance through the still-quivering form of the woman on the stones.

The giant Othman, in flaming silk and polished steel, rode among his black dogs, beating them off. They mounted, swung into line behind him. In a swinging canter they swept down the streets, gory human heads bobbing on their lances—an object lesson for the maddened Cairenes who crouched in their coverts, panting with hot-eyed hate.

The breathless eunuch who brought news of the uprising and its suppression to al Hakim was followed swiftly by another, who prostrated himself before the caliph and cried, "Oh, Lord of the Three Worlds, the emir Zahir el Ghazi is dead! His servants found him murdered in his palace, and beside him the ring of Zaman the black Sworder.

Wherefore the Berbers cry out that he was murdered by order of the emir Othman, and they search for Zaman in el Mansuriya, and fight with the Sudani!"

Zaida, listening behind a curtain, stifled a cry, and clutched at her bosom in brief, passing pain. But al Hakim's inscrutable faraway gaze did not alter; he was wrapped in aloofness, isolated in the contemplation of mystery.

"Let the Memluks separate them," said he. "Shall private feuds interfere with the destiny of God? El Ghazi is dead, but Allah lives. Another man shall be found to lead my troops into Spain. Meanwhile, let the building of ships commence. Let the Sudani handle the mob until they realize their folly and the sin of their heresy. I have recognized my destiny, which is to reveal myself to the world in blood and fire, until all the tribes of the earth know me and bow down before me. You have my leave to go!"

Night was falling on a tense city as Diego de Guzman strode through the streets of the section adjoining el Mansuriya, the quarter of the Sudani. In that section, occupied mostly by soldiers, lights shone and stalls were open by tacit unspoken agreement. All day, revolt had rumbled in the quarters; the mob was like a thousand-headed serpent; stamp it out in one place, and it broke out anew in another, cursing, yelling, and throwing stones. The hoofs of the Sudani had clattered from Zuweyla to the mosque of Ibn Tulun and back again, spattering blood.

Only armed men now traversed the streets. The great wooden, ironbound gates of the quarters were locked, as in times of civil war. Through the lowering arch of the great gate of Zuweyla cantered troops of black horsemen, the torchlight crimsoning their naked scimitars. Their silk cloaks flowed in the wind, their black arms gleamed like polished ebony.

Guzman had not broken his oath to al Afdhal. Sure that the Turk would betray him to the Moslems if he did not seem to comply with the other's demand, the Spaniard had ridden out of the city and into the Mukattam hills, before the sun was high. But he had not sworn he would not return. Sunset had seen him riding into the crumbling suburbs, where thieves and jackals slunk with furtive tread.

Now he moved on foot through the streets, entered the shops where girdled warriors gorged themselves on melons and nuts and meat, and surreptitiously guzzled wine, and he listened to their talk.

"Where are the Berbers?" demanded a moustached Turk, cramming his jaws with a handful of almond cakes.

"They sulk in their quarter," answered another. "They swear that el Ghazi was slain by the Sudani, and display Zaman's ring to prove it. All men know that ring. But Zaman has disappeared. The black emir Othman swears he knows naught of it. But he can not deny the ring. Already a dozen men had been killed in brawls when the caliph ordered us Memluks to beat them apart. By Allah, this has been a day of days!"

"The madness of al Hakim has brought it about," declared another, lowering his voice and glancing warily around. "How long shall we suffer this Shiite dog to lord it over us?"

"Have a care," cautioned his mate. "He is caliph, and our swords are his—as long as es Salih Muhammad so orders it. But if the revolt breaks out afresh, the Berbers are more likely to fight against the Sudani than with them. Men say that al Hakim has taken Zaida, el Ghazi's concubine, into his *harim*, and that angers the Berbers more, making them suspect that El Ghazi was slain, if not by the order of al Hakim, at least with his consent. But *Wellah*, their anger is naught beside that of Zulaikha, whom the caliph has put aside! Her rage, men say, is that of a desert storm."

Guzman waited to hear no more, but, rising, he hastened out of the wineshop. If anyone knew the secrets of the royal palace, that one was Zulaikha. And a discarded mistress is a sure tool for vengeance. Guzman's mission had become more than a private hunt for the life of a personal enemy. Even now, out of the mysterious fastnesses of the caliph's palace rumors crept, and already in the bazaars men spoke of an invasion of Spain. Guzman knew that the ferocious fighting ability of the Spaniards would not, in the end, avail them against such a force as al Hakim might be able to hurl against them. Perhaps only a madman would entertain the idea of world empire; but a madman might accomplish it; and whatever the ultimate fate of Europe, the doom of Castile was sealed if the hordes of Africa rolled up the mountain passes. Guzman thought little of Europe; the lands beyond the Pyrenees were dim and shadowy to him, not much more real than the empires of Alexander and the Caesars. It was Castile of which he thought, and the fierce passionate people of the savage uplands, than which no other blood beat hotly through his veins.

Skirting el Mansuriya, he crossed the canal and made his way to the grove of palms near the shore. Groping in the darkness among the marble ruins, he found and lifted the slab. Again he advanced through pitch blackness and dripping water, stumbled on the other stair, and mounted it. His fingers found and worked a metal bolt, and he emerged into the now unlighted corridor. The house was silent but the reflection of lights elsewhere indicated that it was still occupied, doubtless by the slain emir's servants and women.

Uncertain as to which way led to the outer air, he set off at random, passed through a curtained archway—and found himself confronted by half a dozen black slaves who sprang up glaring, sword in hand. Before he could retreat he heard a shout and rush of feet behind him. Cursing his luck, he ran straight at the bewildered black men. A flickering whirl of steel and he was through, leaving a writhing, bleeding form behind him, and was dashing through a doorway on the other side of the broad chamber. Curved blades were whickering at his back, and as he slammed the door behind him, steel rang on the stout oak, and glittering points showed in the splintering panels. He shot the bolt and whirled, glaring about for an avenue of escape. His gaze fell on a gold-barred window nearby.

With a headlong rush and a straining gasp of effort, he launched himself full into the window. With a splintering crash, the soft bars gave way, the whole casement was torn out before the impact of his hurtling body. He shot through into empty space, just as the door crashed inward and a swarm of howling figures flooded into the room.

5

In the Great East Palace, where slave-girls and eunuchs glided on stealthy bare feet, no echo reverberated of the hell that raged outside the walls. In a chamber whose dome was of gold-filigreed ivory, al Hakim, clad in a white silk robe that made him look even more ghostly and unreal, sat cross-legged on a couch of gemmed ebony, and stared with his wide unblinking eyes at Zaida the Venetian, who knelt before him.

Zaida was no longer clad in the rags of a slave. Her *dolyman* was of crimson Mosul silk, bordered with cloth-of-gold, her girdle of satin sewn with pearls. The fabric of her wide bag drawers was sheer as gossamer, seeming to glow softly with the pink flesh it scarcely veiled. Her earrings were set with great pear-shaped jewels. Her long lashes were touched with kohl, her fingers tipped with henna. She knelt on a cloth-of-gold cushion.

But amidst all this splendor, which outshone anything even this plaything of princes had ever known, the Venetian's eyes were shadowed. For the first time in her life she found herself actually to be a plaything. She had inspired al Hakim's latest madness, but she had not mastered him. A night, an hour, she had expected to bend him to her will. Now he seemed withdrawn from her, and there was an expression in his cold, inhuman eyes which made her shudder.

Suddenly he spoke, ponderously, portentously, like a god voicing doom. "It is not meet that gods mate with mortals."

She started, opened her mouth, then feared to speak.

"Love is human and a weakness," he continued broodingly. "I will cast it from me. Gods are beyond loves. And weakness assails me when I lie in your arms."

"What do you mean, my lord?" she ventured fearfully.

"Even the gods must sacrifice," he answered somberly. "Love of a human is blasphemy to the godhead. I give you up, lest my divinity weaken."

He clapped his hands deliberately, and a eunuch entered on all fours—a newly instituted custom.

"Send in the emir Othman," ordered al Hakim, and the eunuch bumped his head violently against the floor and backed awkwardly out of the presence.

"*No!*" Zaida sprang up in a frenzy. "Oh, my lord, have mercy! You can not give me to that black beast! You can not—"

She was on her knees, catching at his robe, which he drew back from her fingers.

"Woman!" he thundered. "Are you mad? Would you draw doom upon yourself? Would you assail the person of God?"

Othman entered uncertainly, and in evident trepidation; a warrior of barbaric Darfur, he had risen to his present high estate by wild fighting and a brutal form of diplomacy.

Al Hakim pointed to the cowering woman at his feet and spake briefly. "Take her!'

The Sudani never questioned the commands of his monarch. A broad grin split his ebon countenance, and, stooping, he caught up Zaida, who writhed and screamed in his grasp. As he bore her out of the chamber she twisted in his arms, extending her white hands in passionate entreaty. Al Hakim answered not; he sat with hands folded, his gaze detached and impersonal as that of a hashish eater. If he heard the screams of his erstwhile favorite, he gave no sign.

But another heard. Crouching in an alcove, a slim brown-skinned girl watched the grinning Sudani carry his writhing captive up the hall. Scarcely had he vanished when she fled in another direction, garments caught up above her twinkling brown legs.

Othman, the favored of the caliph, alone of all the emirs dwelt in the Great Palace, which was really an aggregation of palaces united in one mighty structure which housed thirty thousand servants of al Hakim. He dwelt in a wing that opened on to the southern quarter of the Beyn el Kasreyn. To reach it, it was not necessary for him to emerge from the palace. Following winding corridors, crossing an occasional open court paved with mosaics and bordered with fretted arches supported on alabaster columns, he came to his own house.

Black swordsmen guarded the door of black teak, banded with arabesqued copper, which separated his quarters from the rest of the palaces. But even as he came in sight of that door, down a broad paneled corridor, a supple form glided from a curtained doorway and barred his way.

"Zulaikha!" The black recoiled in almost superstitious awe; the woman's slim white hands clenched and unclenched in a refinement of passion too subtle and deep for his brutish comprehension; over the filmy *yasmaq* her eyes burned like gems from hell.

"A servant brought me word that al Hakim had discarded the red-haired slut," said the Arab. "Sell her therefore to me! For I owe her a debt that I fain would pay."

"Why should I sell her?" objected the Sudani, fidgeting in animal impatience. "The caliph has given her to me. Stand aside, woman, lest I do you an injury."

"Have you heard what the Berbers shout in the streets?" she asked.

He started, greying slightly. "What is that to me?" he blustered, but his voice was not steady.

"They howl for the head of Othman," she said coolly and with venom. "They call you the murderer of Zahir el Ghazi. What if I went to them and told them that what they suspect is true?"

"But I had naught to do with it!" he exclaimed wildly, like a man caught in an unseen net.

"I can produce men to swear they saw you help Zaman cut him down," she assured him.

"I'll kill you!" he whispered.

She laughed in his face.

"You dare not, black beast of the grasslands! Now will you sell me the red-haired jade, or will you fight the Berbers?"

His hands slipped from their hold and let Zaida fall to the floor.

"Take her and begone!" he muttered, his black skin ashen.

"Take first your pay!" she retorted with vindictive malice, and hurled a handful of coins full in his face. He shrank back like a great black ape, his eyes burning red, his dusky hands opening and closing in helpless bloodlust.

Ignoring him, Zulaikha bent over Zaida, who crouched, dazed with sick helplessness, crushed by the realization of her impotence against this new conqueror, against whom, as a member of her own sex, all the witchery and wiles she had played against men were helpless. Zulaikha gathered the Venetian's red locks in her fingers and, forcing her head brutally back, stared into her eyes with a fierce and hungry possessiveness that turned Zaida's blood to ice.

The Arab clapped her hands and four Syrian eunuchs entered.

"Take her up and bear her to my house," Zulaikha ordered, and they laid hold of the shrinking Venetian and bore her away. Zulaikha followed, her pink nails sinking into her palms, as she breathed softly between her clenching teeth.

6

When Diego de Guzman plunged through the window, he had no idea of what lay in the darkness beneath him. He did not fall far, and he crashed among shrubs that broke his fall. Springing up, he saw his pursuers crowding through the window he had just shattered, hindering one another by their numbers. He was in a garden, a great shadowy place of trees and ghostly blossoms. The next instant he was racing among the shadows, weaving in and out among the shrubbery. His hunters blundered among the trees, running aimlessly and at a loss. Unopposed, he reached the wall, sprang high, caught the coping with one hand, and heaved himself up and over.

He halted and sought to orient himself. He had never been in the streets of el Kahira before, but he had heard the inner city described so often that a mental map of it was in his mind. He knew that he was in the Quarter of the Emirs, and ahead of him, over the flat roofs, loomed a great structure which could be only the Lesser West Palace, a gigantic pleasure house, giving onto the far-famed Garden of Kafur. Fairly sure of his ground, he hurried along the narrow street into which he had fallen, and soon emerged on to the broad thoroughfare which traversed el Kahira from the Gate of el Futuh in the north to the Gate of Zuweyla in the south.

Late as it was, there was much stirring abroad. Armed Memluks rode past him; in the broad Beyn el Kasreyn, the great square which lay between the twin palaces, he heard the jingle of reins on restive horses, and saw a squadron of Sudani troopers sitting their steeds under the torchlight. There was reason for their alertness. Far away he heard tom-toms drumming sullenly among the quarters. Somewhere beyond the walls a dull light began to glow against the stars. The wind brought snatches of wild song and distant yells.

With his soldier's swagger, and saber hilt thrust prominently forward, Guzman passed unnoticed among the mailed and weapon-girded figures that stalked the streets. When he ventured to pluck a bearded Memluk's sleeve and inquire the way to the house of Zulaikha, the Turk gave the

information readily and without surprise. Guzman knew—
as all Cairo knew—that however much the Arab had re-
garded al Hakim as her special property, she had by no
means considered herself the exclusive possession of the
caliph. There were mercenary captains who were as familiar with her chambers as was al Hakim.

Zulaikha's house stood just off the broad street, built
closely adjoining a court of the East Palace, to the gardens
of which, indeed, it was connected, so that Zulaikha, in the
days of her favoritism, could pass between her house and
the palace without violating the caliph's order concerning
the seclusion of women. Zulaikha was no servitor; she was
the daughter of a free shaykh, and she had been al Hakim's
mistress, not his slave.

Guzman did not anticipate any great difficulty in obtain-
ing entrance into her house; she pulled hidden strings of
intrigue and politics, and men of all creeds and conditions
were admitted into her audience chamber, where dancing
girls and opium offered entertainment. That night there
were no dancing girls or guests, but a villainous-looking
Yemenite without question opened the arched door above
which burned a cresset, and showed the false Moor across
a small court, up an outer stair, down a corridor, and into
a broad chamber into which opened a number of fretted
arches hung with crimson velvet tapestries.

The room was empty, under the soft glow of the bronze
lamps, but somewhere in the house sounded the sharp cry
of a woman in pain, accompanied by rich musical laughter,
also in a woman's voice, and indescribably vindictive and
malicious.

But Guzman gave it little heed, for it was at that moment that all hell burst loose outside the walls of el Kahira.

It was a muffled roaring of incredible volume, like the
bellowing of a pent-up torrent at last bursting its dam; but
it was the wild beast howling of many men. The Yemenite
heard too, and went livid under his swarthy skin. Then he
cried out and ran into the corridor, as there sounded the
swift padding of feet, and a laboring breath.

In a nearby chamber, straightening from a task she
found indescribably amusing, Zulaikha heard a strangled
scream outside the door, the swish and chop of a savage
blow, and the thud of a falling body. The door burst open
and Othman rushed in, a wild and terrifying figure, white

eyeballs and bared teeth gleaming in the lamplight, blood dripping from his broad scimitar.

"Dog!" she exclaimed, drawing herself up like a serpent from its coil. "What do you here?"

"The woman you took from me!" he mouthed, ape-like in his passion. "The red-haired woman! Hell is loose in Cairo! The quarters have risen! The streets will swim in blood before dawn! Kill! Kill! Kill! I ride to cut down the Sunnite dogs like bamboo stalks. One more killing in all this slaughter means nothing! Give me the woman before I kill you!"

Drunk with blood-hunger and frustrated lust, the maddened black had forgotten his fear of Zulaikha. The Arab cast a glance at the naked, quivering figure that lay stretched out and bound hand and foot to a divan. She had not yet worked her full will on her rival. What she had already done had been but an amusing prelude to torture, mutilation, and death—agonizing only in its humiliation. All hell could not take her victim from her.

"Ali! Abdullah! Ahmed!" she shrieked, drawing a jeweled dagger.

With a bull-like roar, the huge black lunged. The Arab had never fought men, and her supple quickness, without experience or knowledge of combat, was futile. The broad blade plunged through her body, standing out a foot between her shoulders. With a choked cry of agony and awful surprise she crumpled, and the Sudani brutally wrenched his scimitar free as she fell. At that instant Diego de Guzman appeared at the door.

The Spaniard knew nothing of the circumstances; he only saw a huge black man tearing his sword out of the body of a white woman; and he acted according to his instincts.

Othman, wheeling like a great cat, threw up his dripping scimitar, only to have it beaten stunningly down on his woolly skull beneath Guzman's terrific stroke. He staggered, and the next instant the saber, wielded with all the power of the Spaniard's knotty muscles, clove his left arm from the shoulder, sheared down through his ribs, and wedged deep in his pelvis.

Guzman, grunting and swearing as he twisted his blade out of the prisoning tissue and bone, sweating in fear of an attack before he could free the weapon, heard the rising thunder of the mob, and the hair lifted on his head. He knew that roar—the hunting yell of men, the thunder that has shaken the thrones of the world all down through the ages. He heard the clatter of hoofs on the streets outside, fierce voices shouting commands.

He turned toward the outer corridor when he heard a voice begging for something, and wheeling back into the chamber, saw, for the first time, the naked figure writhing on the divan. Her limbs and body showed neither gash nor bruise, but her cheeks were wet with tears, the red locks that streamed in wild profusion over her white shoulders were damp with perspiration, and her flesh quivered as if from torture.

"Free me!" she begged. "Zulaikha is dead—free me, in God's name!"

With a muttered oath of impatience, he slashed her cords and turned away again, almost instantly forgetting about her. He did not see her rise and glide through a curtained doorway.

Outside a voice shouted, "Othman! Name of Shaitan, where are you? It is time to mount and ride! I saw you run in here! Devil take you, you black dog, where *are* you?"

A mailed and helmeted figure dashed into the chamber, then halted short.

"What—? *Wellah*! You lied to me!"

"Not I!" responded Guzman cheerfully. "I left the city as I swore to do; but I came back."

"Where is Othman?" demanded al Afdhal. "I followed him in here—Allah!" He plucked his moustaches wildly. "By God, the One True God! Oh, cursed Caphar! Why *must* you slay Othman? All the cities have risen, and the Berbers are fighting the Sudani, who had their hands full already. I ride with my men to aid the Sudani. As for you—I still owe you my life, but there is a limit to all things! In Allah's name, get you gone, and never let me see you again!"

Guzman grinned wolfishly. "You are not rid of me so easily this time, *es Salih Muhammad!*"

The Turk started. "What?"

"Why continue this masquerade?" retorted Guzman. "I knew you when we went into the house of Zahir el Ghazi, which was once the house of es Salih Muhammad. Only a master of the house could be so familiar with its secrets. You helped me kill el Ghazi because the Berber had hired Zaman and the others to kill you. Good enough. But that is not all. I came to Egypt to kill el Ghazi; that is done; but now al Hakim plots the ruin of Spain. He must die; and you must aid me in his overthrow."

"You are mad as al Hakim!" exclaimed the Turk.

"What if I went to the Berbers and told them that you aided me to slay their emir?" asked Guzman.

"They would cut you to pieces!"

"Aye, so they would! But they would likewise cut you to pieces. And the Sudani would aid them; neither loves the Turks. Berbers and blacks together will cut down every Turk in Cairo. Then where is your ambition, when your head is off? I will die, yes; but if I set Sudani, Turk, and Berber to slaying each other, perchance the rebellion will whelm them all, and I will have gained in death what I could not in life."

Es Salih Muhammed recognized the grim determination which lay behind the Castilian's words.

"I see I must slay you, after all!" he muttered, drawing his scimitar. The next instant the chamber resounded to the clash of steel.

At the first pass Guzman realized that the Turk was the finest swordsman he had ever met; he was ice where the Spaniard was fire. To his reluctance to kill es Salih was added the knowledge that he was opposed by a greater swordsman than himself. And the thought nerved him to desperate fury, so that the headlong recklessness that had always been his weakness became his strength. His life did not matter; but if he fell in that bloodstained chamber, Castile fell with him.

Outside the walls of el Kahira the mob surged and ravened, torches showered sparks, and steel drank and reddened. Inside the chamber of dead Zulaikha the curved blades sang and whistled. "Smite, Diego de Guzman!" they sang. Spain hangs on your arm. Strike for the glories of yesterday and the splendors of tomorrow. Strike for the thunder of arms, the rustle of banners in the mountain winds, the agony of endeavor, and the blood of martyrdom; strike for the spears of the uplands, the black-haired women, fires on the red hearths, and the trumpets of empires yet to be! Strike for the unborn kingdoms, the pageantry of glory, and the great galleons rolling across a golden sea to a world undreamed! Strike for the wonder that is Spain, aged and ever ageless, the phoenix of nations, rising for ever from the ashes of a dead past to burn among the standards of the world!

Through his parted lips es Salih Muhammad's breath hissed. Under his dark skin grew an ashy hue. Skill nor craft availed him against this blazing-eyed incarnation of fury who came on in an irresistible surge, smiting like a smith on an anvil.

Under the brown-crusted bandage Guzman's wound was bleeding afresh, and the blood poured down his temple, but his sword was like a flaming wheel. The Turk could only parry; he had no opportunity to strike back.

Es Salih Muhammad was fighting for personal ambition; Diego de Guzman was fighting for the future of a nation.

A last gasping heave of thew-wrenching effort, an explosive burst of dynamic power, and the scimitar was beaten from the Turk's hand. He reeled back with a cry, not of pain or fear, but of despair. Guzman, his broad breast heaving from his exertions, turned away.

"I will not cut you down myself," he said. "Nor will I force an oath from you at sword's edge. You would not keep it. I go to the Berbers, and my doom—and yours. Farewell; I would have made you vizir of Egypt!"

"Wait!" panted es Salih, grasping at a hanging for support. "Let us reason this matter! What do you mean?"

"What I say!" Guzman wheeled back from the door, galvanized with a feeling that he had the desperate game in his hand at last. "Do you not realize that at the instant you hold the balance of power? The Sudani and the Berbers fight each other, and the Cairenes fight both! Neither faction can win without your support. The way you throw your Memluks will be the deciding factor. You planned to support the Sudani and crush both the Berbers and the rebels. But suppose you threw in your lot with the Berbers? Suppose you appeared as the *leader of the revolt, the upholder* of the orthodox creed against a blasphemer? El Ghazi is dead; Othman is dead; the mob has no leader. You are the only strong man left in Cairo. You sought honors under al Hakim; greater honors are yours for the asking! Join the Berbers with your Turks, and stamp out the Sudani? The mob will acclaim you as a liberator. Kill al Hakim! Set up another caliph, with yourself as vizir, and real ruler! I will ride at your side, and my sword is yours!"

Es Salih, who had been listening like a man in a dream, gave a sudden shout of laughter, like a drunken man. Real-

ization that Guzman wished to use him as a pawn to crush
a foe of Spain was drowned in the heady wine of personal
ambition.

"*Done!*" he trumpeted. "To horse, brother! You have
shown me the way I sought! Es Salih Muhammad shall yet
rule Egypt!"

7

In the great square in el Mansuriya, the tossing torches
blazed on a maelstrom of straining, plunging figures,
screaming horses, and lashing blades. Men brown, black,
and white fought hand-to-hand, Berber, Sudani, Egyptian,
gasping, cursing, slaying, and dying.

For a thousand years Egypt had slept under the heel of
foreign masters; now she awoke, and crimson was the
awakening.

Like brainless madmen, the Cairenes grappled the black
slayers, dragging them bodily from their saddles, slashing
the girths of the frenzied horses. Rusty pikes clanged
against lances. Fire burst out in a hundred places, mounting into the skies until the herdsmen on Mukattam awoke
and gaped in wonder. From all the suburbs poured wild
and frantic figures, a roaring torrent with a thousand
branches all converging on the great square. Hundreds of
still shapes, in mail or striped kaftans, lay under the tram-
pling hoofs, the stamping feet, and over them the living
screamed and hacked.

The square lay in the heart of the Sudani quarter, into
which had come ravening the blood-mad Berbers while the
bulk of the blacks had been fighting the mob in other parts
of the city. Now, withdrawn in haste to their own quarter,
the ebony swordsmen were overwhelming the Berbers with
sheer numbers, while the mob threatened to engulf both
hordes. The Sudani, under their captain Izz ed din, maintained some semblance of order, which gave them an advantage over the unorganized Berbers and the leaderless
mob.

The maddened Cairenes were smashing and plundering
the houses of the blacks, dragging forth howling women;
the blaze of burning buildings made the square swim in an
ocean of fire.

Somewhere there began the whir of Tatar kettledrums, above the throb of many hoofs.

"The Turks at last," panted Izz ed din. "They have loitered long enough! And where in Allah's name is Othman?"

Into the square raced a frantic horse, foam flying from the bit-rings. The rider reeled in the saddle, gay-hued garments in tatters, ebony skin laced with crimson.

"Izz ed din!" he screamed, clinging to the flying mane with both hands. "*Izz ed din!*"

"Here, fool!" roared the Sudani, catching the other's bridle and hurling the horse back on its haunches.

"Othman is dead!" shrieked the man above the roar of the flames and the rising thunder of the onrushing kettledrums. "The Turks have turned on us! They slay our brothers in the palaces! Aie! They come!"

With a deafening thunder of hoofs and an earth-shaking roll of drums, the squadrons of mailed spearmen burst upon the square, cleaving the waves of carnage, riding down friend and foe alike. Izz ed din saw the dark, exultant face of es Salih Muhammad beneath the blazing arc of his scimitar, and with a roar he reined full at him, his house troops swirling in behind him.

But with a strange war cry a rider in Moorish garb rose in the stirrups and smote, and Izz ed din went down; and over the slashed bodies of his captains stormed the hoofs of the slayers, a dark, roaring river that thundered on into the flame riven night.

On the rocky spurs of Mukattam the herdsmen watched and shivered, seeing the blaze of fire and slaughter from the Gate el Futuh to the mosque of Ibn Tulun; and the clangor of swords was heard as far south as El Fustat, where pallid nobles trembled in their garden-lapped palaces.

Like a crimson foaming, frothing, flame-faceted torrent, the tides of fury overflowed the quarters and gushed through the Gate of Zuweyla, staining the streets of el Kahira, the Victorious. In the great Beyn el Kasreyn, where ten thousand men could be paraded, the Sudani made their last stand, and there they died, hemmed in by helmeted Turks, shrieking Berbers and frantic Cairenes.

It was the mob which first turned its attention to al Hakim. Rushing through the arabesqued bronze doors of the Great East Palace, the ragged hordes streamed howling down the corridors through the Golden Gates into the great Golden Hall, tearing aside the curtain of gilt filigree to reveal an empty golden throne. Silk embroidered tapestries were ripped from the freized walls by grimed and bloody fingers; sardonyx tables were overthrown with a clatter of gold enameled vessels; eunuchs in crimson robes fled squeaking, slave-girls screamed in the hands of the ravishers.

In the Great Emerald Hall, al Hakim stood like a statue on a furstrewn dais. His white hands twitched, his eyes were clouded; he seemed like a drunken man. At the entrance of the hall clustered a handful of faithful servants, beating back the mob with drawn swords. A band of Berbers ploughed through the motley throng and closed with the black slaves, and in that storm of swordstrokes, no man had time to glance at the white, rigid figure on the dais.

Al Hakim felt a hand tugging at his elbow, and looked into the face of Zaida, seeing her as in a dream.

"Come, my lord!" she urged. "All Egypt has risen against you! Think of your own life! Follow me!"

He suffered her to lead him. He moved like a man in a trance, mumbling "But I am God! How can a god know defeat? How can a god die?"

Drawing aside the tapestry she led him into a secret alcove and down a long narrow corridor. Zaida had learned well the secrets of the Great Palace during her brief sojourn there. Through dim spice-scented gardens she led him hurriedly, through a winding street amidst flat-topped houses. She had thrown her *khalat* over him. None of the few folk they met heeded the hastening pair. A small gate, hidden behind clustering palms, let them through the wall. North and east el Kahira was hemmed in by empty desert. They had come out on the eastern side. Behind them and far away down the south rose the roar of flames and slaughter, but about them was only the desert, silence, and the stars. Zaida halted, and her eyes burned in the starlight as she stood unspeaking.

"I am God," muttered al Hakim dazedly. "Suddenly the world was in flames. Yet I am God—"

He scarcely felt the Venetian's strong arms about him in a last terrible embrace. He scarcely heard her whisper, "You gave me into the hands of a black beast! Whereby I fell into the clutches of my rival, who dealt me such shame as men do not dream of! I guided your escape because none but Zaida shall destroy you, al Hakim, fool who thought you were a god!"

Even as he felt the mortal bite of her dagger, he moaned, "Yet I am God—and the gods can not die—" Somewhere a jackal began to yelp.

Back in el Kahira, in the Great East Palace, whose mosaics were fouled with blood, Diego de Guzman, a blood-stained figure, turned to es Salih Muhammad, equally disheveled and stained.

"Where is al Hakim?"

"What matter?" laughed the Turk. "He has fallen; we are lords of Egypt this night, you and I! Tomorrow another will sit in the seat of the caliph, a puppet whose string I pull. Tomorrow I will be vizir, and you—ask what you will! But tonight we rule in naked power, by the sheen of our swords!"

"Yet I would like to drive my saber through al Hakim as a fitting climax to this night's work," answered Guzman.

But it was not to be, though men with thirsty daggers ranged through tapestried halls and arched chambers until to hate and rage began to be added wonder and the superstitious awe which grows into legends of miraculous disappearances, and through mysteries invokes the supernatural. Time turns devils and madmen into saints and *hadjis*; afar in the mountains of Lebanon the Druses await the coming again of al Hakim the Divine. But though they wait until the trumpets have blown for the passing of ten thousand years, they will be no nearer the portals of Mystery. And only the jackals which haunt the hills of Mukattam and the vultures which fold their wings on the towers of Bab el Vezir could tell the ultimate destiny of the man who would be God.

The Track of Bohemond

THE TRACK OF BOHEMOND

As the moon glided from behind a mass of fleecy clouds, etching the shadows of the woods in a silvery glow, the man sprang into a dark clump of bushes, like a hunted thing that fears the disclosing light. As a clink of shod hoofs came plainly to him, he drew further back into his covert, scarcely daring to breathe. In the silence a nightbird called sleepily, and he heard, in the distance, the lazy lap of waters against the shore. The moon slid again behind a drifting cloud, just as the horseman emerged from the trees on the other side of the small glade. The man, hugging his covert, cursed silently. He could make out only a vague moving mass; could hear only the clink of stirrups and the creak of leather. Then the moon came out again, and, with a deep gasp of relief, the hider sprang from among the bushes.

The horses reared and snorted, the rider yelped a startled oath, and a short spear gleamed in his lifted hand. The apparition which had so suddenly sprung to his horse's head was not one calculated to reassure a lonely wayfarer. It was a tall, rangily powerful man, naked but for a loincloth, his steely muscles rippling in the moonlight.

"Back, or I run you through!" snarled the horseman, in Turki. "Who are you, in Satan's name?"

"Roger de Bracy," answered the other, in Norman French. "Speak softly. We are scarce a mile from a Moslem rendezvous, and they may have scouts out. I marvel that you have not been taken. Up the shore, in a small bay screened with tall trees, there are three galleys hidden, and I saw the glitter of arms ashore. This night I escaped from the galley of the famed pirate, the Arab, Yusef ibn Zalim, where I have toiled for months at the oars. He made the rendezvous, for what reason I know not but, fearing treachery of some sort from the Turks, anchored outside the bay. And now he lies at the bottom of the gulf, for I broke my chain, came quietly upon him as he drowsed in the bows, strangled him, and swam ashore."

The horseman grunted, sitting his horse like a statue, etched in the moonlight. He was tall, clad in gray chain mail which did not hide the hard lines of his rangy limbs, an iron cap pushed back carelessly on his steel-hooded head. Even in the uncertain light, the fugitive was impressed by the man's hawk-like, predatory features.

"I think you lie," he said, speaking Norman French with a peculiar accent. "You, a galley slave, with your hair new-cropped and your face freshly-shaven? And what Moslem galleys would dare hide on the European shore, so close to the city?"

"Why, by God," answered the other in evident surprise, "You can not deny that I am a Christian. As to my hair and beard, I think it a poor thing that a cavalier should allow himself to become sloven, even in captivity. One of the captives on board the galley was a Greek barber, and only this morning I prevailed upon him to shear and shave me. As for the other, all men know that the Moslems steal up and down the Bosphorus and the Sea of Marmara almost at will. But we risk our lives standing here babbling. Give me a stirrup and let us be gone."

"I think not," muttered the horseman. "You have seen too much."

And with a powerful heave of his whole frame, he drove the spear straight toward the other's broad chest. So unexpected was the action that it was only the instinctive movement of the victim which saved him. Caught flatfooted, his steel trap coordination yet electrified him a flashing fraction of an instant quicker than the driving steel, which cut the skin on his shoulder as it hissed past him. But it was not blind instinct which caused him to grasp the spear-shaft and jerk back savagely. Rage at the unprovoked attack woke the killing lust in his brain. The avoiding of the blow and the jerk of the spear-shaft were the work of an instant. Overreached and off-balance from the missed stroke, the horseman tumbled headlong from the saddle, full on his antagonist's breast, and they crashed to the ground together, the horseman's carelessly-worn helmet falling from his head. The horse snorted and bolted to the edge of the trees.

The horseman had released the spear as he fell, and now, close-locked, the fighters rolled across the open space and crashed among the bushes. The mailed hand clutched at the sheathed dagger, but Bracy was quicker. With a volcanic heave, he reared himself above his antagonist, clutching a heavy stone on which his fingers had blindly closed.

The dagger was out, gleaming in the moonlight, but before it could drive home the stone crashed with stunning force on the mail-clad head. The flexible coif was not enough protection against such a blow. The pliant links did not part, but they gave, and beneath them the striker felt the skull crunch under the blow. And with fully roused ferocity, the ex-slave struck again and again, until his foeman lay motionless beneath him, blood seeping sluggishly from beneath the iron hood.

Then, panting, he rose, flinging aside the crude weapon, and glared down at the vanquished. Still shaken with fury and surprise, he shook his head bewilderedly. Then a sudden thought came to him, and he wondered that it had not occurred to him before. The horseman had come from the direction of the Moslem camp. Surely it had been impossible for him to have ridden past it unchallenged. He must have been in the camp itself. Then that meant that the fellow was somehow in league with the paynim, and again Roger shook his head. He had learned much of the ways of the East since he had ridden down the Danube in the vanguard of Peter the Hermit. Byzantine and Moslem were not always at each other's throats. Sometimes they dealt together secretly, to the confounding of the westerners. But Roger had never heard of a Crusader turning renegade—and this man, in the armor of a Cross Wearer, was no Greek.

Yielding to urgent necessity, Roger began to strip the dead. The dead man was clean-shaven, with square-cut yellow hair. As far as appearances went, he might have been a Norman, but Bracy remembered his alien accent. The ex-galley slave hurriedly donned the harness, settled the sword belt more firmly about his lean loins, and looked about for the iron cap, which he placed on his tawny locks. All fitted him as if made for him. Inch for inch, the unknown attacker and he had been a perfect match. He stroked the hilt of the long broadsword, and felt like a man again, for the first time in months. The clink of the scabbard against his mail-sheathed thigh reminded him that he was again Sir Roger de Bracy, knight of the Cross, and one of England's surest swords.

No sound save the distant twittering of nightbirds disturbed the silence as he caught the charger, which was calmly grazing at the edge of the woods. As he swung into the saddle, the long months of degradation and grinding toil fell away from him like a cast-off mantle, leaving only a grim determination to pay the debt he owed the worshippers of Muhammad. He smiled bleakly as he remembered the dying gurgles of Yusef ibn Zalim, but his face darkened as another visage rose before him, mocking in the moonlight—a lean hawk face, crowned by a peaked helmet with a heron's feather. Prince Othman, son of Kilidg Arslan, the Red Lion of the Seljuks. The phantom mocked, but there would be another day and, scant in all other things, Norman patience, when laid toward vengeance, was deep and abiding as the North Sea which bred it.

Roger left the spear where it lay, but he unslung the kite-shaped shield which hung at the saddle-bow, and, wary as a wolf, plunged into the shadows of the trees, in the direction in which he had been going before the adventure. There was no insignia on the shield, but on the breast of the hauberk a strange emblem was worked in gold—something that looked like a falcon, and was unmistakably Grecian in its artistry.

The woods through which he rode were now as deserted as if he were the last man on earth. He followed the shoreline as near as he dared, guiding his course by the distant lap of the waves, and the terrain was rolling and uneven. After some three hours, the lights of Constantinople blazed through the trees as he mounted rises, then vanished as he dipped into hollows. It was, he calculated, somewhat past midnight when he rode into the outskirts of the city which, separate from the greater metropolis and yet a part of it, sprawled along the northern bank of the Golden Horn. This was the quarter of the Venetian traders and other foreign merchants—straggling streets of carved wooden buildings and more substantial houses of stone. But before he reached the heart of the city a wall halted him, and the watch at the gate hailed him. A torch in a mailed hand was reached down, to be brandished almost in his face; but before he could name himself, he saw a figure in black velvet lean from the wall and scrutinize him closely. There followed a few low words in Greek, and the gates swung open, to clang to behind him as he reined his steed through. He prepared to ride away down the street, when the velveted figure darted out and caught his rein.

"Light, light!" exclaimed this person impatiently "What is in your mind? Have you forgotten our master's instructions? Here, Manuel, take this steed to the pier

Come with me, my Lord Thorvald. Wait! Someone may recognize you! I had not known you, in those western trappings and without your beard, but for the golden falcon on your hauberk. But someone might—take this silken scarf and mask your features with it."

Sir Roger took it and wrapped it loosely about his coif, so that only his steely eyes were visible. It was apparent that he had been mistaken for the man he had slain. It was almost certain that he was going into danger, but it was as certain that if he declared his identity, he would just as quickly find himself in danger. The name of Thorvald stirred some faint recollection at the back of the Norman's mind, and he instinctively touched the hilt of the sword at his girdle.

The guide led the way through narrow, deserted streets, until Roger knew that they were not far from piers that gave on to the strait, and halted at the door of a squat stone tower, evidently a relic of an earlier, ruder age. Someone looked out through a slit in the door.

"Open, fool!" hissed the man in velvet. "It is Angelus and the lord, Thorvald the Smiter."

Hinges creaked as the door swung inward. Sir Roger followed, in a maze of fantastic speculations. Thorvald the Smiter—so that was the man he had battered to death with a stone in the glade. He had heard of the Norseman who was the grimmest swordsman in the Varangian Guards, that band of mercenaries, northern slayers maintained by the Greeks. He had seen them about the palace of the Emperor—tall, bearded men, in crested helmets and scarlet-edged cloaks and gilded mail. But what was a Varangian captain doing riding from a Turkish rendezvous in the night, clad in the mail of a Crusader?

Roger began to feel that he had stepped into a pit full of hidden snakes in the dark, but he drew the scarf closer about his features, and followed his guide through a short, dark corridor into a small, dimly-lit chamber. Someone was sitting in a great ornate chair, and to this figure the guide bowed almost to the floor, and withdrew, closing the door behind him. The Norman stood, straining his eyes, and as they became accustomed to the dim candlelight, the form in the chair slowly took shape. It was a short, stocky man who sat there, wrapped in a plain dark satin cloak which hid all other details of his costume. A featherless slouch hat and a mask lay on a table close at hand, arguing that the man had come in secrecy, fearing recognition. The knight's eyes were drawn to the other's face; the blue-black beard was carefully curled, the dark locks bound back from the broad forehead with a cloth-of-gold band; beneath it, wide brown eyes gleamed with an innate vitality. Sir Roger started violently. In God's name, into what dark undercurrent of plot and intrigue had he fallen? The man in the chair was Alexius Comnenus, emperor of the Byzantine empire.

"You have come quickly enough, Thorvald," said the emperor—and Sir Roger did not reply, being too busy wondering what mysterious matter had brought the emperor of the East from his marble-pillared palace in the dead of night to an obscure tower in the outer city.

"You ride with a loose rein. The messenger I sent did not tell you why I wished your presence?"

Sir Roger shook his head, at a venture. Alexius nodded.

"I told him to only bid you hasten here. But tell me—in your cruisings among the Black Sea corsairs, have they ever suspected your true identity?"

Again Sir Roger shook his head.

Alexius smiled.

"Sparing of speech as ever, old wolf! It is well. But just now I have work for you even more important than keeping an eye on the Moslem pirates. So I sent for you . . .

"Thorvald, since you went spying among the Turks, the hosts of the Franks have come and gone. They did not come as came Peter and Hermit and Gautier-sans-Avoir: rabbles of paupers and knaves. They came with war-horses, and wagon trains, cavaliers and women, archers, pikemen, and men-at-arms—all afire with zeal for recovering the Holy Sepulcher.

"First came Hugh of Vermandois, brother of the French king, in a ship with a few attendants. I feasted him royally, made him rich gifts, and persuaded him to take oath of allegiance to me. Then came others: St. Gilles of Provence, Godfrey of Bouillon and his brothers, and that devil, Bohemond. All took oaths of fealty except the stubborn Count of Provence—but I fear him not. He is zealous, and all for Jerusalem. Bohemond is another matter; he would cut the throat of Saint Paul to gratify his ambition.

"They took Nicaea for me, but I tricked them out of it, sending Manuel Butumites to make a secret treaty with the Turks, and now the city is garrisoned with my soldiers.

Now the host marches southward, toward Palestine, and in the hills of Asia Minor Kilidg Arslan will doubtless cut all their throats. Yet it may be that they will prevail against him. At least, they will deal him such great blows that he will be no more a menace for Byzantium for years to come. Nay, I fear him less than I fear that devil, Bohemond, whom naught but luck helped me to defeat some twelve years ago when he came up out of Italy with Robert Guiscard.

"Thorvald, I sent for you because there is no man east of the Danube able to stand against you in swordplay. I have laid my plans well, yet Bohemond has slipped through my fingers before. With the corsairs, you have been my eyes and my brain; now you must be my sword. Your task is to see that Bohemond does not leave the field alive when Kilidg Arslan comes up against the Franks. Hew not to the right nor to the left, but aim your strokes at him! This is my command—come what will, be the fortune of war what it may, whoever conquers or loses, lives or dies—*kill Bohemond!*"

The emperor's voice rang vibrantly in the chamber, his dark eyes flashed magnetically. Roger felt the force of the man's dynamic personality like a physical impact.

"The Crusaders have already been a few days on the road," said Alexis, "But they travel slowly, for their cavalry must keep pace with their wagons. It will be easy for you to pass beyond them and reach the Sultan before he joins battle, with the arrangements I have made. Your steed is already on a boat—a fresh steed, that is. The boat lies at the foot of the Green Pier—but Angelus will guide you thither. On the Asiatic side, Ortuk Khan, he whom men call the Rider of the Wind, will meet you and lead you to the Sultan. Theodore Butumites is with Godfrey—" he broke off suddenly, staring at Roger's coif. "By Saint Paul," said he, "there is fresh blood on your mail, Thorvald. Are you wounded?"

His mind was full of whirling conjectures, Roger absently answered, "No."

Instantly he realized his mistake. Alexius started, and his keen eyes flared with suspicion. Every faculty of the man was as sharp as a whetted sword.

"That's not Thorvald's voice!" he snarled, and with a motion quick as a striking hawk he ripped the scarf from the knight's head. Both men leaped to their feet, the emperor recoiling with a scream.

"Spy! This is not Thorvald! Ho, the guard!"

Sir Roger's sword flashed in the candlelight. Alexius leaped back, catlike, and the blade sheared a lock of hair from his head as it hummed past. Instantly, it seemed, the room swarmed with armed men, pouring in from each door. But the sight of the emperor fleeing desperately from the murderous attack of one they supposed to be a loyal servitor, momentarily froze their wits. Roger alone knew exactly what he had to do. No time for another stroke at the emperor, who had sprung behind the great chair, and was shouting for his soldiers to cut down the imposter. The Norman wheeled toward the nearest door, where three men barred his way. The first went down, casque and skull cloven by the knight's shearing stroke, and as the other two sprang in, hacking, Sir Roger ducked and drove in headlong behind his shield. They reeled apart before the impact, and the Norman's bull-like drive carried him through the door and into the corridor. Recovering his balance in full flight, he raced down the short hallway. The outer door had been left unguarded. A quick fumbling at the chains and bolts and he was through, slamming the door in the faces of his yelling pursuers; and he fled down the narrow street, cursing the clang of his mail-shod feet on the flags. He could not hope to evade his attackers, but ahead of him were the broad rows of green marble steps leading down to the water's edge, known as the Green Pier. He knew it of old. At the foot of the steps lay a broad boat, the steersman holding the craft to the lower step by a boathook thrust into a ring set in the marble. A rangy Arab horse was held quiet by grooms, and the brawny oarsmen gaped at his haste, as the knight ran down the steps and sprang into the boat.

"Give way!" he growled. The boatmen hesitated. Up the street came the clamor of pursuit. Steel clanked and torches tossed.

"Push off!" The boatmen saw the glimmer of naked steel in the knight's mailed hand. They were unarmed laborers, not fighters. The steersman disengaged the boathook and, thrusting it against the steps, shoved powerfully. The heavy craft swung out into the current, and the rowers bent to their labor. They moved out into the shadowy, star-mirroring reaches and, looking back, Sir Roger saw mailed figures racing up and down the piers, seeking a boat. But luck was with him; the wharfs had vanished in the distance before he heard, faintly, the clack of oarlocks, and knew that the pursuit had taken to water.

The rowers, eyeing his dripping sword, bent to their oars as strongly as if he had been Alexius himself. The noise of the pursuing boats drew steadily nearer; they dogged his trail throughout that three-mile row, and the last few hundred yards he saw starlight glinting on helmets. But he was still a few score paces ahead when the low prow nudged the Asian shore. Springing to the saddle, he spurred the steed over the side and plunged into the darkness.

There he had the advantage. His pursuers were not mounted, although it was quite possible that there might be steeds for them in the vicinity. He headed eastward at a long swinging gallop. In the darkness, he was aware only of a vague shadowy landscape of low hills and flat stretches, with occasional blurs he took to be herders' huts. Clouds had again obscured the stars, and the moon had long set. He drew rein, moving along almost at a walk in the thick darkness, when suddenly he realized that there was a movement about him. He heard the restive stamp of hoofs and the jingle of trappings. A voice swore in a tongue alien yet hatefully familiar. Turks! He had ridden blindly into them in the darkness. They were all about him, hemming him in. Stealthily, he reached for his sword; then a sibilant voice inquired, "Is it you, lord Thorvald?"

"Who else?" growled the knight, striving to assume the harsh accents of the Norseman.

"Strike a light," muttered another voice. "Best be certain."

There was the clink of flint of steel, and a tiny flame sprang up, illuminating a ring of bearded, hawk-like faces, glinting on polished shoulder-plates, burnished helmets and ring-mail. The tall warrior who held the light leaned forward and eyed Sir Roger intently.

"There is the gold falcon, see?" said the Moslem. "Besides, look at the sword. The face of the Smiter is not so familiar to me that I would know it without the beard, but, by Allah, I would recognize that blade anywhere!"

The light went out. Behind them, toward the shore, came a distant murmur as of many men. Torches tossed erratically. Roger felt the warriors about him stiffen suspiciously, and he heard the stir of scimitars in their sheaths.

"Who moves yonder?" asked the tall Moslem.

"Men the emperor sent to see that I got safely across," answered Sir Roger. "He feared lest the Franks had left spies behind them. Why do we linger here? It is not long until dawn."

"True," muttered the Turk. "And we were better safe in the hills before daylight. You came ahead of time. We were riding to the shore to meet you when you rode in among us. We were lucky that we did not miss each other in this accursed dark. Ride in the midst of us, my lord."

They moved off in a canter that grew into an easy swinging gallop that ate up the miles. As dawn rose, the band, like a flying band of desert ghosts, crossed the shoulder of a blue mountain and vanished in the hills beyond.

Daylight showed the knight his companions: a score of hawk-like riders in the steel and gold and leather of the Seljuks. They rode like the wind, like men who do not have to spare their mounts, and he guessed that relays awaited them in the hills, for already they were beyond the easternmost bounds of Alexius's domain. They had not suspected him, and in that grim masquerade he had made no plans. He had but followed the trend of the tide, caught in the eddy, moving without volition of his own. He knew what he would do if the opportunity arose, but for the moment he was helpless, with only half-facts at his command.

Indeed, the whole course of his life had lain along those lines, he thought morosely, to the tune of the drumming hoofs. Born in a castle built up out of the ruins of a Saxon keep, almost exactly a year after the Battle of Hastings, Sir Roger's impulses and instincts had led him into such a tangle of affairs that he himself despaired of unravelling it. So, he departed from the land of his birth, not much in advance of soldiers sent by the exasperated king. Resentment toward his leige led him into the service of Duke Robert of Normandy, who was continually at loggerheads with his fox-like brother; but Roger's impatient spirit could not endure the procrastinating and wine-guzzling habits of the Duke, however generous Norman swords had carved in southern Italy. He had ridden beside Tancred and shared the yellow fighting-cock's adventures, but Bohemond's everlasting ambition had palled on the English knight. The scene shifted to the Rhineland, where he was a participant in the gory climax of Duke Godfrey's feud with Rudolph of Swabia. Then came the dawn of the Crusades, Urban's trumpet-like invocation, and men selling their lands to buy horses to carry them eastward to salvation and the slaughter of the heathen.

The barons were gathering, but, to the more penniless, they moved too slowly. Besides, there was an unexpressed doubt that there would be enough plunder to go around, once the great lords took the field. A horde of ploughmen, beggars, and vagabonds rallied around Peter the Hermit, kissing the ground on which he walked, and getting their brains kicked out by his pessimistic jackass when they tried to pluck out the animal's gray hairs for holy relics. Peter emulated Urban, and great was his magnetic power. To the gaunt fanatics, likewise, came a sprinkling of poverty-ridden knights and nobles, and the motley horde moved eastward down the Danube, singing hosannas and stealing pigs.

Among these poverty-ridden knights were Roger de Bracy and his brother-at-arms, Gautier-sans-Avoir—the Penniless. They tried to herd the horde, but they might as well have tried to herd the vultures of the Carpathians. The ravenous pilgrims, some eighty thousand strong, passed like a famine through the land of the Hungarians, fought with Alexius's outposts, fell on their knees to greet the spires of Constantinople, and settled themselves down, apparently, to devour all the food in the empire.

When they began to hack sheets of lead from the cathedral roofs to sell in the marketplace, Alexius, in despair, had them ferried across the Bosphorus, and there herds of them straggled away into the hills and managed to get themselves butchered by a raiding band of Turks. Gautier and his comrades, with more valor than discretion, sallied forth to rescue the miserable wretches, and ran into a veritable army of chanting, heron-feathered riders. There died Gautier, on a heap of Turkish corpses, with his mad and gallant gentlemen, and Sir Roger, recovering his senses after a battle-ax, shattering on his casque, had dashed him into darkness, found himself bound with chains along with the remnant of his band, and being marched to Nicaea, where he was sold to a tall, lean vulture in steel and gold: the Arab, Yusef ibn Zalim. His lean ship cruised the shores of the Black Sea, and up and down the Bosphorus from the Black Sea to the Mediterranean; and Roger saw sights, both in the belly of the galley and on the bloodstained deck, which haunted his dreams for the rest of his life. Yet these red visions were not able to dim one scene of horror and madness: his comrade, Gautier, dying among the dead, and a lean, scornful horseman in gilded mail and heron-feathered helmet, rearing his horse to bring down the hoofs crashing in the bloodstained, dying face.

"This Othman, son of Kilidg Arslan, deals with infidels!" The scornful words rang in Roger de Bracy's ears above the wash of waves, the splintering of the oars, and the red clamor of battle.

Now the English knight found himself galloping in company with Turkish reivers, in a grim masquerade, bound for a destination of which he knew nothing, save that it would doubtless bring him face to face with Prince Othman and his grim sire. He kept looking back for signs of pursuit; but if Alexius's soldiers had followed, they had missed the trail.

At noon the riders came upon a squat tower in the hills, where food and drink and fresh horses awaited them. They were in the outlying domain of Kilidg Arslan, the Red Lion of Islam, but as yet they had seen no villages, only ruins, relics of ancient Roman rule. They spent scant time at their meal, but swung to the saddle and spurred up their mounts again.

And all through the hot, dry summer afternoon they swung through the rugged hills at a gallop, pushing their horses unmercifully. Roger had kept his eyes open for outriders of the Crusaders, or signs of their march, but he realized that they must be riding to the north of the Cross Wearers' line of march. He asked no questions, nor did Ortuk Khan vouchsafe any information. He rode along humming a song about a warrior whose skill at racing had gained for him the name of the Rider of the Wind. Roger sensed that this matter was the Seljuk's one weakness and vanity.

At moonrise, and again when the moon had set, they came again upon a relay of fresh horses in the hills, with a dusty courier, with whom Ortuk Khan talked long. After the latter talk, he seated himself crosslegged on the ground, and signed for the men to prepare the meal.

"We are within striking distance of our objective," said he to Roger. "We have covered in hours what took the Cross Wearers days to traverse. We are now but three hours riding from the camp of the infidels. At dawn we will go forward, and join in the battle."

Roger had been puzzling in his mind as to how Alexius meant to wipe out Bohemond without destroying the rest of the Crusaders, and he ventured a question. "Repeat to me the trap the Red Lion has set for the Cross Wearers."

"This it is," answered Ortuk Khan readily. "Maimoun—Bohemond—and his people march ahead of the main body of the infidels. This night they lie in camp where the hills slope down into the plain of Doryleum, awaiting the coming up of Senjhil—St. Gilles—and the rest.

"But Alexius has given these others a guide to lead them astray. You see yonder peak which stands up in the night above the other hills? Were you to ride due south on a straight line from that peak for five hours, you would come upon their camp.

"At dawn, the Red Lion will ride in from the east, and crush Maimoun and his iron men between his hands. Then he will move on Senjhil and the others and sweep them from the earth."

So Alexius was hand-and-glove with the Seljuk, as far as destroying Bohemond went; it had been obvious from the beginning. The traitorous guide mentioned by Ortuk Khan must be Theodore Butumites. Alexius had said the Greek was with St. Gilles. Roger looked long at the peak pointed out to him by the Turk, and fixed the landmarks of the country firmly in his mind. Doryleum was three hours' ride to the east; the camp of the others five hours' ride to the south. On the eastern hills was crawling the first faint whitening of dawn. The Turks were bestirring themselves, saddling their horses and buckling their armor.

"Ortuk Khan," said Sir Roger casually, rising and laying his hand on the mane of the lean Turkoman steed which had been given him, "dawn is lifting and we must quickly be on our way to join the Red Lion. But, to breathe our steeds, I will race you to yonder knoll."

The Turk smiled. "It is still three hours' hard riding to Doryleum, my lord, and our steeds will have much work to do after we reach the field."

"It is only a few hundred paces to the knoll," answered Sir Roger. "I have heard much of your skill at racing, and wished to have the honor of striving against you. Of course, there are many stones and boulders, and the footing is perilous. If you fear the attempt—"

Ortuk Khan's face darkened.

"That was ill said, oh man men call the Smiter. The folly of one makes fools of wise men. Yet mount, and I will do this childish thing."

They swung to their saddles, reined back their mounts even with each other; then, at a word, were off like bolts from a crossbow. The steel-clad warriors watched the race with interest.

"The footing is not so unstable as the Frank said," quoth one. "Look, their flight is as that of falcons. Ortuk Khan draws ahead."

"But the Smiter is close on his heels!" exclaimed another. "Look, they near the knoll—what is this? The Frank has drawn his sword! It flashes in the dawn-light—Allah!"

A yell of astounded fury rose from the lean warriors. Riding hard, the Norman had disappeared around the knoll; behind him a riderless horse raced away from the still form which lay in a crimson pool among the rocks. The Rider of the Wind had ridden his last race.

Shaking the red drops from his blade, Sir Roger gave the Turkoman horse the rein. He did not look back, though he strained his ears for the drum of pursuing hoofs. Guiding his course by the peak, he passed through the hills like a flying ghost. A short time after sunrise, he crossed a broad track, with marks of broad wagon wheels and the prints of myriad feet and hoofs. The road of Bohemond. Among these prints were fresher hoofprints, unshod, smaller. The prints of Turkish steeds. So the scouts of the Seljuks dogged the Norman column closely.

It was past the middle of the morning when Roger rode into the vast, wideflung camp of the Crusaders. His none-too-tender heart warmed at the familiar sights: knights with falcons on their wrists and giant hounds trailing them, yellow-haired women laughing under canopied pavilions, young esquires burnishing the armor of their lords. It was like a bit of Europe transferred to the bleak hills of Asia Minor. Two hundred thousand people camped here, their fires and tents spreading out over the valley. Some of the pavilions had been taken down, some of the oxen harnessed to the wagons, but there was an air of waiting. Men-at-arms leaned on their pikes, pages wandered through the low bushes, whistling to their hounds. It was as if all the west had streamed eastward. Roger saw flaxen-haired Rhinelanders, black-bearded Spaniards and Provencals,

French, Germans, Austrians. The clatter of a score of different tongues reached him.

The English knight reined through the throngs which stared at his dusty mail and sweaty horse, and halted before the pavilions whose richer colors betokened the leaders of the expedition. He saw them coming forth from their tents in full armor: Godfrey of Bouillon, and his brothers, Eustace and Baldwin of Boulogne; a stocky gray-bearded figure which must be Raymond of St. Gilles, Count of Toulouse. With them was a figure in ornate armor, the burnished plates contrasting with the gray mesh mail coats of the westerners; Roger knew the man must be Theodore Butumites, brother of the new-made duke of Nicaea, and officer of the Greek cataphracts.

The Turkoman charger snorted and tossed its head up and down, froth flying from the bit, as Roger slid to earth. Norman-like, the knight wasted no words.

"My lords," he said bluntly, without preliminary salutation, "I have come to tell you that a battle is forward, and if you would take part, you had best hasten."

"A battle?" It was Eustace of Boulogne, keen as a hunting hound on the scent. "Who fights?"

"Bohemond confronts the Red Lion, even as we stand here."

The barons looked at each other uncertainly, and Butumites laughed.

"The man is mad. How could Kilidg Arslan fall upon Bohemond without passing us? And we have seen no Turks."

"Where is Bohemond?" asked Raymond.

"In the plain of Doryleum, some six hours' hard riding to the north."

"What!" It was an exclamation of unbelief. "How could that be? The lord Theodore has led us in a direct route, through valleys Bohemond missed. The Normans are somewhere behind us, and Theodore has sent his Byzantine scouts to find them and bring them hither, since it is evident that they have become lost in the hills. We are awaiting them before we take up the march."

"It is you who are lost," snapped Sir Roger. "Theodore Butumites is a spy and a traitor, sent by Alexius to lead you astray, while Kilidg Arslan crushes Bohemond—"

"Dog, your life for that!" shouted the fiery Greek, strid-

ing forward, his hand on his sword. Roger fronted him
grimly, gripping his own hilt, but the barons intervened.

"These are serious accusations you bring, friend," said
Godfrey. "What proofs have you of these words?"

"Why, in God's name," exclaimed Roger. "have you not
seen that the Greek has swung further and further south?
The Normans took the straighter course—it is you who
have wandered from the route. Bohemond marched south-
east by south; you have traveled due south. If you follow
this course long enough, you may fetch the Mediterranean,
but you will scarce come to the Holy Land!"

"Who is this rogue?" exclaimed Butumites angrily.

"Duke Godfrey knows me," retorted the Norman. "I am
Roger de Bracy."

"By the saints!" exclaimed Godfrey, a smile lighting his
worn face. "I had thought to recognize you, Roger! But
you have changed—you have changed. My lords," he
turned to the others, "this gentleman is known to me afore-
time—nay, he rode with me into the Lateran, when I—"

He checked himself with the strange aversion he always
felt toward speaking of what he considered his sacrilege in
killing Duke Rudolph in the holy confines.

"But we know him not," answered St. Gilles, with the
caution that always ate at him like a worm in a beam.
"And he comes with a strange tale—he would lead us on a
wild chase, with naught but his own word—"

"God's thunder!" cried Roger, his short Norman patience exhausted. "Shall we gabble here while the Turks
cut Bohemond's throat? It is my word against the Greek's,
and I demand trial—the gauge of combat to decide between us!"

"Well spoken!" exclaimed Ademar, the pope's legate, a
tall man who wore the chain mail of a knight. Such scenes
warmed his heart, which was that of a warrior. "As mouth-
piece of our Holy Father, I declare the righteousness of
such course."

"Well, and let us be at it!" exclaimed Roger, burning
with impatience. "Choose your weapons, Greek!"

Butumites glanced over his dusty mail, and the light-
limbed, sweat-covered steed, and smiled secretly.

"Dare you run a course with sharpened spears?"

This was a matter at which the Franks were more expe-
rienced than the Greeks, but Butumites was of larger-boned
frame than most of his race, well able to compete with the

westerners in physical strength, and he had had experience jousting with the western knights while they lay at Alexius's court. He glanced at his giant black warhorse, accoutered with heavy trappings of silk, steel, and lacquered leather, and smiled again. But Godfrey interposed.

"Nay, masters, this is but a sorry thing, seeing that Sir Roger has come hither on a weary steed, and that more fit for racing than fighting. Nay, Roger, you shall take my steed and lance, and my casque, too."

Butumites shrugged his shoulders. In an instant his crushing advantage had been swept away, but he was still confident. At any rate, he preferred lances to sword strokes, having no desire to encounter the stroke of the great sword that hung at Roger's hip. He had fought Normans before.

Roger took the long, heavy spear, and mounted the steed held by Godfrey's esquires, but refused the heavy helmet, a massive, pot-like affair, without a movable vizor, but with a slit for the eyes. The joust had not then attained its later conventions and formalities; at that early date, a lance-running was either a duel with sharpened weapons or simply a form of training for more serious warfare. A rude course had been formed by the crowd, pressing in on both sides, leaving a broad lane open. In this clear space, the foes trotted apart for a short distance, wheeled, couched their lances, and awaited the signal.

The trumpet blared, and the great horses thundered toward each other. The shining black armor and plumed casque of the Byzantine contrasted strongly with the dusty gray armor and plain iron bassinet of the Norman. Roger knew that Butumites would aim his lance directly at his unprotected face, and he bent low, glaring at his foe above the upper rim of his heavy shield. The hosts gave tongue as the knights shocked together with a rending crash. Both lances shivered to the handgrips, and the horses were hurled back on their haunches. But Roger kept his seat, though half-stunned by the terrible impact, while Butumites was dashed from his saddle as though by a thunderbolt. He lay where he had fallen, his burnished, steel-clad limbs crumpled in the dust, blood oozing from his cracked helmet.

Roger reined in his rearing steed and slid to earth dazedly, his head still ringing. The breaking lance of the Byzantine, glancing from the rim of his shield, had torn his basinet from his head, and all but ripped loose the tendons of his neck. He advanced rather stiffly to the group which had formed about the prostrate Greek. The casque with its nodding plumes had been lifted off, and Butumites looked up at the faces above him with glazed eyes. It was evident that the man was dying. His breastplate was shattered, and his whole breastbone caved inward. Ademar leaned above him, rosary in hand, muttering rapidly.

"My son, have you any confession?"

The dying lips worked, but only a dry rattle came from them. With a terrible effort, the Greek muttered, "Doryleum—Kilidg Arslan—Bohemond—" Blood gushed from his lips and he stiffened, a still figure of burnished metal, steel-sheathed limbs falling awry.

Godfrey went into instant action.

"To horse!" he shouted. "A steed for Sir Roger! Bohemond needs aid, and by the favor of God, he shall not call in vain!"

The throng yelped and the scene became a medley of confusion, knights mounting, men-at-arms buckling on their armor.

"Wait!" exclaimed St. Gilles. "We can not go racing over these hills, wagons and footmen—someone must guard the supplies—"

"Do you this thing, my lord Raymond," said Godfrey, afire with impatience. "Get the wagons under way, and follow with them and the footmen. My horsemen and I will push forward. Roger, lead the way!"

Gates of Empire

GATES OF EMPIRE

The clank of the sour sentinels on the turrets, the gusty uproar of the spring winds, were not heard by those who revelled in the cellar of Godfrey de Courtenay's castle; and the noise these revellers made was bottled up deafeningly within the massive walls.

A sputtering candle lighted those rugged walls, damp and uninviting, flanked with wattled casks and hogsheads over which stretched a veil of dusty cobwebs. From one barrel the head had been knocked out, and leathern drinking-jacks were immersed again and again in the foamy tide, in hands that grew increasingly unsteady.

Agnes, one of the serving-wenches, had stolen the massive iron key to the cellar from the girdle of the steward; and rendered daring by the absence of their master, a small but far from select group were making merry with characteristic heedlessness of the morrow.

Agnes, seated on the knee of the varlet Peter, beat erratic time with a jack to a ribald song both were bawling in different tunes and keys. The ale slopped over the rim of the wobbling jack and down Peter's collar, a circumstance he was beyond noticing.

The other wench, fat Marge, rolled on her bench and slapped her ample thighs in uproarious appreciation of a spicy tale just told by Giles Hobson. This individual might have been the lord of the castle from his manner, instead of a vagabond rapscallion tossed by every wind of adversity. Tilted back on a barrel, booted feet propped on another, he loosened the belt that girdled his capacious belly in its worn leather jerkin, and plunged his muzzle once more into the frothing ale.

"Giles, by Saint Withold his beard," quoth Marge, "madder rogue never wore steel. The very ravens that pick your bones on the gibbet tree will burst their sides a-laughing. I hail ye—prince of all bawdy liars!"

She flourished a huge pewter pot and drained it as stoutly as any man in the realm.

At this moment another reveller, returning from an errand, came into the scene. The door at the head of the stairs admitted a wobbly figure in close-fitting velvet. Through the briefly opened door sounded noises of the night—slap of hangings somewhere in the house, sucking and flapping in the wind that whipped through the crevices; a faint disgruntled hail from a watchman on a tower. A gust of wind whooped down the stair and set the candle to dancing.

Guillaume, the page, shoved the door shut and made his way with groggy care down the rude stone steps. He was not so drunk as the others, simply because, what of his extreme youth, he lacked their capacity for fermented liquor.

"What's the time, boy?" demanded Peter.

"Long past midnight," the page answered, groping unsteadily for the open cask. "The whole castle is asleep, save for the watchmen. But I heard a clatter of hoofs through the wind and rain; methinks 'tis Sir Godfrey returning."

"Let him return and be damned!" shouted Giles, slapping Marge's fat haunch resoundingly. "He may be lord of the keep, but at present we are keepers of the cellar! More ale! Agnes, you little slut, another song!"

"Nay, more tales!" clamored Marge. "Our mistress's brother, Sir Guiscard de Chastillon, has told grand tales of Holy Land and the infidels, but by Saint Dunstan, Giles' lies outshine the knight's truths!"

"Slander not a—hic!—holy man as has been on pilgrimage and Crusade," hiccuped Peter. "Sir Guiscard has seen Jerusalem, and foughten beside the King of Palestine—how many years?"

"Ten year come May Day, since he sailed to Holy Land," said Agnes. "Lady Eleanor had not seen him in all that time, till he rode up to the gate yesterday morn. Her husband, Sir Godfrey, never has seen him."

"And wouldn't know him?" mused Giles, "nor Sir Guiscard him?"

He blinked, raking a broad hand through his sandy mop. He was drunker than even he realized. The world spun like a top and his head seemed to be dancing dizzily on his shoulders. Out of the fumes of ale and a vagrant spirit, a madcap idea was born.

A roar of laughter burst gustily from Giles's lips. He reeled upright, spilling his jack in Marge's lap and bringing a burst of rare profanity from her. He smote a barrelhead with his open hand, strangling with mirth.

"Good lack!" squawked Agnes. "Are you daft, man?"

"A jest!" The roof reverberated to his bull's bellow. "Oh, Saint Withold, a jest! Sir Guiscard knows not his brother-in-law, and Sir Godfrey is now at the gate. Hark ye!"

Four heads, bobbing erratically, inclined toward him as he whispered, as if the rude walls might hear. An instant's bleary silence was followed by boisterous guffaws. They were in the mood to follow the maddest course suggested to them. Only Guillaume felt some misgivings, but he was swept away by the alcoholic fervor of his companions.

"Oh, a devil's own jest!" cried Marge, planting a loud, moist kiss on Giles's ruddy cheek. "On, rogues, to the sport!"

"*En avant!*" bellowed Giles, drawing his sword and waving it unsteadily, and the five weaved up the stairs, stumbling, blundering, and lurching against one another. They kicked open the door, and shortly were running erratically up the wide hall, giving tongue like a pack of hounds.

The castles of the Twelfth Century, fortresses rather than mere dwellings, were built for defense, not comfort.

The hall through which the drunken band was hallooing was broad, lofty, windy, strewn with rushes, now but faintly lighted by the dying embers in a great ill-ventilated fireplace. Rude, sail-like hangings along the walls rippled in the wind that found its way through. Hounds, sleeping under the great table, woke yelping as they were trodden on by blundering feet, and added their clamor to the din.

This din roused Sir Guiscard de Chastillon from dreams of Acre and the sun-drenched plains of Palestine. He bounded up, sword in hand, supposing himself to be beset by Saracen raiders, then realized where he was. But events seemed to be afoot. A medley of shouts and shrieks clamored outside his door, and on the stout oak panels boomed a rain of blows that bade fair to burst the portal inward. The knight heard his name called loudly and urgently.

Putting aside his trembling squire, he ran to the door and cast it open. Sir Guiscard was a tall, gaunt man, with a great beak of a nose and cold grey eyes. Even in his shirt he was a formidable figure. He blinked ferociously at the group limned dimly in the glow from the coals at the other end of the hall. There seemed to be women, children, a fat man with a sword.

This fat man was bawling, "Succor, Sir Guiscard, succor! The castle is forced, and we are all dead men! The robbers of Horsham Wood are within the hall itself!"

Sir Guiscard heard the unmistakable tramp of mailed feet, saw vague figures coming into the hall—figures on whose steel the faint light gleamed redly. Still mazed by slumber, but ferocious, he went into furious action.

Sir Godfrey de Courtenay, returning to his keep after many hours of riding through foul weather, anticipated only rest and ease in his own castle. Having vented his irritation by roundly cursing the sleepy grooms who shambled up to attend his horses, and were too bemused to tell him of his guest, he dismissed his men-at-arms and strode into the donjon, followed by his squires and the gentlemen of his retinue. Scarcely had he entered when the devil's own bedlam burst loose in the hall. He heard a wild stampede of feet, crash of overturned benches, baying of dogs, and an uproar of strident voices, over which one bull-like bellow triumphed.

Swearing amazedly, he ran up the hall, followed by his knights, when a ravening maniac, naked but for a shirt, burst on him, sword in hand, howling like a werewolf.

Sparks flew from Sir Godfrey's basinet beneath the madman's furious strokes, and the lord of the castle almost succumbed to the ferocity of that onslaught before he could draw his own sword. He fell back, bellowing for his men-at-arms. But the madman was yelling louder than he, and from all sides swarmed other lunatics in shirts who assailed Sir Godfrey's dumfounded gentlemen with howling frenzy.

The castle was in an uproar—lights flashing up, dogs howling, women screaming, men cursing, and over all the clash of steel and the stamp of mailed feet.

The conspirators, sobered by what they had raised, scattered in all directions, seeking hiding-places—all except Giles Hobson. His state of intoxication was too magnificent to be perturbed by any such trivial scene. He admired his handiwork for a space, then, finding swords flashing too close to his head for comfort, withdrew, and following some instinct, departed for a hiding-place known to him of old. There he found with gentle satisfaction that he had all the time retained a cobwebbed bottle in his hand. This he emptied, and its contents, coupled with what had already found its way down his gullet, plunged him into extinction for an amazing period. Tranquilly he snored under the straw, while events took place above and around him, and matters moved not slowly.

There in the straw Friar Ambrose found him just as dusk was falling after a harassed and harrying day. The friar, ruddy and well paunched, shook the unpenitent one into bleary wakefulness.

"The saints defend us!" said Ambrose. "Up to your old tricks again! I thought to find you here. They have been searching the castle all day for you; they searched these stables, too. Well that you were hidden beneath a very mountain of hay."

"They do me too much honor," yawned Giles. "Why should they search for me?"

The friar lifted his hands in pious horror.

"Saint Denis is my refuge against Sathanas and his works! Is it not known how you were the ringleader in that madcap prank last night that pitted poor Sir Guiscard against his sister's husband?"

"Saint Dunstan!" quoth Giles, expectorating dryly. "How I thirst! Were any slain?"

"No, by the providence of God. But there is many a broken crown and bruised rib this day. Sir Godfrey nigh fell at the first onset, for Sir Guiscard is a woundy swordsman. But our lord being in full armor, he presently dealt Sir Guiscard a shrewd cut over the pate, whereby blood did flow in streams, and Sir Guiscard blasphemed in a manner shocking to hear. What had then chanced, God only knows, but Lady Eleanor, awakened by the noise, ran forth in her shift, and, seeing her husband and her brother at swords' points, she ran between them and bespoke them in words not to be repeated. Verily, a flailing tongue hath our mistress when her wrath is stirred.

"So understanding was reached, and a leech was fetched for Sir Guiscard and such of the henchmen as had suffered scathe. Then followed much discussion, and Sir Guiscard had recognized you as one of those who banged on his door. Then Guillaume was discovered hiding, as from a guilty conscience, and he confessed all, putting the blame on you. Ah me, such a day as it has been!

"Poor Peter in the stocks since dawn, and all the villeins and serving-wenches and villagers gathered to clod him—

they but just now left off, and a sorry sight he is, with nose a-bleeding, face skinned, an eye closed, and broken eggs in his hair and dripping over his features. Poor Peter!

"And as for Agnes, Marge, and Guillaume, they have had whipping enough to content them all a lifetime. It would be hard to say which of them has the sorest posterior. But it is you, Giles, the masters wish. Sir Guiscard swears that only your life will anyways content him."

"Hmmmm," ruminated Giles. He rose unsteadily, brushed the straw from his garments, hitched up his belt, and stuck his disreputable bonnet on his head at a cocky angle.

The friar watched him gloomily. "Peter stocked, Guillaume birched, Marge and Agnes whipped—what should be your punishment?"

"Methinks I'll do penance by a long pilgrimage," said Giles.

"You'll never get through the gates," predicted Ambrose.

"True," sighed Giles. "A friar may pass at will, where an honest man is halted by suspicion and prejudice. As further penance, lend me your robe."

"My robe?" exclaimed the friar. "You are a fool—"

A heavy fist *clunked* against his fat jaw, and he collapsed with a whistling sigh.

A few minutes later a lout in the outer ward, taking aim with a rotten egg at the dilapidated figure in the stocks, checked his arm as a robed and hooded shape emerged from the stables and crossed the open space with slow steps. The shoulders drooped as from a weight of weariness, the head was bent forward; so much so, in fact, that the features were hidden by the hood.

The lout doffed his shabby cap and made a clumsy leg.

"God go wi' 'ee, good faither," he said.

"*Pax vobiscum*, my son," came the answer, low and muffled, from the depths of the hood.

The lout shook his head sympathetically as the robed figure moved on, unhindered, in the direction of the postern gate.

"Poor Friar Ambrose," quoth the lout. "He takes the sin o' the world so much to heart; there 'ee go, fair bowed down by the wickedness o' men."

He sighed, and again took aim at the glum countenance that glowered above the stocks.

Through the blue glitter of the Mediterranean wallowed a merchant galley, clumsy, broad in the beam. Her square sail hung limp on her one thick mast. The oarsmen, sitting on the benches which flanked the waist deck on either side, tugged at the long oars, bending forward and heaving back in machine-like unison. Sweat stood out on their sunburnt skin, their muscles rolled evenly. From the interior of the hull came a chatter of voices, the complaint of animals, a reek as of barnyards and stables. This scent was observable some distance to leeward. To the south the blue waters spread out like molten sapphire. To the north, the gleaming sweep was broken by an island that reared up white cliffs crowned with dark green. Dignity, cleanliness, and serenity reigned over all, except where that smelly, ungainly tub lurched through the foaming water, by sound and scent advertising the presence of man.

Below the waist-deck passengers, squatted among bundles, were cooking food over small braziers. Smoke mingled with a reek of sweat and garlic. Horses, penned in a narrow space, whinnied wretchedly. Sheep, pigs and chickens added their aroma to the smells.

Presently, amidst the babble below decks, a new sound floated up to the people above—members of the crew, and the wealthier passengers who shared the *patrono's* cabin. The voice of the *patrono* came to them, strident with annoyance, answered by a loud rough voice with an alien accent.

The Venetian captain, prodding among the butts and bales of the cargo, had discovered a stowaway—a fat, sandy-haired man in worn leather, snoring bibulously among the barrels.

Ensued an impassioned oratory in lurid Italian, the burden of which at last focused in a demand that the stranger pay for his passage.

"Pay?" echoed that individual, running thick fingers through unkempt locks. "What should I pay with, Thinshanks? Where am I? What ship is this? Where are we going?"

"This is the *San Stefano*, bound for Cyprus from Palermo."

"Oh, yes," muttered the stowaway. "I remember. I came aboard at Palermo—lay down beside a wine cask between the bales—"

The *patrono* hastily inspected the cask and shrieked with new passion.

"Dog! You've drunk it all!"

"How long have we been at sea?" demanded the intruder.

"Long enough to be out of sight of land," snarled the other. "Pig, how can a man lie drunk so long—"

"No wonder my belly's empty," muttered the other. "I've lain among the bales, and when I woke, I'd drink till I fell asleep again. Hmmm!"

"Money!" clamored the Italian. "Bezants for your fare!"

"Bezants!" snorted the other. I haven't a penny to my name."

"Then overboard you go," grimly promised the *patrono*. "There's no room for beggars aboard the *San Stefano*."

That struck a spark. The stranger gave vent to a war-like snort, and tugged at his sword.

"Throw me overboard into all that water? Not while Giles Hobson can wield blade. A free-born Englishman is as good as any velvet-breeched Italian. Call your bullies and watch me bleed them!"

From the deck came a loud call strident with sudden fright. "Galleys off the starboard bow! Saracens!"

A howl burst from the *patrono's* lips and his face went ashy. Abandoning the dispute at hand, he wheeled and rushed up on deck. Giles Hobson followed and gaped about him at the anxious brown faces of the rowers, the frightened countenances of the passengers—Latin priests, merchants and pilgrims. Following their gaze, he saw three long low galleys shooting across the blue expanse toward them. They were still some distance away, but the people on the *San Stefano* could hear the faint clash of cymbals, see the banners stream out from the mast heads. The oars dipped into the blue water, came up shining silver.

"Put her about and steer for the island!" yelled the *patrono*. "If we can reach it, we may hide and save our lives. The galley is lost—and all the cargo! Saints defend me!" He wept and wrung his hands, less from fear than from disappointed avarice.

The *San Stefano* wallowed cumbrously about and waddled hurriedly toward the white cliffs jutting in the sunlight. The slim galleys came up, shooting through the waves like water snakes. The space of dancing blue between the *San Stefano* and the cliffs narrowed, but more swiftly narrowed the space between the merchant and the raiders. Arrows began to arch through the air and patter on the deck. One struck and quivered near Giles Hobson's boot, and he gave back as if from a serpent. The fat Englishman mopped perspiration from his brow. His mouth was dry, his head throbbed, his belly heaved. Suddenly he was violently seasick.

The oarsmen bent their backs, gasped, heaved mightily, seeming almost to jerk the awkward craft out of the water. Arrows, no longer arching, raked the deck. A man howled; another sank down without a word. An oarsman flinched from a shaft through his shoulder, and faltered in his stroke. Panic-stricken, the rowers began to lose rhythm. The *San Stefano* lost headway and rolled more wildly, and the passengers sent up a wail. From the raiders came yells of exultation. They separated in a fan-shaped formation meant to envelop the doomed galley.

On the merchant's deck the priests were shriving and absolving.

"Holy Saints grant me—" gasped a gaunt Pisan, kneeling on the boards—convulsively he clasped the feathered shaft that suddenly vibrated in his breast, then slumped sidewise and lay still.

An arrow thumped into the rail over which Giles Hobson hung, quivering near his elbow. He paid no heed. A hand was laid on his shoulder. Gagging, he turned his head, lifted a green face to look into the troubled eyes of a priest.

"My son, this may be the hour of death; confess your sins and I will shrive you."

"The only one I can think of," gasped Giles miserably, "is that I mauled a priest and stole his robe to flee England in."

"Alas, my son," the priest began, then cringed back with a low moan. He seemed to bow to Giles; his head inclining still further, he sank to the deck. From a dark welling spot on his side jutted a Saracen arrow.

Giles gaped about him; on either hand a long slim galley was sweeping in to lay the *San Stefano* aboard. Even as he looked, the third galley, the one in the middle of the triangular formation, rammed the merchant ship with a deafening splintering of timber. The steel beak cut through the bulwarks, rending apart the stern cabin. The concussion rolled men off their feet. Others, caught and crushed in the collision, died howling awfully. The other raiders ground alongside, and their steel-shod prows sheared through the banks of oars, twisting the shafts out of the oarsmen's hands, crushing the ribs of the wielders.

The grappling hooks bit into the bulwarks, and over the rail came dark, naked men with scimitars in their hands, their eyes blazing. They were met by a dazed remnant who fought back desperately.

Giles Hobson fumbled out his sword, strode groggily forward. A dark shape flashed at him out of the melée. He got a dazed impression of glittering eyes, and a curved blade hissing down. He caught the stroke on his sword, staggering from the spark-showering impact. Braced on wide straddling legs, he drove his sword into the pirate's belly. Blood and entrails gushed forth, and the dying corsair dragged his slayer to the deck with him in his throes.

Feet booted and bare stamped on Giles Hobson as he strove to rise. A curved dagger hooked at his kidneys, caught in his leather jerkin, and ripped the garment from hem to collar. He rose, shaking the tatters from him. A dusky hand locked in his ragged shirt, a mace hovered over his head. With a frantic jerk, Giles pitched backward, to a sound of rending cloth, leaving the torn shirt in his captor's hand. The mace met empty air as it descended, and the wielder went to his knees from the wasted blow. Giles fled along the blood-washed deck, twisting and ducking to avoid struggling knots of fighters.

A handful of defenders huddled in the door of the forecastle. The rest of the galley was in the hands of the triumphant Saracens. They swarmed over the deck, down into the waist. The animals squealed piteously as their throats were cut. Other screams marked the end of the women and children dragged from their hiding-places among the cargo.

In the door of the forecastle the blood-stained survivors parried and thrust with notched swords. The pirates hemmed them in, yelping mockingly, thrusting forward their pikes, drawing back, springing in to hack and slash.

Giles sprang for the rail, intending to dive and swim for the island. A quick step behind him warned him in time to wheel and duck a scimitar. It was wielded by a stout man of medium height, resplendent in silvered chain mail and chased helmet, crested with egret plumes.

Sweat misted the fat Englishman's sight; his wind was short; his belly heaved, his legs trembled. The Moslem cut at his head. Giles parried, struck back. His blade clanged against the chief's mail. Something like a white-hot brand seared his temple, and he was blinded by a rush of blood. Dropping his sword, he pitched headfirst against the Saracen, bearing him to the deck. The Moslem writhed and cursed, but Giles's thick arms clamped desperately about him.

Suddenly a wild shout went up. There was a rush of feet across the deck. Men began to leap over the rail, to cast loose the boarding-irons. Giles's captive yelled stridently, and men raced across the deck toward him. Giles released him, ran like a bulky cat along the bulwarks, and scrambled up over the roof of the shattered poop cabin. None heeded him. Men naked but for *tarbooshes* hauled the mailed chieftain to his feet and rushed him across the deck while he raged and blasphemed, evidently wishing to continue the contest. The Saracens were leaping into their own galleys and pushing away. And Giles, crouching on the splintered cabin roof, saw the reason.

Around the western promontory of the island they had been trying to reach came a squadron of great red dromonds, with battle-castles rearing at prow and stern. Helmets and spearheads glittered in the sun. Trumpets blared, drums boomed. From each mast-head streamed a long banner bearing the emblem of the Cross.

From the survivors aboard the *San Stefano* rose a shout of joy. The galleys were racing southward. The nearest dromond swung ponderously alongside, and brown faces framed in steel looked over the rail.

"Ahoy, there!" rang a stern-voiced command. "You are sinking; stand by to come aboard."

Giles Hobson started violently at that voice. He gaped up at the battle-castle towering above the *San Stefano*. A helmeted head bent over the bulwark, a pair of cold grey eyes met his. He saw a great beak of a nose, a scar seaming the face from the ear down the rim of the jaw.

Recognition was mutual. A year had not dulled Sir Guiscard de Chastillon's resentment.

"So!" The yell rang bloodthirstily in Giles Hobson's ears. "At last I have found you, rogue—"

Giles wheeled, kicked off his boots, ran to the edge of the roof. He left it in a long dive, shot into the blue water with a tremendous splash. His head bobbed to the surface, and he struck out for the distant cliffs in long pawing strokes.

A mutter of surprise rose from the dromond, but Sir Guiscard smiled sourly.

"A bow, varlet," he commanded.

It was placed in his hands. He nocked the arrow, waited until Giles's dripping head appeared again in a shallow trough between the waves. The bowstring twanged, the arrow flashed through the sunlight like a silver beam. Giles Hobson threw up his arms and disappeared. Nor did Sir Guiscard see him rise again, though the knight watched the waters for some time.

To Shawar, vizir of Egypt, in his palace in el Fustat, came a gorgeously robed eunuch who, with many abased supplications, as the due of the most powerful man in the caliphate, announced: "The Emir Asad ed din Shirkuh, lord of Emesa and Rahba, general of the armies of Nour ed din, Sultan of Damascus, has returned from the ships of el Ghazi with a Nazarene captive, and desires audience."

A nod of acquiescence was the vizir's only sign, but his slim white fingers twitched at his jewel-encrusted white girdle—sure evidence of mental unrest.

Shawar was an Arab, a slim, handsome figure, with the keen dark eyes of his race. He wore the silken robes and pearl-sewn turban of his office as if he had been born to them—instead of to the black felt tents from which his sagacity had lifted him.

The Emir Shirkuh entered like a storm, booming forth his salutations in a voice more fitted for the camp than for the council chamber. He was a powerfully-built man of medium height, with a face like a hawk's. His *khalat* was of watered silk, worked with gold thread, but like his voice, his hard body seemed more fitted for the harness of war than the garments of peace. Middle age had dulled none of the restless fire in his dark eyes.

With him was a man whose sandy hair and wide blue eyes contrasted incongruously with the voluminous bag trousers, silken *khalat* and turned-up slippers which adorned him.

"I trust that Allah granted you fortune upon the sea, *ya khawand?*" courteously inquired the vizir.

"Of a sort," admitted Shirkuh, casting himself down on the cushions. "We fared far, Allah knows, and at first my guts were like to gush out of my mouth with the galloping of the ship, which went up and down like a foundered camel. But later Allah willed that the sickness should pass.

"We sank a few wretched pilgrims' galleys and sent to hell the infidels therein—which was good, but the loot was wretched stuff. But look ye, lord vizir, did you ever see a Caphar like to this man?"

The man returned the vizier's searching stare with wide, guileless eyes.

"Such as he I have seen among the Franks of Jerusalem," Shawar decided.

Shirkuh grunted and began to munch grapes with scant ceremony, tossing a bunch to his captive.

"Near a certain island we sighted a galley," he said, between mouthfuls, "and we ran upon it and put the folk to the sword. Most of them were miserable fighters, but this man cut his way clear, and would have sprung overboard had I not intercepted him. By Allah, he proved himself strong as a bull! My ribs are yet bruised from his hug.

"But in the midst of the mêlée up galloped a herd of ships full of Christian warriors, bound—as we later learned—for Ascalon; Frankish adventurers seeking their fortune in Palestine. We put the spurs to our galleys, and as I looked back I saw the man I had been fighting leap overboard and swim toward the cliffs. A knight on a Nazarene ship shot an arrow at him and he sank, to his death, I supposed.

"Our water butts were nearly empty. We did not run far. As soon as the Frankish ships were out of sight over the skyline, we beat back to the island for fresh water. And we found, fainting on the beach, a fat, naked, red-haired man whom I recognized as he whom I had fought. The arrow had not touched him; he had dived deep and swum far under the water. But he had bled much from a cut I had given him on the head, and was nigh dead from exhaustion.

"Because he had fought me well, I took him into my cabin and revived him, and in the days that followed he learned the speech we of Islam hold with the accursed Nazarenes. He told me that he was a bastard son of the king of England, and that enemies had driven him from his father's court, and were hunting him over the world. He swore the king his father would pay a mighty ransom for him, so I make you a present of him. For me, the pleasure of the cruise is enough. To you shall go the ransom the *malik* of England pays for his son. He is a merry companion, who can tell a tale, quaff a flagon, and sing a song as well as any man I have ever known."

Shawar scanned Giles Hobson with new interest. In that rubicund countenance he failed to find any evidence of royal parentage, but reflected that few Franks showed royal lineage in their features: ruddy, freckled, light-haired, the western lords looked much alike to the Arab.

He turned his attention again to Shirkuh, who was of more importance than any wandering Frank, royal or common. The old war-dog, with shocking lack of formality, was humming a Kurdish war song under his breath as he poured himself a goblet of Shiraz wine—the Shiite rulers of Egypt were no stricter in their morals than were their Mameluke successors.

Apparently Shirkuh had no thought in the world except to satisfy his thirst, but Shawar wondered what craft was revolving behind that bluff exterior. In another man Shawar would have despised the Emir's restless vitality as an indication of an inferior mentality. But the Kurdish right hand man of Nour ed din was no fool. The vizier wondered if Shirkuh had embarked on that wild-goose chase with el Ghazi's corsairs merely because his restless energy would not let him be quiet, even during a visit to the caliph's court, or if there was a deeper meaning behind his voyaging. Shawar always looked for hidden motives, even in trivial things. He had reached his position by ignoring no possibility of intrigue. Moreover, events were stirring in the womb of Destiny in that early spring of 1167 A.D.

Shawar thought of Dirgham's bones rotting in a ditch near the chapel of Sitta Nefisa, and he smiled and said, "A thousand thanks for your gifts, my lord. In return a jade goblet filled with pearls shall be carried to your chamber. Let this exchange of gifts symbolize the everlasting endurance of our friendships."

"Allah fill thy mouth with gold, lord," boomed Shirkuh, rising; "I go to drink wine with my officers, and tell them lies of my voyagings. Tomorrow I ride for Damascus. Allah be with thee!"

"And with thee, *ya khawand*."

After the Kurd's springy footfalls had ceased to rustle the thick carpets of the halls, Shawar motioned Giles to sit beside him on the cushions.

"What of your ransom?" he asked, in the Norman French he had learned through contact with the Crusaders.

"The king my father will fill this chamber with gold," promptly answered Giles. "His enemies have told him I was dead. Great will be the joy of the old man to learn the truth."

So saying, Giles retired behind a wine goblet and racked his brain for bigger and better lies. He had spun this fantasy for Shirkuh, thinking to make himself sound too valuable to be killed. Later—well, Giles lived for today, with little thought of the morrow.

Shawar watched, in some fascination, the rapid disappearance of the goblet's contents down his prisoner's gullet.

"You drink like a French baron," commented the Arab.

"I am the prince of all topers," answered Giles modestly—and with more truth than was contained in most of his boastings.

"Shirkuh, too, loves wine," went on the vizier. "You drank with him?"

"A little. He wouldn't get drunk, lest we sight a Christian ship. But we emptied a few flagons. A little wine loosens his tongue."

Shawar's narrow dark head snapped up; that was news to him.

"He talked? Of what?"

"Of his ambitions."

"And what are they?" Shawar held his breath.

"To be Caliph of Egypt," answered Giles, exaggerating the Kurd's actual words, as was his habit. Shirkuh had talked wildly, though rather incoherently.

"Did he mention me?" demanded the vizier.

"He said he held you in the hollow of his hand," said Giles, truthfully, for a wonder.

Shawar fell silent; somewhere in the palace a lute twanged and a black girl lifted a weird whining song of the South. Fountains splashed silverly, and there was a flutter of pigeons' wings.

"If I send emissaries to Jerusalem, his spies will tell him," murmured Shawar to himself. "If I slay or constrain him, Nour ed din will consider it cause for war."

He lifted his head and stared at Giles Hobson.

"You call yourself king of topers; can you best the Emir Shirkuh in a drinking-bout?"

"In the palace of the king my father," said Giles, "in one night I drank fifty barons under the table, the least of which was a mightier toper than Shirkuh."

"Would you win your freedom without ransom?"

"Aye, by Saint Withold!"

"You can scarcely know much of Eastern politics, being but newly come into these parts. But Egypt is the keystone of the arch of empire. It is coveted by Amalric, king of Jerusalem, and Nour ed din, sultan of Damascus. Ibn Ruzzik, and after him Dirgham, and after him, I, have played one against the other. By Shirkuh's aid I overthrew Dirgham; by Amalric's aid, I drove out Shirkuh. It is a perilous game, for I can trust neither.

"Nour ed din is cautious. Shirkuh is the man to fear. I think he came here professing friendship in order to spy me out, to lull my suspicions. Even now his army may be moving on Egypt.

"If he boasted to you of his ambitions and power, it is a sure sign that he feels secure in his plots. It is necessary that I render him helpless for a few hours; yet I dare not do him harm without true knowledge of whether his hosts are actually on the march. So this is your part."

Giles understood and a broad grin lit his ruddy face, and he licked his lips sensuously.

Shawar clapped his hands and gave orders, and presently, at request, Shirkuh entered, carrying his silk-girdled belly before him like an emperor of India.

"Our royal guest," purred Shawar, "has spoken of his prowess with the winecup. Shall we allow a Caphar to go home and boast among his people that he sat above the Faithful in anything? Who is more capable of humbling his pride than the Mountain Lion?"

"A drinking-bout?" Shirkuh's laugh was gusty as a sea blast. "By the beard of Muhammad, it likes me well! Come, Giles ibn Malik, let us to the quaffing!"

A procession began, of slaves bearing golden vessels brimming with sparkling nectar. . . .

During his captivity on el Ghazi's galley, Giles had become accustomed to the heady wine of the East. But his blood was boiling in his veins, his head was singing, and the gold-barred chamber was revolving to his dizzy gaze before Shirkuh, his voice trailing off in the midst of an incoherent song, slumped sidewise on his cushions, the gold beaker tumbling from his fingers.

Shawar leaped into frantic activity. At his clasp Sudanese slaves entered, naked giants with gold earrings and silk loinclouts.

"Carry him into the alcove and lay him on a divan," he ordered. "Lord Giles, can you ride?"

Giles rose, reeling like a ship in a high wind.

"I'll hold to the mane," he hiccuped. "But why should I ride?"

"To bear my message to Amalric," snapped Shawar. "Here it is, sealed in a silken packet, telling him that Shirkuh means to conquer Egypt, and offering him payment in return for aid. Amalric distrusts me, but he will listen to one of the royal blood of his own race, who tells him of Shirkuh's boasts."

"Aye," muttered Giles groggily, "Royal Blood; my grandfather was a horse-boy in the royal stables."

"What did you say?" demanded Shawar, not understanding, then went on before Giles could answer. "Shirkuh has played into our hands. He will lie senseless for hours, and while he lies there, you will be riding for Palestine. He will not ride for Damascus tomorrow; he will be sick of overdrunkenness. I dared not imprison him, or even drug his wine. I dare make no move until I reach an agreement with Amalric. But Shirkuh is safe for the time being, and you will reach Amalric before he reaches Nour ed din. Haste!"

In the courtyard outside sounded the clink of harness, the impatient stamp of horses. Voices blurred in swift whispers. Footfalls faded away through the halls. Alone in the alcove, Shirkuh unexpectedly sat upright. He shook his head violently, buffeted it with his hands as if to clear away the clinging cobwebs. He reeled up, catching at the arras for support. But his beard bristled in an exultant grin. He seemed bursting with a triumphant whoop he could scarcely restrain. Stumblingly he made his way to a gold-barred window. Under his massive hands the thin gold rods twisted and buckled. He tumbled through, pitching headfirst to the ground in the midst of a great rose bush. Oblivious of bruises and scratches, he rose, careening like a ship on a tack, and oriented himself. He was in a broad garden; all about him waved great white blossoms; a breeze shook the palm leaves, and the moon was rising.

None halted him as he scaled the wall, though thieves skulking in the shadows eyed his rich garments avidly as he lurched through the deserted streets.

By devious ways he came to his own quarters and kicked his slaves awake.

"Horses, Allah curse you!" His voice crackled with exultation.

Ali, his captain of horse, came from the shadows:

"What now, lord?"

"The desert and Syria beyond!" roared Shirkuh, dealing him a terrific buffet on the back. "Shawar has swallowed the bait! Allah, how drunk I am! The world reels—but the stars are mine!

"That bastard Giles rides to Amalric—I heard Shawar give him his instructions as I lay in feigned slumber. We have forced the vizir's hand! Now Nour ed din will not hesitate, when his spies bring him news from Jerusalem of the marching of the iron men! I fumed in the caliph's court, checkmated at every turn by Shawar, seeking a way. I went into the galleys of the corsairs to cool my brain, and Allah gave into my hands a red-haired tool! I filled the lord Giles full of 'drunken' boastings, hoping he would repeat them to Shawar, and that Shawar would take fright and send for Amalric—which would force our overly cautious sultan to act. Now follow marching and war and the glutting of ambition. But let us ride, in the devil's name!"

A few minutes later the Emir and his small retinue were clattering through the shadowy streets, past gardens that slept, a riot of color under the moon, lapping six-storied palaces that were dreams of pink marble and lapis lazuli and gold.

At a small, secluded gate, a single sentry bawled a challenge and lifted his pike.

"Dog!" Shirkuh reined his steed back on its haunches and hung over the Egyptian like a silk-clad cloud of death. "It is Shirkuh, your master's guest!"

"But my orders are to allow none to pass without written order, signed and sealed by the vizir," protested the soldier. "What shall I say to Shawar—"

"You will say naught," prophesied Shirkuh. "The dead speak not."

His scimitar gleamed and fell, and the soldier crumpled, cut through the helmet and head.

"Open the gate, Ali," laughed Shirkuh. "It is Fate that rides tonight—Fate and Destiny!"

In a cloud of moon-bathed dust they whirled out of the gate and over the plain. On the rocky shoulder of Mukattam, Shirkuh drew rein to gaze back over the city, which lay like a legendary dream under the moonlight, a waste of masonry and stone and marble, splendor and squalor merging in the moonlight, magnificence blent with ruin. To the south the dome of Imam esh Shafi'y shone beneath the moon; to the north loomed up the gigantic pile of the Castle of el Kahira, its walls carved blackly out of the white moonlight. Between them lay the remains and ruins of three capitals of Egypt; palaces with their mortar yet undried reared beside crumbling walls haunted only by bats.

Shirkuh laughed, and yelled with pure joy. His horse reared and his scimitar glittered in the air.

"A bride in cloth-of-gold! Await my coming, oh Egypt, for when I come again, it will be with spears and horsemen, to seize ye in my hands!"

Allah willed it that Amalric, king of Jerusalem, should be in Darum, personally attending to the fortifying of that small desert outpost, when the envoys from Egypt rode through the gates. A restless, alert, and wary king was Amalric, bred to war and intrigue.

In the castle hall the Egyptian emissaries salaamed before him like corn bending before a wind, and Giles Hobson, grotesque in his dusty silks and white turban, louted awkwardly and presented the sealed packet of Shawar.

Amalric took it with his own hands and read it, striding absently up and down the hall, a gold-maned lion, stately, yet dangerously supple.

"What talk is this of royal bastards?" he demanded suddenly, staring at Giles, who was nervous but not embarrassed.

"A lie to cozen the paynim, your majesty," admitted the Englishman, secure in his belief that the Egyptians did not understand Norman French. "I am no illegitimate of the blood, only the honest-born younger son of a baron of the Scottish marches."

Giles did not care to be kicked into the scullery with the rest of the varlets. The nearer the purple, the richer the pickings. It seemed safe to assume that the king of Jerusalem was not over-familiar with the nobility of the Scottish border.

"I have seen many a younger son who lacked coat-armor, war-cry, and wealth, but was none the less worthy," said Amalric. "You shall not go unrewarded. Messer Giles, know you the import of this message?"

"The wazeer Shawar spoke to me at some length," admitted Giles.

"The ultimate fate of Outremer hangs in the balance," said Amalric. "If the same man holds both Egypt and Syria, we are caught in the jaws of the vise. Better for Shawar to rule in Egypt, than Nour ed din. We march for Cairo. Would you accompany the host?"

"In sooth, lord," began Giles, "it has been a wearisome time—"

"True," broke in Amalric. " 'Twere better that you ride on to Acre and rest from your travels. I will give you a letter for the lord commanding there. Sir Guiscard de Chastillon will give you service—"

Giles started violently. "Nay, lord," he said hurriedly, "duty calls, and what are weary limbs and an empty belly beside duty? Let me go with you and do my devoir in Egypt!"

"Your spirit likes me well, Messer Giles," said Amalric with an approving smile. "Would that all the foreigners who come adventuring in Outremer were like you."

"An they were," murmured an immobile-faced Egyptian to his mate, "not all the wine-vats of Palestine would suffice. We will tell a tale to the vizir concerning this liar."

But lies or not, in the grey dawn of a young spring day the iron men of Outremer rode southward, with the great banner billowing over their helmeted heads, and their spear-points coldly glinting in the dim light.

There were not many; the strength of the Crusading kingdoms lay in the quality, not the quantity, of their defenders. Three hundred and seventy five knights took the road to Eygpt: nobles of Jerusalem, barons whose castles guarded the eastern marches, Knights of Saint John in their white surcoats, grim Templars, adventurers from beyond the sea, their skins yet ruddy from the cold sun of the north.

With them rode a swarm of Turcoples, Christianized Turks, wiry men on lean ponies. After the horseman lumbered the wagons, attended by the rag-and-tag camp followers, the servants, ragamuffins, and trulls that tag after any host. With shining, steel-sheathed, banner-crowned van, and rear trailing out into picturesque squalor, the army of Jerusalem moved across the land.

The dunes of the Jifar knew again the tramp and shod of horses, the clink of mail. The iron men were riding again the old road of war, the road their fathers had ridden so oft before them.

Yet when at last the Nile broke the monotony of the level land, winding like a serpent feathered with green palms, they heard the strident clamor of cymbals and *nakirs*, and saw egret feathers moving among gay-striped pavilions that bore the colors of Islam. Shirkuh had reached the Nile before them, with seven thousand horsemen.

Mobility was always an advantage possessed by the Moslems. It took time to gather the cumbrous Frankish host, time to move it.

Riding like a man possessed, the Mountain Lion had reached Nour ed din, told his tale, and then, with scarcely a pause, had raced southward again with the troops he had held in readiness since the first Egyptian campaign. The thought of Amalric in Egypt had sufficed to stir Nour ed din to action. If the Crusaders made themselves masters of the Nile, it meant the eventual doom of Islam.

Shirkuh's was the dynamic vitality of the nomad. Across the desert by Wadi el Ghizlan he had driven his riders until even the tough Seljuks reeled in their saddles. Into the teeth of a roaring sandstorm he had plunged, fighting like a madman for each mile, each second of time. He had crossed the Nile at Atfih, and now his riders were regaining their breath, while Shirkuh watched the eastern skyline for the moving forest of lances that would mark the coming of Amalric.

The king of Jerusalem dared not attempt a crossing in the teeth of his enemies; Shirkuh was in the same case. Without pitching camp, the Franks moved northward along the river bank. The iron men rode slowly, scanning the sullen stream for a possible crossing.

The Moslems broke camp and took up the march, keep-

ing pace with the Franks. The *fellaheen*, peeking from their
mud huts, were amazed by the sight of two hosts moving
slowly in the same direction without hostile demonstration,
with the river between.

So they came at last into sight of the towers of el Kahira.

The Franks pitched their camp close to the shores of
Birket el Habash, near the gardens of el Fustat, whose six-
storied houses reared their flat roofs among oceans of
palms and waving blossoms. Across the river, Shirkuh encamped at Gizeh, in the shadow of the scornful colossus
reared by cryptic monarchs forgotten before his ancestors
were born.

Matters fell at a deadlock. Shirkuh, for all his impetuos-
ity, had the patience of the Kurd, imponderable as the
mountains which bred him. He was content to play a waiting game, with the broad river between him and the terrible swords of the Europeans.

Shawar waited on Amalric with pomp and parade and
the clamor of *nakirs*, and he found the lion wary as he was
indomitable. Two hundred thousand *dinars* and the caliph's
hand on the bargain, that was the price he demanded for
Egypt. And Shawar knew he must pay. Egypt slumbered as
she had slumbered for a thousand years, inert alike under
the heel of Macedonian, Roman, Arab, Turk, or Fatimid.
The *fellah* toiled in his field, and scarcely knew to whom
he paid his taxes. There was no land of Egypt: it was a
myth, a cloak for a despot. Shawar was Egypt; Egypt was
Shawar; the price of Egypt was the price of Shawar's head.

So the Frankish ambassadors went to the hall of the caliph.

Mystery ever shrouded the person of the Incarnation of
Divine Reason. The spiritual center of the Shiite creed
moved in a maze of mystic inscrutability, his veil of supernatural awe increasing as his political power was usurped
by plotting viziers. No Frank had ever seen the caliph of
Egypt.

Hugh of Cæsarea and Geoffrey Fulcher, Master of the
Templars, were chosen for the mission, blunt war-dogs,
grim as their own swords. A group of mailed horsemen
accompanied them.

They rode through the flowering gardens of el Fustat,
past the chapel of Sitta Nefisa, where Dirgham had died
under the hands of the mob; through winding streets which

covered the ruins of el Askar and el Katai; past the Mosque of Ibn Tulun, and the Lake of the Elephant, into the teeming streets of El Mansuriya, the quarter of the Sudanese, where weird native citterns twanged in the houses, and swaggering black men, gaudy in silk and gold, stared childishly at the grim horsemen.

At the Gate Zuweyla the riders halted, and the Master of the Temple and the lord of Cæsarea rode on, attended by only one man—Giles Hobson. The fat Englishman wore good leather and chain mail, and a sword at his thigh, though the portly arch of his belly somewhat detracted from his warlike appearance. Little thought was being taken in those perilous times of royal bastards or younger sons; but Giles had won the approval of Hugh of Cæsarea, who loved a good tale and a bawdy song.

At Zuweyla gate Shawar met them with pomp and pageantry and escorted them through the bazaars and the Turkish quarter, where hawklike men from beyond the Oxus stared and silently spat. For the first time, Franks in armor were riding through the streets of el Kahira.

At the gates of the Great East Palace the ambassadors gave up their swords, and followed the vizir through dim tapestry-hung corridors and gold arched doors where tongueless Sudanese stood like images of black silence, sword in hand. They crossed an open court bordered by fretted arcades supported by marble columns; their iron-clad feet rang on mosaic paving. Fountains jetted their silver sheen into the air, peacocks spread their iridescent plumage, parrots fluttered on gold threads. In broad halls, jewels glittered for eyes of birds wrought of silver or gold. So they came at last to the vast audience room, with its ceiling of carved ebony and ivory. Courtiers in silks and jewels knelt facing a broad curtain heavy with gold and sewn with pearls that gleamed against its satin darkness like stars in a midnight sky.

Shawar prostrated himself thrice to the carpeted floor. The curtains were swept apart, and the wondering Franks gazed on the gold throne, where, in robes of white silk, sat al Adhid, Caliph of Egypt.

They saw a slender youth, dark almost to negroid, whose hands lay limp, whose eyes seemed already shadowed by ultimate sleep. A deadly weariness clung about him, and he listened to the representations of his vizir as one who heeds a tale too often told.

But a flash of awakening came to him when Shawar suggested, with extremest delicacy, that the Franks wished his hand upon the pact. A visible shudder passed through the room. Al Adhid hesitated, then extended his gloved hand. Sir Hugh's voice boomed through the breathless hall.

"Lord, the good faith of princes is naked; troth is not clothed."

All about came a hissing intake of breath. But the Caliph smiled, as at the whims of a barbarian, and, stripping the glove from his hand, laid his slender fingers in the bearlike paw of the Crusader.

All this Giles Hobson observed from his discreet position in the background. All eyes were centered on the group clustered about the golden throne. From near his shoulder a soft hiss reached Giles's ear. Its feminine note brought him quickly about, forgetful of kings and caliphs. A heavy tapestry was drawn slightly aside, and in the sweet-smelling gloom, a slender white hand waved invitingly. Another scent made itself evident, a luring perfume, subtle yet unmistakable.

Giles turned silently and pulled aside the tapestry, straining his eyes in the semi-darkness. There was an alcove behind the hangings, and a narrow corridor meandering away. Before him stood a figure whose vagueness did not conceal its lissomeness. A pair of eyes glowed and sparkled at him, and his head swam with the power of that diabolical perfume.

He let the tapestry fall behind him. Through the hangings the voices in the throne room came vague and muffled.

The woman spoke not; her little feet made no sound on the thickly carpeted floor over which he stumbled. She invited, yet retreated; she beckoned, yet she withheld herself. Only when, baffled, he broke into earnest profanity, she admonished him with a finger to her lips and a warning: "Ssssh!"

"Devil take you, wench!" he swore, stopping short. "I'll follow you no more. What manner of game is this, anyway? If you don't want to deal with me, why did you wave at me? Why do you beckon and then run away? I'm going back to the audience hall and may the dogs bite your—"

"Wait!" The voice was liquid sweet.

She glided close to him, laying her hands on his shoulders. What light there was in the winding, tapestried corridor was behind her, outlining her supple figure through her filmy garments. Her flesh shone like dim ivory in the purple gloom.

"I could love you," she whispered.

"Well, what detains you?" he demanded uneasily.

"Not here; follow me." She glided out of his groping arms and drifted ahead of him, a lithely swaying ghost among the velvet hangings.

He followed, burning with impatience and questing not at all for the reason of the whole affair, until she came out into an octagonal chamber, almost as dimly lighted as had been the corridor. As he pushed after her, a hanging slid over the opening behind him. He gave it no heed. Where he was he neither knew nor cared. All that was important to him was the supple figure that posed shamelessly before him, veilless, naked arms uplifted and slender fingers intertwined behind her nape, over which fell a mass of hair that was like black burnished foam.

He stood, struck dumb with her beauty. She was like no other woman he had ever seen; the difference was not only in her dark eyes, her dusky tresses, her long kohl-tinted lashes, or the warm ivory of her roundly slender limbs. It was in every glance, each movement, each posture, that made voluptuousness an art. Here was a woman cultured in the arts of pleasure, a dream to madden any lover of the fleshpots of life. The English, French, and Venetian women he had nuzzled seemed slow, stolid, frigid beside this vibrant image of sensuality. A favorite of the Caliph! The implication of the realization sent the blood pounding suffocatingly through his veins. He panted for breath.

"Am I not fair?" Her breath, scented with the perfume that sweetened her body, fanned his face. The soft tendrils of her hair brushed against his cheek. He groped for her, but she eluded him with disconcerting ease. "What will you do for me?"

"Anything!" he swore ardently, and with more sincerity than he usually voiced the vow.

His hand closed on her wrist and he dragged her to him; his other arm bent about her waist, and the feel of her resilient flesh made him drunk. He pawed for her lips with his, but she bent supplely backward, twisting her head this way and that, resisting him with unexpected strength; the lithe pantherish strength of a dancing-girl. Yet even while she resisted him, she did not repulse him.

"Nay," she laughed, and her laughter was the gurgle of a silver fountain; "first there is a price!"

"Name it, for the love of the Devil!" he gasped. "Am I a frozen saint? I can not resist you forever!" He had released her wrist and was pawing at her shoulder straps.

Suddenly she ceased to struggle; throwing both arms about his thick neck, she looked into his eyes. The depths of hers, dark and mysterious, seemed to drown him; he shuddered as a wave of something akin to fear swept over him.

"You are high in the council of the Franks!" she breathed. "We know you disclosed to Shawar that you are a son of the English king. You came with Amalric's ambassadors. You know his plans. Tell what I wish to know, and I am yours! What is Amalric's next move?"

"He will build a bridge of boats and cross the Nile to attack Shirkuh by night," answered Giles without hesitation.

Instantly she laughed, with mockery and indescribable malice, struck him in the face, twisted free, sprang back, and cried out sharply. The next moment the shadows were alive with rushing figures as from the tapestries leaped naked black giants.

Giles wasted no time in futile gestures toward his empty belt. As great dusky hands fell on him, his massive fist smashed against bone, and the Negro dropped with a fractured jaw. Springing over him, Giles scudded across the room with unexpected agility. But to his dismay he saw that the doorways were hidden by the tapestries. He groped frantically among the hangings; then a brawny arm hooked throttlingly about his throat from behind, and he felt himself dragged backward and off his feet. Other hands snatched him, white eyeballs and teeth glimmered in the semi-darkness. He lashed out savagely with his foot and caught a big black in the belly, curling him up in agony on the floor. A thumb felt for his eye and mangled it between his teeth, bringing a whimper of pain from the owner. But a dozen pairs of hands lifted him, smiting and kicking. He heard a grating, sliding noise, felt himself swung up violently and hurled downward—a black opening in the floor rushed up to meet him. An earsplitting yell burst from him, and then he was rushing headlong down a walled shaft, up which sounded the sucking and bubbling of racing water.

He hit with a tremendous splash and felt himself swept irresistibly onward. The well was wide at the bottom. He had fallen near one side of it, and was being carried toward the other, in which, he had light enough to see as he rose blowing and snorting above the surface, another black orifice gaped. Then he was thrown with stunning force against the edge of that opening; his legs and hips were sucked through, but his frantic fingers, slipping from the mossy stone lip, encountered something and clung on. Looking wildly up, he saw, framed high above him in the dim light, a cluster of woolly heads rimming the mouth of the well. Then abruptly all light was shut out as the trap was replaced, and Giles was conscious only of utter blackness and the rustle and swirl of the racing water that dragged relentlessly at him.

This, Giles knew, was the well into which were thrown foes of the Caliph. He wondered how many ambitious generals, plotting viziers, rebellious nobles, and importunate *harim* favorites had gone whirling through that black hole to come into the light of day again only floating as carrion on the bosom of the Nile. It was evident that the well had been sunk into an underground flow of water that rushed into the river, perhaps miles away.

Clinging there by his fingernails in the dank, rushing blackness, Giles Hobson was so frozen with horror that it did not even occur to him to call on the various saints he ordinarily blasphemed. He merely hung on to the irregularly round, slippery object his hands had found, frantic with the fear of being torn away and whirled down that black slimy tunnel, feeling his arms and fingers growing numb with the strain, and slipping gradually but steadily from their hold.

His last ounce of breath went from him in a wild cry of despair, and—miracle of miracles—it was answered. Light flooded the shaft, a light dim and gray, yet in such contrast with the former blackness that it momentarily dazzled him. Someone was shouting, but the words were unintelligible amidst the rush of the black waters. He tried to shout back, but he could only gurgle. Then, mad with fear lest the trap should shut again, he achieved an inhuman screech that almost burst his throat.

Shaking the water from his eyes and craning his head backward, he saw a human head and shoulders blocked in the open trap far above him. A rope was dangling down toward him. It swayed before his eyes, but he dared not let go long enough to seize it. In desperation, he mounted for it, gripped it with his teeth, then let go and snatched, even as he was sucked into the black hole. His numbed fingers slipped along the rope. Tears of fear and helplessness rolled down his face. But his jaws were locked desperately on the strands, and his corded neck muscles resisted the terrific strain.

Whoever was on the other end of the rope was hauling like a team of oxen. Giles felt himself ripped bodily from the clutch of the torrent. As his feet swung clear, he saw, in the dim light, that to which he had been clinging: a human skull, wedged somehow in a crevice of the slimy rocks.

He was drawn rapidly up, revolving like a pendant. His numbed hands clawed stiffly at the rope, his teeth seemed to be tearing from their sockets. His jaw muscles were knots of agony, his neck felt as if it were being racked.

Just as human endurance reached its limit, he saw the lip of the trap slip past him, and he was dumped on the floor at its brink.

He grovelled in agony, unable to unlock his jaws from about the hemp. Someone was massaging the cramped muscles with skilful fingers, and at last they relaxed with a stream of blood from the tortured gums. A goblet of wine was pressed to his lips and he gulped it loudly, the liquid slopping over and spilling on his slime-smeared mail. Some one was tugging at it, as if fearing lest he injure himself by guzzling, but he clung on with both hands until the beaker was empty. Then only he released it, and, with a loud gasping sigh of relief, looked up into the face of Shawar. Behind the vizir were several giant Sudani, of the same type as those who had been responsible for Giles's predicament.

"We missed you from the audience hall," said Shawar. "Sir Hugh roared treachery, until a eunuch said he saw you follow a woman slave off down a corridor. Then the lord Hugh laughed and said you were up to your old tricks, and rode away with the lord Geoffrey. But I knew the peril you ran in dallying with a woman in the Caliph's palace; so I searched for you, and a slave told me he had heard a frightful yell in this chamber. I came, and entered just as a black was replacing the carpet above the trap. He sought to flee, and died without speaking." The vizir indicated a sprawling form that lay near, head lolling on half-severed neck. "How came you in this state?"

"A woman lured me here," answered Giles, "and set blackamoors upon me, threatening me with the well unless I revealed Amalric's plans."

"What did you tell her?" The vizir's eyes burned so intently on Giles that the fat man shuddered slightly and hitched himself further away from the yet-open trap.

"I told them nothing! Who am I to know the king's plans, anyway? Then they dumped me into that cursed hole, though I fought like a lion and maimed a score of the rogues. Had I but had my trusty sword—"

At a nod from Shawar the trap was closed, the rug drawn over it. Giles breathed a sigh of relief. Slaves dragged the corpse away.

The vizar touched Giles's arm, and led the way through a corridor concealed by the hangings.

"I will send an escort with you to the Frankish camp. There are spies of Shirkuh in this palace, and others who love him not, yet hate me. Describe me this woman—the eunuch saw only her hand."

Giles groped for adjectives, then shook his head.

"Her hair was black, her eyes moonfire, her body alabaster."

"A description that would fit a thousand women of the Caliph," said the vizir. "No matter; get you gone, for the night wanes and Allah only knows what morn will bring."

The night was indeed late as Giles Hobson rode into the Frankish camp surrounded by Turkish *memluks* with drawn sabers. But a light burned in Amalric's pavilion, which the wary monarch preferred to the palace offered him by Shawar; and thither Giles went, confident of admittance as a teller of lusty tales who had won the king's friendship.

Amalric and his barons were bent above a map as the fat man entered, and they were too engrossed to notice his entry, or his bedraggled appearance.

"Shawar will furnish us men and boats," the king was saying; "they will fashion the bridge, and we will make the attempt by night—"

An explosive grunt escaped Giles's lips, as if he had been hit in the belly.

"What, Sir Giles the Fat!" exclaimed Amalric, looking up; "are you but now returned from your adventuring in Cairo? You are fortunate still to have head on your shoulders. Eh—what ails you, that you sweat and grow pale? Where are you going?"

"I have taken an emetic," mumbled Giles over his shoulder.

Beyond the light of the pavilion he broke into a stumbling run. A tethered horse started and snorted at him. He caught the rein, grasped the saddle peak; then, with one foot in the stirrup, he halted. Awhile he meditated, then at last, wiping cold sweat beads from his face, he returned with slow and dragging steps to the king's tent.

He entered unceremoniously and spoke forthwith: "Lord, is it your plan to throw a bridge of boats across the Nile?"

"Aye, so it is," declared Amalric.

Giles uttered a loud groan and sank down on a bench, his head in his hands. "I am too young to die!" he lamented. "Yet I must speak, though my reward be a sword in the belly. This night Shirkuh's spies trapped me into speaking like a fool. I told them the first lie that came into my head—and Saint Withold defend me, I spoke the truth unwittingly. I told them you meant to build a bridge of boats!"

A shocked silence reigned. Geoffrey Fulcher dashed down his cup in a spasm of anger. "Death to the fat fool!" he swore, rising.

"Nay!" Amalric smiled suddenly. He stroked his golden beard. "Our foe will be expecting the bridge, now. Good enough. Hark ye!"

And, as he spoke, grim smiles grew on the lips of the barons, and Giles Hobson began to grin and thrust out his belly, as if his fault had been virtue, craftily devised.

All night the Saracen host had stood at arms; on the opposite bank fires blazed, reflected from the rounded walls and burnished roofs of el Fustat. Trumpets mingled with the clang of steel. The Emir Shirkuh, riding up and down the bank along which his mailed hawks were ranged, glanced toward the eastern sky, just tinged with dawn. A wind blew out of the desert.

There had been fighting along the river the day before, and all through the night drums had rumbled and trumpets blared their threat. All day Egyptians and naked Sudani had toiled to span the dusky flood with boats chained together, end to end. Thrice they had pushed toward the western bank, under the cover of their archers in the barges, only to falter and shrink back before the clouds of Turkish arrows. Once the end of the boat bridge had almost touched the shore, and the helmeted riders had spurred their horses into the water to slash at the shaven heads of the workers. Shirkuh had expected an onslaught of the knights across the frail span, but it had not come. The men in the boats had again fallen back, leaving their dead floating in the muddily churning wash.

Shirkuh decided that the Franks were lurking behind walls, saving themselves for a supreme effort, when their allies should have completed the bridge. The opposite bank was clustered with swarms of naked figures, and the Kurd expected to see them begin the futile task once more.

As dawn whitened the desert, there came a rider who rode like the wind, sword in hand, turban unbound, blood dripping from his beard.

"Woe to Islam!" he cried. "The Franks have crossed the river!"

Panic swept the Moslem camp; men jerked their steeds from the river bank, staring wildly northward. Only Shirkuh's bull-like voice kept them from flinging away their swords and bolting.

The Emir's profanity was frightful. He had been fooled and tricked. While the Egyptians held his attention with their useless labor, Amalric and the iron men had marched northward, crossed the prongs of the Delta in ships, and were now hastening vengefully southward. The Emir's spies had had neither time nor opportunity to reach him. Shawar had seen to that.

The Mountain Lion dared not await attack in this unsheltered spot. Before the sun was well up, the Turkish host was on the march; behind them the rising light shone on spear-points that gleamed in a rising cloud of dust.

This dust irked Giles Hobson, riding behind Amalric and his councillors. The fat Englishman was thirsty; dust settled greyly on his mail; gnats bit him, sweat got into his eyes, and the sun, as it rose, beat mercilessly on his basinet; so he hung it on his saddle peak and pushed back his linked

coif, daring sunstroke. On either side of him leather
creaked and worn mail clinked. Giles thought of the ale-
pots of England, and cursed the man whose hate had
driven him around the world.

And so they hunted the Mountain Lion up the valley of
the Nile, until they came to el Baban, the Gates, and found
the Saracen host drawn up for battle in the gut of the low
sandy hills.

Word came back along the ranks, putting new fervor
into the knights. The clatter of leather and steel seemed
imbued with new meaning. Giles put on his helmet and,
rising in his stirrups, looked over the ironclad shoulders in
front of him.

To the left were the irrigated fields on the edge of which
the host was riding. To the right was the desert. Ahead of
them the terrain was broken by the hills. On these hills,
and in the shallow valleys between, bristled the banners of
the Turks, and their *nakirs* blared. A mass of the host was
drawn up in the plain between the Franks and the hills.

The Christians had halted: three hundred and seventy-
five knights, plus half a dozen more who had ridden all the
way from Acre and reached the host only an hour before,
with their retainers. Behind them, moving with the baggage, their allies halted in straggling lines: a thousand Turcoples, and some five thousand Egyptians, whose gaudy
garments outshone their courage.

"Let us ride forward and smite those on the plain,"
urged one of the foreign knights, newly come to the East.

Amalric scanned the closely massed ranks and shook his
head. He glanced at the banners that floated among the
spears on the slopes on either flank where the kettledrums
clamored.

"That is the banner of Saladin in the center," he said.
"Shirkuh's house troops are on yonder hill. If the center
expected to stand, the Emir would be there. No, messers, I
think it is their wish to lure us into a charge. We will wait
their attack, under cover of the Turcoples' bows. Let them
come to us; they are in a hostile land, and must push the
war."

The rank and file had not heard his words. He lifted his
hand, and, thinking it preceded an order to charge, the forest of lances quivered and sank in rest. Amalric, realizing
the mistake, rose in his stirrups to shout his command to

fall back, but before he could speak, Giles's horse, restive, shouldered that of the knight next to him. This knight, one of those who had joined the host less than an hour before, turned irritably; Giles looked into a lean, beaked face, seamed by a livid scar.

"Ha!" Instinctively, the ogre caught at his sword.

Giles's action was also instinctive. Everything else was swept out of his mind at the sight of that dread visage which had haunted his dreams for more than a year. With a yelp he sank his spurs into his horse's belly. The beast neighed shrilly and leaped, blundering against Amalric's warhorse. That highstrung beast reared and plunged, got the bit between its teeth, broke from the ranks, and thundered out across the plain.

Bewildered, seeing their king apparently charging the Saracen host singlehanded, the men of the Cross gave tongue and followed him. The plain shook as the great horses stampeded across it, and the spears of the ironclad riders crashed splinteringly against the shields of their enemies.

The movement was so sudden it almost swept the Moslems off their feet. They had not expected a charge so instantly to follow the coming up of the Christians. But the allies of the knights were struck by confusion. No orders had been given, no arrangement made for battle. The whole host was disordered by that premature onslaught. The Turcoples and Egyptians wavered uncertainly, drawing up about the baggage wagons.

The whole first rank of the Saracen center went down, and over their mangled bodies rode the knights of Jerusalem, swinging their great swords. An instant the Turkish ranks held; then they began to fall back in good order, marshalled by their commander, a slender, dark, self-contained young officer, Salah ed din, Shirkuh's nephew.

The Christians followed. Amalric, cursing his mischance, made the best of a bad bargain, and so well he plied his trade that the harried Turks cried out on Allah and turned their horses' heads from him.

Back into the gut of the hills the Saracens retired, and turning there, under cover of slope and cliff, darkened the air with their shafts. The headlong force of the knights' charge was broken in the uneven ground, but the iron men came on grimly, bending their helmeted heads to the rain.

Then on the flanks kettledrums roared into fresh clamor. The riders of the right wing, led by Shirkuh, swept down the slopes and struck the horde which clustered loosely about the baggage train. That charge swept the unwarlike Egyptians off the field in headlong flight. The left wing began to close in to take the knights on the flank, driving before it the troops of the Turcoples. Amalric, hearing the kettledrums behind and on either side of him as well as in front, gave the order to fall back, before they were completely hemmed in.

To Giles Hobson it seemed the end of the world. He was deafened by the clang of swords and the shouts. He seemed surrounded by an ocean of surging steel and billowing dust clouds. He parried blindly and smote blindly, hardly knowing whether his blade cut flesh or empty air. Out of the defiles horsemen were moving, chanting exultantly. A cry of *"Yala-l-Islam!"* rose above the thunder—Saladin's war-cry, that was in later years to ring around the world. The Saracen center was coming into the battle again.

Abruptly the press slackened, broke; the plain was filled with flying figures. A strident ululation cut the din. The Turcoples' shafts had stayed the Saracens' left wing just long enough to allow the knights to retreat through the closing jaws of the vise. But Amalric, retreating slowly, was cut off with a handful of knights. The Turks swirled about him, screaming in exultation, slashing and smiting with mad abandon. In the dust and confusion the ranks of the iron men fell back, unaware of the fate of their king.

Giles Hobson, riding through the field like a man in a daze, came face to face with Guiscard de Chastillon.

"Dog!" croaked the knight. "We are doomed, but I'll send you to hell ahead of me!"

His sword went up, but Giles leaned from his saddle and caught his arm. The fat man's eyes were bloodshot; he licked his dust-stained lips. There was blood on his sword and his helmet was dinted.

"Your selfish hate and my cowardice have cost Amalric the field this day," Giles croaked. "There he fights for his life; let us redeem ourselves as best as we may."

Some of the glare faded from Chastillon's eyes; he twisted about, stared at the plumed heads that surged and eddied about a cluster of iron helmets; and he nodded his steel-clad head.

They rode together into the mêlée. Their swords hissed and crackled on mail and bone. Amalric was down, pinned under his dying horse. Around him whirled the eddy of battle, where his knights were dying under a sea of hacking blades.

Giles fell rather than jumped from his saddle, gripped the dazed king, and dragged him clear. The fat Englishman's muscles cracked under the strain, a groan escaped his lips. A Seljuk leaned from the saddle, slashed at Amalric's unhelmeted head. Giles bent his head, took the blow on his own crown; his knees sagged and sparks flashed before his eyes. Guiscard de Chastillon rose in his stirrups, swinging his sword with both hands. The blade crunched through mail, gritted through bone. The Seljuk dropped, shorn through the spine. Giles braced his legs, heaved the king up, slung him over his saddle.

"Save the king!" Giles did not recognize that croak as his own voice.

Geoffrey Fulcher loomed through the crush, dealing great strokes. He seized the rein of Giles' steed; half a dozen reeling, blood-dripping knights closed about the frantic horse and its stunned burden. Nerved to desperation, they hacked their way clear. The Seljuks swirled in behind them to be met by Guiscard de Chastillon's flailing blade.

The waves of wild horsemen and flying blades broke on him. Saddles were emptied and blood spurted. Giles rose from the red-splashed ground among the lashing hoofs. He ran in among the horses, stabbing at bellies and thighs. A sword stroke knocked off his helmet. His blade snapped under a Seljuk's ribs.

Guiscard's horse screamed awfully and sank to the earth. His grim rider rose, spurting blood at every joint of his armor. Feet braced wide on the blood-soaked earth, he wielded his great sword until the steel wave washed over him and he was hidden from view by waving plumes and rearing steeds.

Giles ran at a heron-feathered chief, gripped his leg with his naked hands. Blows rained on his coif, bringing fire-shot darkness, but he hung grimly on. He wrenched the Turk from his saddle, fell with him, groping for his throat.

Hoofs pounded about him, a steed shouldered against him, knocking him rolling in the dust. He clambered painfully to his feet, shaking the blood and sweat from his eyes. Dead men and dead horses lay heaped in a ghastly pile about him.

A familiar voice reached his dulled ears. He saw Shirkuh sitting his white horse, gazing down at him. The Mountain Lion's beard bristled in a grin.

"You have saved Amalric," said he, indicating a group of riders in the distance, closing in with the retreating host; the Saracens were not pressing the pursuit too closely. The iron men were falling back in good order. They were defeated, not broken. The Turks were content to allow them to retire unmolested.

"You are a hero, Giles ibn Malik," said Shirkuh.

Giles sank down on a dead horse and dropped his head in his hands. The marrow of his legs seemed turned to water, and he was shaken with a desire to weep.

"I am neither a hero nor the son of a king," said Giles. "Slay me and be done with it."

"Who spoke of slaying?" demanded Shirkuh. "I have just won an empire in this battle, and I would quaff a goblet in token of it. Slay you? By Allah, I would not harm a hair of such a stout fighter and noble toper. You shall come and drink with me in celebration of a kingdom won, when I ride into el Kahira in triumph."

The Road of Azrael

THE ROAD OF AZRAEL

I

Towers reel as they burst asunder,
Streets run red in the butchered
*   town;*
Standards fall and the lines go under
And the iron horsemen ride me down.
Out of the strangling dust around me
Let me ride for my hour is nigh,
From the walls that prison, the hoofs
*   that ground me,*
To the sun and the desert wind to die.

Allaho Akbar! There is no God but God. These happenings I, Kosru Malik, chronicle that men may know truth thereby. For I have seen madness beyond human reckoning, aye, I have ridden the road of Azrael that is the Road of Death, and have seen mailed men fall like garnered grain; and here I detail the truths of that madness and of the doom of Kizilshehr the Strong, the Red City, which has faded like a summer cloud in the blue skies.

Thus was the beginning. As I sat in peace in the camp of Muhammad Khan, sultan of Kizilshehr, conversing with divers warriors on the merits of the verses of one Omar Khayyam, a tentmaker of Nishapur and a doughty toper, suddenly I was aware that one came close to me, and I felt anger burn in his gaze, as a man feels the eyes of a hungry tiger upon him. I looked up, and as the firelight took his bearded face, I felt my own eyes blaze with an old hate. For it was Moktra Mirza, the Kurd, who stood above me, and there was an old feud between us. I have scant love for any Kurd, but this dog I hated. I had not known he was in the camp of Muhammad Khan, whither I had ridden alone at dusk, but where the lion feasts, there the jackals gather.

No word passed between us. Moktra Mirza had his hand on his blade, and when he saw he was perceived, he drew with a rasp of steel. But he was slow as an ox. Gathering my feet under me. I shot erect, my scimitar springing to my hand, and as I leaped I struck, and the keen edge sheared through his neck cords.

Even as he crumpled, gushing blood, I sprang across the fire and ran swiftly through the maze of tents, hearing a clamor of pursuit behind me. Sentries patrolled the camp, and ahead of me I saw one on a tall bay, who sat gaping at me. I wasted no time, but, running up to him, I seized him by the leg and cast him from the saddle.

The bay horse reared as I swung up, and was gone like an arrow, I bending low on the saddle-peak for fear of shafts. I gave the bay his head, and in an instant we were past the horse-lines and the sentries, who gave tongue like a pack of hounds, and the fires were dwindling behind us.

We struck the open desert, flying like the wind, and my heart was glad. The blood of my foe was on my blade, a good steed between my knees, the stars of the desert above me, the night wind in my face. A Turk need ask no more.

The bay was a better horse than the one I had left in the camp, and the saddle was a goodly one, richly brocaded and worked in Persian leather.

For a time I rode with a loose rein, then, as I heard no sound of pursuit, I slowed the bay to a walk, for who rides on a weary horse in the desert dices with Death. Far behind me I saw the twinkling of the campfires and wondered that a hundred Kurds were not howling on my trail. But so swiftly had the deed been done, and so swiftly had I fled, that the avengers were bemused and though men followed, not with hate, they missed my trail in the dark, I learned later.

I had ridden west by blind chance, and now I came on to the old caravan route that once led from Edessa to Kizilshehr and Shiraz. Even then it was almost abandoned because of the Frankish robbers. It came to me that I would ride to the caliphs and lend them my sword, so I rode leisurely across the desert which here is very broken land, flat, sandy levels giving way to rugged stretches of ravines and low hills, and these again running out into plains. The breezes from the Persian Gulf cooled me and even while I listened for the drum of hoofs behind me, I dreamed of the days of my early childhood when I rode, night-herding the ponies, on the great upland plains far to the East, beyond the Oxus.

And then, after some hours, I heard the sound of men and horses, but from in front of me. Far ahead I made out in the dim starlight, a line of horsemen and a lurching bulk I knew to be a wagon such as the Persians use to transport their wealth and their harems. Some caravan bound for Muhammad's camp, or for Kizilshehr beyond, I thought, and did not wish to be seen by them, who might put the avengers on my trail.

So I reined aside into a broken maze of gullies, and, sitting my steed behind a huge boulder, I watched the travelers. They approached my hiding place and I, straining my eyes in the vague light, saw that they were Seljuk Turks, heavily armed. One, who seemed a leader, sat his horse in a manner somehow familiar to me, and I knew I had seen him before. I decided that the wagon must contain some princess, and wondered at the fewness of the guards. There were not above thirty of them, enough to resist the attack of nomad raiders, no doubt, but certainly not enough to beat off the Franks who were wont to swoop down on Moslem wayfarers. And this puzzled me, because men, horses, and wagon had the look of long travel, as if from beyond the Caliphate. And beyond the Caliphate lay a waste of Frankish robbers.

Now the wagon was abreast of me, and one of the wheels creaking in the rough ground lurched into a depression and hung there. The mules, after the manner of mules, lunged once and then ceased pulling, and the rider who seemed familiar rose up with a torch and cursed. By the light of the torch I recognized him—one Abdullah Bey, a Persian noble high in the esteem of Muhammad Khan—a tall, lean man and a somber one, more Arab than Persian.

Now the leather curtains of the wagon parted and a girl looked out—I saw her young face by the flare of the torch. But Abdullah Bey thrust her back angrily and closed the curtains. Then he shouted to his men, a dozen of whom dismounted and put their shoulders to the wheel. With much grunting and cursing they lifted the wheel free, and soon the wagon lurched on again, and it and the horsemen faded and dwindled in my sight until all were shadows far out on the desert.

And I took up my journey again, wondering; for in the light of the torch I had seen the unveiled face of the girl in the wagon, and she was a Frank, and one of great beauty. What was the meaning of Seljuks on the road from Edessa, commanded by a Persian nobleman, and guarding a girl of the Nazarenes? I concluded that these Turks had captured her in a raid on Edessa or the Kingdom of Jerusalem and were taking her to Kizilshehr or Shiraz to sell to some emir, and so dismissed the matter from my mind.

The bay was fresh, and I had a mind to put a long way between me and the Persian army, so I rode slowly but steadily all night. And in the first white blaze of dawn, I met a horseman riding hard out of the west.

His steed was a long-limbed roan that reeled from fatigue. The rider was an iron man—clad in close-meshed mail from head to foot, with a heavy vizorless helmet on his head. And I spurred my steed to a gallop, for this was a Frank—and he was alone and on a tired horse.

He saw me coming and he cast his long lance into the sand and drew his sword, for he knew his steed was too weary to charge. And as I swooped down, as a hawk swoops on its prey, I suddenly gave a shout and, lowering my blade, set my steed back on his haunches, almost beside the Frank.

"Now by the beard of the Prophet," said I, "we are well met, Sir Eric de Cogan!"

He gazed at me in surprise. He was no older than I, broad-shouldered, long-limbed, and yellow-haired. Now his face was haggard and weary, as if he had ridden hard without sleep, but it was the face of a warrior, as his body was that of a warrior. I lack but an inch and a fraction of six feet in height, as the Franks reckon a man's stature, but Sir Eric was half a head taller.

"You know me," said he, "but I do not remember you."

"Ha!" quoth I, "we Saracens look all alike to you Franks? But I remember you, by Allah! Sir Eric, do you not remember the taking of Jerusalem and the Moslem boy you protected from your own warriors?"

Aye, I remembered! I was but a youth, newly come to Palestine, and I slipped through the beseiging armies into the city the very dawn it fell. I was not used to street-fighting. The noise, the shouting and the crashing of the shattered gates, bewildered me, and the dust and the foul smells of the strange city stifled me and maddened me. The Franks came over the walls and red Purgatory broke in the streets of Jerusalem. Their iron horsemen rode over the ruins of the gates, and their horses tramped fetlock deep in blood. The Crusaders shouted hosannas and slew like blood-mad tigers, and the mangled bodies of the faithful choked the streets.

In a blind red whirl and chaos of destruction and delirium, I found myself slashing vainly against giants who
seemed built of solid iron. Slipping in the filth of a blood-
running gutter, I hacked blindly in the dust and smoke,
and then the horsemen rode me down and trampled me. As
I staggered up, bloody and dazed, a great bellowing mon-
ster of a man strode on foot out of the carnage swinging an
iron mace. I had never fought Franks and did not then
know the power of the terrible blows they deal in hand-to-
hand fighting. In my youth and pride and inexperience I
stood my ground and sought to match blows with the
Frank, but that whistling mace shivered my sword to bits,
shattered my shoulder-bone, and dashed me half dead into
the bloodstained dust.

Then the giant bestrode me, and, as he swung up his
mace to dash out my brains, the bitterness of death took
me by the throat. For I was young, and in one blinding
instant I saw again the sweet upland grass and the blue of
the desert sky, and the tents of my tribe by the blue Oxus.
Aye—life is sweet to the young.

Then out of the whirling smoke came another—a
golden-haired youth of my own age, but taller. His sword
was red to the hilt, but his eyes were haunted. He cried out
to the great Frank, and though I could not understand, I
knew, vaguely, as one knows in a dream, that the youth
asked that my life be spared—for his soul was sick with the
slaughter. But the giant foamed at the mouth and roared
like a beast, as he again raised his mace—and the youth
leaped like a panther and thrust his long straight sword
through his throat, so the giant fell down and died in the
dust beside me.

Then the youth knelt at my side and made to staunch
my wounds, speaking to me in halting Arabic. But I mumbled, "This is no place for a Chagatai to die. Set me on a
horse and let me go. These walls shut out the sun, and the
dust of the streets chokes me. Let me die with the wind and
the sun in my face."

We were nigh the outer wall, and all gates had been
shattered. The youth caught one of the riderless horses
which raced through the streets and lifted me into the saddle. And I let the reins lie along the horse's neck, and he
went from the city as an arrow goes from a bow, for he,
too, was desert-bred and he yearned for the open lands. I
rode as a man rides in a dream, clinging to the saddle,

and knowing only that the walls and the dust and the blood of the city no longer stifled me, and that I would die in the desert after all, which is the place for a Chagatai to die. And so I rode until all knowledge went from me.

2

Shall the grey wolf slink at the mastiff's
heel?
Shall the ties of blood grow weak
and dim?—
By smoke and slaughter, by fire and
steel,
He is my brother—I ride with him.

Now, as I gazed into the clear grey eyes of the Frank, all this came back to me, and my heart was glad.

"What!" said he, "are you that one whom I set on a horse and saw ride out of the city gate to die in the desert?"

"I am he—Kosru Malik," said I. "I did not die—we Turks are harder than cats to kill. The good steed, running at random, brought me into an Arab camp, and they dressed my wounds and cared for me through the months I lay helpless of my wounds. Aye—I was more than half dead when you lifted me on the Arab horse, and the shrieks and red sights of the butchered city swam before me like a dim nightmare. But I remembered your face, and the lion on your shield.

"When I might ride again, I asked men of the Frankish youth who bore the lion-shield, and they told me it was Sir Eric de Cogan of that part of Frankistan that is called England, newly come to the East but already a knight. Ten years have passed since that crimson day, Sir Eric. Since then I have had fleeting glances of your shield gleaming like a star in the mist, in the forefront of battle, or glittering on the walls of towns we beseiged, but until now I have not met you face to face.

"And my heart is glad, for I would pay you the debt I owe you."

His face was shadowed. "Aye—I remember it all. You are in truth that youth. I was sick—sick—triply sick of bloodshed. The Crusaders went mad once they were within the walls. When I saw you, a lad of my own age, about to be butchered in cold blood by one I knew to be a brute and a vandal, a swine and a desecrator of the Cross he wore, my brain snapped."

"And you slew one of your own race to save a Saracen," said I. "Aye—my blade has drunk deep in Frankish blood since that day, my brother, but I can remember a friend as well as an enemy. Whither do you ride? To seek a vengeance? I will ride with you."

"I ride against your own people, Kosru Malik," he warned.

"My people? Bah! Are Persians my people? The blood of a Kurd is scarcely dry on my scimitar. And I am no Seljuk."

"Aye," he agreed," I have heard that you are a Chagatai."

"Aye, so," said I. "By the beard of the Prophet, on whom peace, Tashkent and Samarkand and Khiva and Bokhara are more to me than Trebizond and Shiraz and Antioch. You let blood of your breed to succor me—am I a dog that I should shirk my obligations? Nay, brother, I ride with thee!"

"Then turn your steed on the track you have come and let us be on," he said, as one who is consumed with wild impatience. "I will tell you the whole tale, and a foul tale it is, and one which I shame to tell, for the disgrace it puts on a man who wears the Cross of Holy Crusade.

"Know, then, that in Edessa dwells one William de Brose, Seneschal to the Count of Edessa. To him lately has come from France his young niece Ettaire. Now harken, Kosru Malik, to the tale of man's unspeakable infamy! The girl has vanished and her uncle would give me no answer as to her whereabouts. In desperation I sought to gain entrance to his castle, which lies in the disputed land beyond Edessa's southeastern border, but was apprehended by a man-at-arms close in the council of Brose. To this man I gave a death wound, and as he died, fearful of damnation, he gasped out the whole vile plot.

"William de Brose plots to wrest Edessa from his lord, and to this end has received secret envoys from Muhammad Khan, sultan of Kizilshehr. The Persian has promised to come to the aid of the rebels when the time comes.

Edessa will become part of the Kizilshehr sultanate and Brose will rule there as a sort of satrap.

"Doubtless each plans to trick the other eventually—Muhammad demanded from Brose a sign of good faith. And Brose, the beast unspeakable, as a token of good will sends Ettaire to the sultan!"

Sir Eric's iron hand was knotted in his horse's mane, and his eyes gleamed like a roused tiger's.

"Such was the dying soldier's tale," he continued. "Already Ettaire had been sent away with an escort of Seljuks—with whom Brose intrigues as well. Since I learned this I have ridden hard—by the saints, you would swear I lied were I to tell you how swiftly I have covered the long weary miles between this spot and Edessa! Days and nights have merged into one dim haze, so I hardly remember myself how I have fed myself and my steed, how or when I have snatched brief moments of sleep, or how I have eluded or fought my way through hostile lands. This steed I took from a wandering Arab when my own fell from exhaustion—surely Ettaire and her captors cannot be far ahead of me."

I told him of the caravan I had seen in the night, and he cried out with fierce eagerness but I caught his rein. "Wait, my brother," I said, "your steed is exhausted. Besides, now the maid is already with Muhammad Khan."

Sir Eric groaned.

"But how can that be? Surely they cannot yet have reached Kizilshehr."

"They will come to Muhammad ere they come to Kizilshehr," I answered. "The sultan is out with his hawks, and they are camped on the road to the city. I was in their camp last night."

Sir Eric's eyes were grim. "Then all the more reason for haste. Ettaire shall not bide in the clutches of the paynim while I live—"

"Wait!" I repeated. "Muhammad Khan will not harm her. He may keep her in the camp with him, or he may send her on to Kizilshehr. But for the time being she is safe. Muhammad is out on sterner business than lovemaking. Have you wondered why he is encamped with his slayers?"

Sir Eric shook his head.

"I supposed the Kharesmians were moving against him."

"Nay, since Muhammad tore Kizilshehr from the empire, the Shah has not dared attack him, for he has turned Sunnite and claims protection of the Caliphate. And for this reason many Suljuks and Kurds flock to him. He has high ambitions. He sees himself the Lion of Islam. And this is but the beginning. He may yet revive the powers of Islam, with himself at the head.

"But now he waits the coming of Ali bin Sulieman, who has ridden up from Araby with five hundred desert hawks and swept a raid far into the borders of the sultanate. Ali is a thorn in Muhammad's flesh, but now he has the Arab in a trap. He has been outlawed by the Caliphs—if he rides to the west their warriors will cut him to pieces. A single rider, like yourself, might get through, not five hundred men. Ali must ride south to gain Arabia—and Muhammad is between with a thousand men. While the Arabs were looting and burning on the borders, the Persians cut in behind them with swift marches.

"Now let me venture to advise you, my brother. Your horse has done all he may, nor will it aid us or the girl to go riding into Muhammad's camp and be cut down. But less than a league yonder lies a village where we can eat and rest our horses. Then, when your steed is fit for the road again, we will ride to the Persian camp and steal the girl from under Muhammad's nose."

Sir Eric saw the wisdom of my words, though he chafed fiercely at the delay, as is the manner of Franks, who can endure any hardship but that of waiting and who have learned all things but patience.

But we rode to the village, a squalid, miserable cluster of huts, whose people had been oppressed by so many different conquerors that they no longer knew what blood they were. Seeing the unusual sight of Frank and Saracen riding together, they at once assumed that the two conquering nations had combined to plunder them. Such being the nature of humans, who would think it strange to see wolf and wildcat combine to loot the rabbit's den.

When they realized we were not about to cut their throats they almost died of gratitude and immediately brought us food of their best—and sorry stuff it was—and cared for our steeds as we directed. As we ate we conversed; I had heard much of Sir Eric de Cogan, for his name is known to every man in Outremer, as the Franks call it, whether Caphar or Believer, and the name of Kosru Malik is not smoke for the wind to blow from men's ears.

He knew me by reputation, though he had never linked the name with the lad he saved from his people when Jerusalem was sacked.

We had no difficulty in understanding each other now, for he spoke Turki like a Seljuk, and I had long learned the speech of the Franks, especially the tongue of those Franks who are called Normans. These are the leaders and the strongest of the Franks—the craftiest, fiercest, and most cruel of all the Nazarenes. Of such was Sir Eric, though he differed from most of them in many ways. When I spoke of this he said it was because he was half Saxon. This people, he said, once ruled the isle of England, that lies west of Frankistan, and the Normans had come from a land called France, and conquered them, as the Seljuks conquered the Arabs, nearly half a century before. They had intermarried with the conquered, said Sir Eric, and he was the son of a Saxon princess and a knight who rode with William the Conqueror, the emir of the Normans.

He told me—and from weariness fell asleep in the telling—of the great battle which the Normans call Senlac and the Saxons Hastings, in which the emir William overcame his foes, and deeply did I wish that I had been there, for there is no fairer sight to me than to see Franks cutting each other's throats.

3

> *Pent between tiger and wolf,*
> *Only our lives to lose—*
> *The dice will fall as the gods decide,*
> *But who knows what may first betide?*
> *And blind are all of the roads we ride—*
> *Choose, then, my brother, choose!*

As the sun dipped westward Sir Eric woke and cursed himself for his sloth, and we mounted and rode at a canter back along the way I had come, and over which the trail of the caravan was still to be seen. We went warily for it was in my mind that Muhammad would have outriders to see that Ali bin Sulieman did not slip past him. And indeed, as dusk began to fall, we saw the last light of day glint on spear-tips and steel caps to the north and west, but we went with care and escaped notice. At about midnight we came upon the site of the Persian camp but it was deserted and the tracks led southeastward.

"Scouts have relayed word by signal smokes that Ali bin Sulieman is riding hard for Araby," said I, "and Muhammad has marched to cut him off. He is keeping well in touch with his foes."

"Why does the Persian ride with only a thousand men?" asked Sir Eric. "Two to one is no great odds against men like the Bedouins."

"To trap the Arab, speed is necessary," said I. "The sultan can shift his thousand riders as easily and swiftly as a chess player moves his piece. He has sent riders to harry Ali and herd him toward the route across which lies Muhammad with his thousand hard-bitten slayers. We have seen, far away, all evening, signal smokes hanging like serpents along the skyline. Wherever the Arabs ride, men send up smoke, and these smokes are seen by other scouts far away, who likewise send up smoke that may be seen by Muhammad's outriders."

Sir Eric had been searching among the tracks with flint, steel, and tinder, and now he announced: "Here is the track of Ettaire's wagon. See—the left hind wheel has been broken at some time and mended with rawhide—the mark in the tracks shows plainly. The stars give light enough to show if a wagon turned off from the rest. Muhammad may keep the girl with him, or he may send her on to his harem at Kizilshehr."

So we rode on swiftly, keeping good watch, and no wagon train turned off. From time to time Sir Eric dismounted and sought with flint and steel until he found the mark of the hidebound wheel again. So we progressed, and just before the darkness that precedes the dawn, we came to the camp of Muhammad Khan which lay in a wide reach of level desert land at the foot of a jagged tangle of bare, gully-torn hills.

At first I thought the thousand of Muhammad had become a mighty host, for many fires blazed on the plain, straggling in a vast half-circle. The warriors were wide awake, many of them, and we could hear them singing and shouting as they feasted and whetted their scimitars and strung their bows. From the darkness that hid us from their eyes, we could make out the bulks of steeds standing nearby in readiness, and many riders went to and fro between the fires for no apparent reason.

"They have Ali bin Sulieman in a trap," I muttered. "All this show is to fool scouts—a man watching from those hills would swear ten thousand warriors camped here. They fear he might try to break through in the night."

"But where are the Arabs?"

I shook my head in doubt. The hills beyond the plain loomed dark and silent. No single gleam betrayed a fire among them. At that point the hills jutted far out into the plains, and none could ride down from them without being seen.

"It must be that scouts have reported Ali is riding hither, through the night," said Sir Eric, "and they wait to cut him off. But look! That tent—the only one pitched in camp—is that not Muhammad's? They have not put up the tents of the emirs because they feared a sudden attack. The warriors keep watch or sleep beneath the wagons. And look— that smaller fire which flickers furthest from the hills, somewhat apart from the rest. A wagon stands beside it, and would not the sultan place Ettaire furtherest from the direction in which the enemy comes? Let us see to that wagon."

So the first step in the madness was taken: On the western side the plain was broken with many deep ravines. In one of these we left out horses and in the deepening darkness stole forward on foot. Allah willed it that we should not be ridden down by any of the horsemen who constantly patrolled the plain, and presently it came to pass that we lay on our bellies a hundred paces from the wagon, which I now recognized as indeed the one I had passed the night before.

"Remain here," I whispered. "I have a plan. Bide here, and if you hear a sudden outcry or see me attacked, flee, for you can do no good by remaining."

He cursed me beneath his breath, as is the custom of Franks when a sensible course is suggested to them, but when I swiftly whispered my plan, he grudgingly agreed to let me try it.

So I crawled away for a few yards, then rose and walked boldly to the wagon. One warrior stood on guard, with shield and drawn scimitar, and I hoped it was one of the Seljuks who had brought the girl, since if it were so, he might not know me, or that my life was forfeit in the camp.

But when I approached I saw that, though indeed a Turk, he was a warrior of the sultan's own bodyguard. But he had already seen me, so I walked boldly up to him, seeking to keep my face turned from the fire.

"The sultan bids me bring the girl to his tent," I said gruffly, and the Seljuk glared at me uncertainly.

"What talk is this?" he growled. "When her caravan arrived at the camp, the sultan took time only to glance at her, for much was afoot, and word had come of the movements of the Arab dogs. Earlier in the night he had her before him, but sent her away, saying her kisses would taste sweeter after the dry fury of battle. Well meseemeth he is sorely smitten with the infidel hussy, but is it likely he would break the sleep he snatches now—"

"Would you argue with the royal order?" I asked impatiently. "Do you burn to sit on a stake, or yearn to have your hide flayed from you? Harken and obey!"

But his suspicions were aroused. Just as I thought him about to step back and wake the girl, like a flash he caught my shoulder and swung me around so that the firelight shone full on my face.

"Ha!" he barked like a jackal. "Kosru Malik—!"

His blade was already glittering above my head. I caught his arm with my left hand and his throat with my right, strangling the yell in his gullet. We plunged to earth together and wrestled and tore like a pair of peasants, and his eyes were starting from his head when he drove his knee into my groin. The sudden pain made me relax my grip for an instant, and he ripped his sword-arm free, and the blade shot for my throat like a gleam of light. But in that instant there was a sound like an axe driven deep into a tree trunk, the Seljuk's whole frame jerked convulsively, blood and brains spattered in my face, and the scimitar fell harmlessly on my mailed chest. Sir Eric had come up while we fought and seeing my peril, split the warrior's skull with a single blow of his long straight sword.

I rose, drawing my scimitar, and looked about; the warriors still reveled by the fires a bowshot away; seemingly, no one had heard or seen that short fierce fight in the shadow of the wagon.

"Swift! The girl, Sir Eric!" I hissed, and stepping quickly to the wagon he drew aside the curtain and said softly, "Ettaire!"

She had been wakened by the struggle and I heard a low

cry of joy and love as two white arms went about Sir Eric's
mailed neck and over his shoulder I saw the face of the girl
I had passed on the road to Edessa.

They whispered swiftly to one another and then he lifted
her out and set her gently down. Allah—little more than a
child she was as I could see by the firelight—slim and frail,
with deep eyes, grey like Sir Eric's, but soft instead of cold
and steely. Comely enough, though a trifle slight to my
way of thinking. When she saw the firelight on my dark
face and drawn scimitar she cried out sharply and shrank
back against Sir Eric, but he soothed her.

"Be not afraid," said he. "This is our good friend, Kosru
Malik, the Chagatai. Let us go swiftly; any moment the
sentries may ride past this fire."

Her slippers were soft and she was but little used to
treading the desert. Sir Eric bore her like a child in his
mighty arms as we stole back to the ravine where we had
left the horses. It was the will of Allah that we reached
them without mishap, but even as we rode up out of the
ravine, the Frank holding Ettaire before him, we heard the
rattle of hoofs hard by.

"Ride for the hills," muttered Sir Eric. "There is a large
band of riders close at our heels, doubtless reinforcements.
If we turn back we will ride into them. Perchance we can
reach the hills before dawn breaks, then we can turn back
the way we wish to go."

So we thundered out on the plain in the last darkness
before dawn, made still darker by a thick, clammy fog,
with the tramp of hoofs and the jingle of armor and reins
close at our heels. I did not think they were reinforcements,
but a band of scouts, since they did not turn in to the fires
but made straight out across the levels toward the hills,
driving us before them, though they knew it not. Surely, I
thought, Muhammad knows that hostile eyes are on him,
hence this milling to and fro of riders to give an impression
of great numbers.

The hoofs dwindled behind us as the scouts turned aside
or rode back to the lines. The plain was alive with small
groups of horsemen, who rode to and fro like ghosts in the
deep darkness. On each side we heard the stamp of their
horses and the rattle of their arms. Tenseness gripped us.
Already there was a hint of dawn in the sky, though the
heavy fog veiled all. In the darkness the riders mistook us

for their comrades, so far, but quickly the early light would betray us.

Once a band of horsemen swung close and hailed us; I answered quickly in Turki and they reined away satisfied. There were many Seljuks in Muhammad's army, yet had they come a pace closer they would have made out Sir Eric's stature and Frankish apparel. As it was, the darkness and the mists clumped all objects into shadowy masses, for the stars were dimmed and the sun was not yet.

Then the noises were all behind us, the mists thinned in light that flowed suddenly across the hills in a white tide, stars vanished, and the vague shadows about us took the forms of ravines, boulders, and cactus. Then it was full dawn, but we were among the defiles, out of sight of the plains, which were still veiled in the mists that had forsaken the higher levels.

Sir Eric tilted up the white face of the girl and kissed her tenderly.

"Ettaire," said he, "we are encompassed by foes, but now my heart is light."

"And mine, my lord!" she answered, clinging to him. "I knew you would come! Oh, Eric, did the pagan lord speak truth when he said mine own uncle gave me into slavery?"

"I fear so, little Ettaire," said he gently. "His heart is blacker than night."

"What was Muhammad's word to you?" I broke in.

"When I first was taken to him, upon reaching the Moslem camp," she answered, "there was much confusion and haste, for the infidels were breaking camp and preparing to march. The sultan looked on me and spoke kindly to me, bidding me not fear. When I begged to be sent back to my uncle, he told me I was a gift from my uncle. Then he gave orders that I be given tender care and rode on with his generals. I was put back in the wagon, and thereafter stayed there, sleeping a little, until early last night when I was again taken to the sultan. He talked with me a space, and offered me no indignity, though his talk frightened me. For his eyes glowed fiercely on me, and he swore he would make me his queen—that he would build a pyramid of skulls in my honor and fling the turbans of shahs and caliphs at my feet. But he sent me back to my wagon, saying that when he next came to me, he would bring the head of Ali bin Sulieman for a bridal gift."

"I like it not," said I uneasily. "This is madness—the

talk of a Tatar chief rather than that of a civilized Moslem ruler. If Muhammad has been fired with love for you, he will move all Hell to take you."

"Nay," said Sir Eric, "I—"

And at that moment a half score of ragged figures leaped from the rocks and seized our reins. Ettaire screamed and I made to draw my scimitar; it is not meet that a dog of the Bedouin seize thus the rein of a son of Turan. But Sir Eric caught my arm. His own sword was in its sheath, but he made no move to draw it, speaking instead in sonorous Arabic, as a man speaks who expects to be obeyed, "We are well met, children of the tents; lead us, therefore, to Ali bin Sulieman, whom we seek."

At this the Arabs were taken somewhat aback and they gazed at each other.

"Cut them down," growled one. "They are Muhammad's spies."

"Aye," gibed Sir Eric, "Spies ever carry their womenfolk with them. Fools! We have ridden hard to find Ali bin Sulieman. If you hinder us, your hides will answer. Lead us to your chief."

"Aye," snarled one they called Yurzed, who seemed to be a sort of *beg* or lesser chief among them. "Ali bin Sulieman knows how to deal with spies. We will take you to him, as sheep are taken to the butcher. Give up thy swords, sons of evil!"

Sir Eric nodded to my glance, drawing his own long blade and delivering it hilt first.

"Even this was to come to pass," said I bitterly. "Lo, I eat dust—take my hilt, dog—would it was the point I was passing through thy ribs."

Yurzed grinned like a wolf. "Be at ease, Turk—time thy steel learnt the feel of a man's hand."

"Handle it carefully," I snarled. "I swear, when it comes back into my hands I will bathe it in swine's blood to cleanse it of the pollution of thy filthy fingers."

I thought the veins in his forehead would burst with fury, but with a howl of rage he turned his back on us, and we perforce followed him, with his ragged wolves holding tight to our reins.

I saw Sir Eric's plan, though we dared not speak to each other. There was no doubt but that the hills swarmed with Bedouins. To seek to hack our way through them were madness. If we joined forces with them, we had a chance to live, scant though it was. If not—well, these dogs love a Turk little and a Frank none.

On all sides we caught glimpses of hairy men in dirty garments, watching us from behind rocks or from among ravines, with hard, hawk-like eyes; and presently we came to a sort of natural basin where some five hundred splendid Arab steeds sought the scanty grass that straggled there. My very mouth watered. By Allah, these Bedouin be dogs and sons of dogs, but they breed good horseflesh!

A hundred or so warriors watched the horses—tall, lean men, hard as the desert that bred them, with steel caps, round bucklers, mail shirts, long sabers, and lances. No sign of fire was seen and the men looked worn and evil, as with hunger and hard riding. Little loot had they of that raid! Somewhat apart from them on a sort of knoll sat a group of older warriors, and there our captors led us.

Ali bin Sulieman we knew at once; like all his race he was tall and wide-shouldered, tall as Sir Eric, but lacking the Frank's massiveness, built with the savage economy of a desert wolf. His eyes were piercing and menacing, his face lean and cruel. Sir Eric did not wait for him to speak. "Ali bin Sulieman," said the Frank, "we have brought you two good swords."

Ali bin Sulieman snarled as if Sir Eric had suggested cutting his throat.

"What is this?" he snapped, and Yurzed spake, saying, "These Franks and this dog of a Turk we found in the fringe of the hills, just at the lifting of dawn. They came from toward the Persian camp. Be on your guard, Ali bin Sulieman; Franks are crafty in speech, and this Turk is no Seljuk, meseemeth, but some devil from the East."

"Aye," Ali grinned ferociously, "we have notables among us! The Turk is Kosru Malik the Chagatai, whose trail the ravens follow. And unless I am mad, that shield is the shield of Sir Eric de Cogan."

"Trust them not," urged Yurzed. "Let us throw their heads to the Persian dogs."

Sir Eric laughed and his eyes grew cold and hard, as is the manner of Franks when they stare into the naked face of Doom.

"Many shall die first, though our swords be taken from us," quoth he, "and, chief of the desert, ye have no men to waste. Soon ye will need all the swords ye have, and they may not suffice. You are in a trap."

Ali tugged at his beard, and his eyes were evil and hard.

"If ye be a true man, tell me whose host is that upon the plain."

"That is the army of Muhammad Khan, sultan of Kizil-shehr."

Those about Ali cried out mockingly and angrily and Ali cursed.

"You lie! Muhammad's wolves have harried us for a day and a night. They have hung at our flanks like jackals dogging a wounded stag. At dusk we turned on them and scattered them; then when we rode into the hills, lo, on the other side we saw a great host encamped. How can that be Muhammad?"

"Those who harried you were no more than outriders," replied Sir Eric, "light cavalry sent by Muhammad to hang on your flanks and herd you into his trap like so many cattle. The country is up behind you; you cannot turn back. Nay, the only way is through the Persian ranks."

"Aye, so," said Ali with bitter irony. "Now I know you speak like a friend; shall five hundred men cut their way through ten thousand?"

Sir Eric laughed. "The mists of morning still veil yon plain. Let them rise and you will see no more than a thousand men."

"He lies," broke in Yurzed, for whom I was beginning to cherish a hearty dislike, "all night the plain was full of the tramp of horsemen and we saw the blaze of a hundred fires."

"To trick you," said Eric, "to make you believe you looked on a great army. The horsemen rode the plain, partly to create the impression of vast numbers, partly to prevent scouts from slipping too close to the fires. You have to deal with a master at stratagems. When did you come into these hills?"

"Sometime after dark, last night," said Ali.

"And Muhammad arrived at dusk. Did you not see the signal smokes behind and about you as you rode? They were lighted by scouts to reveal to Muhammad your movements. He timed his march perfectly and arrived in time to build his fires and catch you in his trap. You might have ridden through them last night, and many escaped. Now you must fight by daylight, and I have no doubt but that more Persians are riding this way. See, the mist clears;

come with me to yon eminence and I will show you I speak truth."

The mist indeed had cleared from the plain, and Ali cursed as he looked down on the wide-flung camp of the Persians, who were beginning to tighten cinch and armor strap, and see to their weapons, judging from the turmoil in camp.

"Trapped and tricked," he cursed. "And my own men growl behind my back. There is no water nor much grass in these hills. So close those cursed Kurds pressed us, that we, who thought them the vanguard of Muhammad's army, have had no time to rest or eat for a day and a night. We have not even built fires for lack of aught to cook. What of the five hundred outriders we scattered at dusk, Sir Eric? They fled at the first charge, the crafty dogs."

"No doubt they have reformed and lurk somewhere in your rear," said Sir Eric. "Best that we mount and strike the Persians swiftly, before the heat of the growing day weakens your hungry men. If those Kurds come in behind us, we are caught in the nutcracker."

Ali nodded and gnawed his beard, as one lost in deep thought. Suddenly he spake. "Why do you tell me this? Why join yourselves to the weaker side? What guile brought you into my camp?"

Sir Eric shrugged his shoulders. "We were fleeing Muhammad. This girl is my betrothed, whom one of his emirs stole from me. If they catch us, our lives are forfeit."

Thus he spake, not daring to divulge the fact that it was Muhammad himself who desired the girl, nor that she was the niece of William de Brose, lest Ali buy peace from the Persian by handing us over to him.

The Arab nodded absently, but he seemed well pleased. "Give them back their swords," said he. "I have heard that Sir Eric de Cogan keeps his word. We will take the Turk on trust."

So Yurzed reluctantly gave us back our blades. Sir Eric's weapon was a true Crusader's sword—long, heavy, and double-edged, with a wide crossguard. Mine was a scimitar forged beyond the Oxus—the hilt set in jewels, the blade of fine blue steel of goodly length, not too curved for thrusting nor too straight for slashing, not too heavy for swift and cunning work yet not too light for mighty blows.

Sir Eric drew the girl aside and said softly, "Ettaire, God knows what is best. It may be that you and I and Kosru

Malik die here. We must fight the Persians and God alone knows what the outcome may be. But any other course had cut our throats."

"Come what may, my dear lord," said she, with her soul shining in her eyes, "if it find me by your side, I am content."

"What manner of warriors are these Bedouin, my brother?" asked Sir Eric.

"They are fierce fighters," I answered. "But they will not stand. One of them in single combat is a match for a Turk, and more than a match for a Kurd or a Persian, but the melee of a serried field is another matter. They will charge like a blinding blast from the desert, and if the Persians break and the smell of victory touches the Arabs' nostrils, they will be irresistible. But if Muhammad holds firm and withstands their first onslaught, then you and I had better break away and ride, for these man are hawks who give over if they miss their prey at the first swoop."

"But will the Persians stand?" asked Sir Eric.

"My brother," said I, "I have no love for these Irani. They are called cowards, sometimes; but a Persian will fight like a blood-maddened devil when he trusts his leader. Too many false chiefs have disgraced the ranks of Persia. Who wishes to die for a sultan who betrays his men? The Persians will stand; they trust Muhammad, and there are many Turks and Kurds to stiffen the ranks. We must strike them hard and shear straight through."

The hawks were gathering from the hills, assembling in the basin and saddling their steeds. Ali bin Sulieman came striding over to where we sat and stood glowering down at us. "What thing do ye discuss amongst yourselves?"

Sir Eric rose, meeting the Arab eye to eye. "This girl is my betrothed, stolen from me by Muhammad's men, and stolen back again by me, as I told you. Now I am hard put to find a place of safety for her. We cannot leave her in the hills; we cannot take her with us when we ride down into the plains."

Ali looked at the girl as if he had seen her for the first time, and I saw lust for her born in his eyes. Aye, her white face was a spark to fire men's hearts.

"Dress her as a boy," he suggested. "I will put a warrior to guard her, and give her a horse. When we charge, she shall ride in the rear ranks, falling behind. When we engage the Irani, let her ride like the wind and circle the Persian

camp if she may, and flee southward—toward Araby. If
she is swift and bold she may win free, and her guard will
cut down any stragglers who may seek to stop her. But
with the whole Iranian host engaged with us, it is not likely
that two horsemen fleeing the battle will be noticed."

Ettaire turned white when this was explained to her, and
Sir Eric shuddered. It was indeed a desperate chance, but
the only one. Sir Eric asked that I be allowed to be her
guard, but Ali answered that he could spare another man
better—doubtless he distrusted me, even if he trusted Sir
Eric, and feared I might steal the girl for myself. He would
agree to naught else, but that we both ride at his side, and
we could but agree. As for me, I was glad; I, a hawk of the
Chagatai, to be a woman's watchdog when a battle was
forward! A youth named Yussef was detailed for her duty,
and Ali gave the girl a fine black mare. Clad in Arabian
garments, she did in sooth look like a slim young Arab,
and Ali's eyes burned as he looked on her. I knew that did
we break through the Persians, we would still have the
Arab to fight if we kept the girl.

The Bedouins were mounted and restless. Sir Eric kissed
Ettaire, who wept and clung to him, then he saw that she
was placed well behind the last rank, with Yussef at her
side, and he and I took our places beside Ali bin Sulieman.
We trotted swiftly through the ravines and debouched upon
the broken hillsides.

There is no God but God! With the early morning sun
blazing on the eastern hills we thundered down the defiles
and swept out on to the plain where the Persian army had
just formed. By Allah, I will remember that charge when I
lie dying! We rose like men who ride to feast with Death,
with our blades in hands and the wind in our teeth and the
reins flying free.

And like a blast from Hell we smote the Persian ranks
which reeled to the shock. Our howling fiends slashed and
hacked like madmen and the Kizilshehri went down before
them like garnered grain. Their saberplay was too swift and
desperate for the eye to follow—like the flickering of summer lightning. I swear that a hundred Persians died in the
instant of impact when the lines met and our flying squadron hacked straight into the heart of the Persian host.
There the ranks stiffened and held, though sorely beset, and
the clash of steel rose to the skies. We had lost sight of

Ettaire and there was no time to look for her; her fate lay in the lap of Allah.

I saw Muhammad sitting his great white stallion in the midst of his emirs, as coolly as if he watched a parade—yet the flickering blades of our screaming devils were a scant spear-cast from him. His lords thronged about him—Kai Kedra, the Seljuk, Abdullah Bey, Mirza Khan, Dost Said, Mechmet Atabeg, Ahmed el Ghor, himself an Arab, and Yar Akbar, a hairy giant of a renegade Afghan, accounted the strongest man in Kizilshehr.

Sir Eric and I hewed our way through the lines, shoulder to shoulder, and I swear by the Prophet, we left only empty saddles behind us. Aye, our steeds' hoofs trod headless corpses! Yet somehow Ali bin Sulieman won through to the emirs before us. Yurzed was close at his heels, but Mirza Khan cut off his head with a single stroke and the emirs closed about Ali bin Sulieman, who yelled like a blood-mad panther and stood up in his stirrups, smiting like a madman.

Three Persian men-at-arms he slew, and he dealt Mirza Khan such a blow that it stunned and unhorsed him, though his helmet saved the Persian's brain. Abdullah Bey reined in from behind and thrust his scimitar point through the Arab's mail and deep into his back, and Ali reeled, but ceased not to ply his long saber.

By this time Sir Eric and I had hacked a way to his side. Sir Eric rose in his saddle and, shouting the Frankish war-cry, dealt Abdullah Bey such a stroke that helmet and skull shattered together and the emir went headlong from his saddle. Ali bin Sulieman laughed fiercely, and though at this instant Dost Said hewed through mail shirt and shoulder-bone, he spurred his steed headlong into the press. The great horse screamed and reared, and leaning downward, Ali sheared through the neck cords of Dost Said, and lunged at Muhammad Khan through the melee. But he over-reached as he struck and Kai Kedra gave him his death stroke.

A great cry went up from the hosts. Arabs and Persians, who had seen the deed, and I felt the whole Arabian line give and slacken. I thought it was because Ali bin Sulieman had fallen, but then I heard a great shouting on the flanks and above the din of carnage, the drum of galloping hoofs. Mechmet Atabeg was pressing me close and I had no time to snatch a glance. But I felt the Arab lines melting and crumbling away, and mad to see what was forward, I took a desperate chance, matching my quickness against the quickness of Mechmet Atabeg, and killed him. Then I chanced a swift look. From the north, down from the hills we had just quitted, thundered a squadron of hawk-faced men—the Kurds that had been following the Roualli.

At that sight the Arabs broke and scattered like a flight of birds. It was every man for himself and the Persians cut them down as they ran. In a trice the battle changed from a close-locked struggle to a loose maze of flight and single combats that steamed out over the plain. Our charge had carried Sir Eric and I deep into the heart of the Persian host. Now when the Kizilshehri broke away to pursue their foes, it left but a thin line between us and the open desert to the south.

We struck in the spurs and burst through. Far ahead of us we saw two horsemen riding hard, and one rode the tall black mare the Arabs had given Ettaire. She and her guard had won through, but the plain was alive with horsemen who flew and horsemen who pursued.

We fled after Ettaire, and as we swept past the group that guarded Muhammad Khan, we came so close that I saw the boldness and fearlessness of his brown eyes. Aye—there I looked on the face of a born king.

Men opposed us and men pursued us, but they who followed were left behind and they who barred our way died. Nay, the slayers soon turned to easier prey—the flying Arabs.

So we passed over the battle-strewn plain and we saw Ettaire rein in her mount and gaze back toward the field of battle while Yussef strove to urge her on. But she must have seen us, for she threw up her arm—and then a band of Kurds swept down on them from the side—camp followers, jackals who followed Muhammad for loot. We heard a scream and saw the swift flicker of steel, and Sir Eric groaned and rowelled his steed until it screamed and leaped madly ahead of my bay, and we swept up on the struggling group.

The Arab Yussef had wrought well; from one Kurd had he struck off the left arm at the shoulder, and he had broken his scimitar in the breast of another. Now as we rode up his horse went down, but as he fell, the Arab dragged a Kurd out of the saddle and rolling about on the ground, they butchered each other with their curved daggers.

The other Kurds, by some chance, had pulled Ettaire down, instead of slashing off her head, thinking her to be a boy. Now, as they tore her garments and exposed her face in their roughness, they saw she was a girl and fair, and they howled like wolves. And as they howled, we smote them.

By the Prophet, a madness was over Sir Eric; his eyes blazed terribly from a face white as death, and his strength was beyond that of mortal man. Three Kurds he slew with three blows and the rest cried out and gave way, screaming that a devil was among them. And in fleeing one passed too near me and I cut off his head to teach him manners.

And now Sir Eric was off his horse and had gathered the terrified girl in his arms, while I looked to Yussef and the Kurd and found them both dead. And I discovered another thing—I had a lance thrust in my thigh, and how or when I received it, I know not, for the fire of battle makes men insensible to wounds. I staunched the blood and bound it up as best I could with strips torn from my garments.

"Haste in the name of Allah!" said I to Sir Eric with some irritation, as it seemed he would fondle the girl and whisper pet names to her all morning. "We may be set upon any moment. Set the woman on her horse and let us begone. Save your love-making for a more opportune time."

"Kosru Malik," said Sir Eric, as he did as I advised, "you are a firm friend and a mighty fighter, but have you ever loved?"

"A thousand times," said I, "I have been true to half the women in Samarkand. Mount, in God's name, and let us ride!"

4

"I gasped, 'A kingdom waits my lord,
    her love is but her own,
'A day shall mar, a day shall cure for
    her, but what of thee?
'Cut loose the girl—he follows fast—cut
    loose and ride alone!'
Then Scindhia 'twixt his blistered lips,
'My queens' queen shall she be!' "
                              —Kipling

And so we rose out of that shambles to avoid any stray bands of pillagers—for all the countryside rises when a battle is fought and they care not whom they rob—we rode south and a little east, intending to swing back toward westward when we had put a goodly number of leagues between us and the victorious Kizilshehri.

We rode until past the noon hour, when we found a spring and halted there to rest the horses and to drink. A little grass grew there, but of food for ourselves we had none, and neither Sir Eric nor I had eaten since the day before, nor slept in two nights. But we dared not sleep with the hawks of war on the wing and none too far away, though Sir Eric made the girl lie down, in the shade of a straggling tamarisk, and snatch a small nap.

An hour's rest and we rode on again, slowly, to save the horses. Again, as the sun slanted westward, we paused awhile in the shade of some huge rocks and rested again, and this time Sir Eric and I took turns at sleeping, and though neither of us slept over half an hour, it refreshed us marvellously. Again we took up the trail, swinging in a wide arc to westward.

It was almost nightfall when I began to realize the madness that had fallen on Muhammad Khan. There came to me the strange restless feeling all desert-bred men know—the sensation of pursuit. Dismounting, I laid my ear to the ground. Aye, many horsemen were riding hard, though still far away. I told Sir Eric, and we hastened our pace, thinking it perhaps a band of fleeing Arabs.

We swung back to the east again, to avoid them, but when dusk had fallen I listened to the ground again, and again caught the faint vibration of many hoofs.

"Many riders!" I muttered. "By Allah, Sir Eric, we are being hunted."

"Is it us they pursue?" asked Sir Eric.

"Who else?" I made answer. "They follow our trail as hunting dogs follow a wounded wolf. Sir Eric, Muhammad is mad. He lusts after the maid, fool that he is, to thus risk throwing away an empire for a puling girl-child. Sir Eric, women are more plentiful than sparrows, but warriors like thyself are few. Let Muhammad have the girl. 'Twere no disgrace—a whole army hunts us."

His jaw set like iron and he said only, "Ride away and save thyself."

"By the blood of Allah," said I softly, "None but thou could use those words to me and live."

He shook his head. "I meant no insult by them, my brother; no need for thou, too, to die."

"Spur up the horses, in God's name," I said wearily. "All Franks are mad."

And so we rode on through the gathering twilight, into the light of the stars, and all the while, far behind us, vibrated the faint but steady drum of many hoofs. Muhammad had settled to a steady grinding gait, I believed, and I knew he would gain slowly on us, for his steeds were the less weary. How he learned of our flight I never knew. Perhaps the Kurds who escaped Sir Eric's fury brought him word of us; perhaps a tortured Arab told him.

Thinking to elude him, we swung far to the east, and just before dawn I no longer caught the vibration of the hoofs. But I knew our respite was short; he had lost our trail, but he had Kurds in his ranks who could track a wolf across bare rocks. Muhammad would have us ere another sun set.

At dawn we topped a rise and saw before us, spreading to the skyline, the calm waters of the Green Sea—the Persian Gulf. Our steeds were done; they staggered and tossed their heads, legs wide braced. In the light of dawn I saw my comrades' drawn and haggard faces. The girl's eyes were shadowed and she reeled with weariness, though she spoke no word of complaint. As for me, with a single half-hour's sleep for three nights, all seemed dim and like a dream at times, till I shook myself into wakefulness. But Sir Eric was iron, brain and spirit and body. An inner fire drove him and spurred him on, and his soul blazed so brightly that it overcame the weakness and weariness of his body. Aye, but it is a hard road, the road of Azrael!

We came upon the shores of the sea, leading our stumbling mounts. On the Arab side the shores of the Green Sea are level and sandy, but on the Persian side they are high and rocky. Many broken boulders lined the steep shores, so that the steeds had much ado to pick their way among them.

Sir Eric found a nook between two great boulders and bade the girl sleep a little, while I remained by her to keep watch. He himself would go along the shore and see if he might find a fisher's boat, for it was his intention that we should go out on the face of the sea in an effort to escape the Persians. He strode away along the rocks, straight and tall and very gallant in appearance, with the early light glinting on his armor.

The girl slept the sleep of utter exhaustion, and I sat nearby with my scimitar across my knees and pondered the madness of Franks and sultans. My leg was sore and stiff from the spear thrust, I was athirst and dizzy for sleep and from hunger, and saw naught but death for all ahead.

At last I found myself sinking into slumber in spite of myself, so, the girl being fast asleep, I rose and limped about, that the pain from my wound might keep me awake. I made my way about a shoulder of the cliff a short distance away—and a strange thing came suddenly to pass.

One moment I was alone among the rocks, the next instant a huge warrior had leaped from behind them. I knew in a flashing instant that he was some sort of a Frank, for his eyes were light and they blazed like a tiger's, and his skin was very white, while from under his helmet flowed flaxen locks. Flaxen, likewise, was his thick beard, and from his helmet branched the horns of a bull so at first glance I thought him some fantastic demon of the wilderness.

All this I perceived in an instant, as with a deafening roar the giant rushed upon me, swinging a heavy, flaring-edge axe in his right hand. I should have leaped aside, smiting as he missed, as I had done against a hundred Franks before. But the fog of half-sleep was on me and my wounded leg was stiff.

I caught his swinging axe on my buckler and my forearm snapped like a twig. The force of that terrific stroke dashed me earthward, but I caught myself on one knee and thrust upward, just as the Frank loomed above me. My scimitar-point caught him beneath the beard and rent his jugular, yet even so, staggering drunkenly and spurting blood, he gripped his axe with both hands, and with legs wide braced, heaved the axe high above his head. But life went from him ere he could strike.

Then, as I rose, fully awake now from the pain of my broken arm, men came from the rocks on all sides and made a ring of gleaming steel about me. Such men I had never seen. Like him I had slain, they were tall and massive with red or yellow hair and beards and fierce light eyes. But they were not clad in mail from head to foot like the Crusaders. They wore horned helmets, and shirts of scale mail which came almost to their knees but left their throats and arms bare, and most of them wore no other armor at all. They held on their left arms heavy kite-shaped shields, and in their right hands wide-edged axes. Many wore heavy golden armlets, and chains of gold about their necks.

Surely such men had never before trod the sands of the East. There stood before them, as a chief stands, a very tall Frank, whose hauberk was of silvered scales. His helmet was wrought with rare skill, and instead of an axe he bore a long heavy sword in a richly worked sheath. His face was as a man that dreams, but his strange light eyes were wayward as the gleams of the sea.

Beside him stood another, stranger than he; this man was very old, with a wild white beard and white elf locks. Yet his giant frame was unbowed, and his thews were as oak and iron. Only one eye he had, and it held a strange gleam, scarcely human. Aye, he seemed to reckon little of what went about him, for his lion-like head was lifted and his strange eye stared through and beyond that on which it rested, into the deeps of the world's horizons.

Now I saw that the end of the road was come for me. I flung down my scimitar and folded my arms.

"God gives," said I, and waited for the stroke.

And then there sounded a swift clank of armor, and the warriors whirled as Sir Eric burst roughly through the ring and faced them. Thereat a sullen roar went up and they pressed forward. I caught up my scimitar to stand at Sir Eric's back, but the tall Frank in the silvered mail raised his hand and spoke in a strange tongue, whereat all fell silent. Sir Eric answered in his own tongue. "I cannot understand Norse. Can any of you speak English or Norman French?"

"Aye," answered the tall Frank, whose height was half a head more than Sir Eric's. "I am Skel Thorwald's son, of Norway, and these are my wolves. This Saracen has slain one of my carles. Is he your friend?"

"Friend and brother-at-arms," said Sir Eric. "If he slew, he had just reason."

"He sprang on me like a tiger from ambush," said I wearily. "They are your breed, brother. Let them take my head if they will; blood must pay for blood. Then they will save you and the girl from Muhammad."

"Am I a dog?" growled Sir Eric, and to the warriors he said, "Look at your wolf, think you he struck a blow after his throat was cut? Yet here is Kosru Malik with a broken arm. Your wolf smote first; a man may defend his life."

"Take him, then, and go your ways," said Skel Thorwald's son slowly. "We would not take an unfair advantage of the odds, but I like not your pagan."

"Wait!" exclaimed Sir Eric. "I ask your aid! We are hunted by a Moslem lord as wolves hunt deer. He seeks to drag a Christian girl into his harem—"

"Christian!" rumbled Skel Thorwald's son. "But ten days agone I slew a horse to Thor."

I saw a slow desperation grow in Sir Eric's deep-lined face.

"I thought even you Norse had forsaken your pagan gods," said he, "but let it rest—if there be manhood among ye, aid us, not for my sake nor the sake of my friend, but for the sake of the girl who sleeps among those rocks."

At that, from among the rest thrust himself a warrior of my height and of mighty build. More than fifty winters he had known, yet his red hair and beard were untouched by grey, and his blue eyes blazed as if a constant rage flamed in his soul.

"Aye!" he snarled. "Aid ye ask, you Norman dog! You, whose breed overran the heritage of my people—whose kinsmen rode fetlock deep in good Saxon blood—now you howl for aid and succor like a trapped jackal in this naked land. I will see you in Hell before I lift axe to defend you or yours."

"Nay, Hrothgar," the ancient white-bearded giant spoke for the first time, and his voice was like the call of a deep-throated trumpet. "This knight is alone among we many. Entreat him not harshly."

Hrothgar seemed abashed, angry, yet wishful to please the old one.

"Aye, my king," he muttered half sullenly, half apologetically.

Sir Eric started: "King?"

"Aye!" Hrothgar's eyes blazed anew; in truth he was a man of constant spleen. "Aye—the monarch your cursed William tricked and trapped, and beat by a trick to cast from his throne. There stands Harold, the son of Godwin, rightful king of England!"

Sir Eric doffed his helmet, staring as if at a ghost.

"But I do not understand," he stammered. "Harold fell

at Senlac—Edith Swan-necked found him among the slain—"

Hrothgar snarled like a wounded wolf, while his eyes flamed and flickered with blue lights of hate.

"A trick to cozen tricksters," he snarled. "That was an unknown chief of the west, Edith showed to the priests. I, a lad of ten, was among those that bore King Harold from the field by night, senseless and blinded."

His fierce eyes grew gentler and his rough voice strangely soft.

"We bore him beyond the reach of the dog William, and for months he lay nigh unto death. But he lived, though the Norman arrow had taken his eye and a sword-slash across the head had left him strange and fey."

Again the lights of fury flickered in the eyes of Hrothgar.

"Forty-three years of wandering and harrying on the Viking's path!" he rasped. "William robbed the king of his kingdom, but not of men who would follow and die for him. See ye these Vikings of Skel Thorwald's son? Northmen, Danes, Saxons who would not bide under the Norman heel—we are Harold's kingdom! And you, you French dog, beg us for aid! Ha!"

"I was born in England—" began Sir Eric.

"Aye," sneered Hrothgar, "under the roof of a castle wrested from some good Saxon thane and given to a Norman thief!"

"But kin of mine fought at Senlac beneath the Golden Dragon, as well as on William's side," protested Sir Eric. "On the distaff side I am of the blood of Godric, earl of Wessex—"

"The more shame to you, renegade mongrel," raved the Saxon. "I—"

The swift patter of small feet sounded on the rocks. The girl had wakened, and, frightened by the rough voices, had come seeking her lover. She slipped through the mailed ranks and ran into Sir Eric's arms, panting and staring wildly about in terror at the grim slayers. The Northmen fell silent.

Sir Eric turned beseechingly toward them. "You would not let a child of your own breed fall into the hands of the pagans? Muhammad Khan, sultan of Kizilshehr is close on our heels—scarce an hour's ride away. Let us go into your galley and sail away with you—"

"We have no galley," said Skel Thorwald's son. "In the

night we ventured too close inshore, and a hidden reef ripped the guts out of her. I warned Asgrimm Raven that no good would come of sailing out of the broad ocean into this narrow sea, which witches make green fire at night—"

"And what could we, a scant hundred, do against a host?" broke in Hrothgar. "We could not aid you if we would—"

"But you, too, are in peril," said Sir Eric. "Muhammad will ride you down. He has no love for Franks."

"We will buy our peace by delivering to him you and the girl and the Turk, bound hand and foot," replied Hrothgar. "Asgrimm Raven cannot be far away; we lost him in the night, but he will be scouring the coast to find us. We had dared not light a signal fire lest the Saracens see it. But now we will buy peace of this Eastern lord—"

"Peace!" Harold's voice was like the deep mellow call of a great golden bell. "Have done, Hrothgar. That was not well said."

He approached Sir Eric and the girl, and they would have knelt before him, but he prevented it, and lightly laid his corded hand on Ettaire's head, tilting gently back her face so that her great pleading eyes looked up at him. And I called on the Prophet beneath my breath, for the ancient one seemed unearthly, with his great height and the strange mystic gleam of his eye, and his white locks like a cloud about his mailed shoulders.

"Such eyes had Editha," said he softly. "Aye, child, your face bears me back half a century. You shall not fall into the hands of the heathen while the last Saxon king can lift a sword. I have drawn my blade in many a less worthy brawl on the red roads I have walked. I will draw it again, little one."

"This is madness!" cried out Hrothgar. "Shall kites pick the bones of Godwin's son because of a French girl?"

"God's splendor!" thundered the ancient. "Am I king or dog?"

"You are king, my liege," sullenly growled Hrothgar, dropping his eyes. "It is yours to give command—even in madness we follow."

Such is the devotion of savage men!

"Light the beacon-fire, Skel Thorwald's son," said Harold. "We will hold the Moslem hard till the coming of Asgrimm Raven, God willing. What are thy names, thine and this warrior of the East?"

Sir Eric told him, and Harold gave orders. And I was amazed to see them obeyed without question. Skel Thorwald's son was chief of these men, but he seemed to grant Harold the due of a veritable monarch—he whose kingdom was lost and dead in the mists of time.

Sir Eric and Harold set my arm, binding it close to my body. Then the Vikings brought food and a barrel of stuff they called ale, which had been washed ashore from the broken ship, and while we watched the signal smoke go up we ate and drank ravenously. And new vigor entered into Sir Eric. His face was drawn and haggard from lack of sleep and the strain of flight and battle, but his eyes blazed with indomitable light.

"We have scant time to arrange our battlelines, your majesty," said he, and the old king nodded.

"We cannot meet them in this open place. They would league us on all sides and ride us down. But I noted a very broken space not far from here—"

So we went to this place. A Viking had found a hollow in the rocks where water had gathered, and we gave the weary horses to drink and left them there, drooping in the shade of the cliffs. Sir Eric helped the girl along, and would have given me a hand but I shook my head as I limped along. And Hrothgar came and slipped his mighty arm beneath my shoulders and so aided me, for my wounded leg was numb and stiff.

"A mad game, Turk," he growled.

"Aye," I answered, as one in a dream. "We be all madmen and ghosts on the Road of Azrael. Many have died for the yellow-haired girl. More will die ere the road is at an end. Much madness have I seen in the days of my life, but never aught to equal this."

5

*We shall not see the hills again where
    the grey cloud limns the oak,
We who die in a naked land to succour
    an alien folk;
Well—we have followed the Viking-path
    with a king to lead us forth—*

And scalds will thunder our victories in
the washael halls of the North.
  —*the Song of Skel Thorwald's son*

Already the drum of many hoofs was in our ears. We took our stand in a wide cleft of a cliff, with the broken, boulder-strewn beach at our backs. The land in front of us was a ravine-torn waste, over which the horses could not charge. The Franks massed themselves in the wide cleft, shoulder to shoulder, wide shields overlapping. At the tip of this shield-wall stood King Harold with Skel Thorwald's son on one hand and Hrothgar on the other.

Sir Eric had found a sort of ledge in the cliff, behind and above the heads of the warriors, and here he placed the girl.

"You must bide with her, Kosru Malik," said he. "Your arm is broken, your leg stiff; you are not fit to stand in the shield-wall."

"God gives," said I, "but my heart is heavy, and the tang of bitterness is in my mouth. I had thought to fall beside you, my brother."

"I give her in your trust," said he, and clasping the girl to him, he held her hungrily a moment, then dropped from the ledge and strode away, while she wept and held out her white arms after him.

I drew my scimitar and laid it across my knees. Muhammad might win the fight, but when he came to take the girl he would find only a headless corpse. She would not fall into his hands alive.

Aye, I gazed on that slim white bit of flesh and swore in wonder and amazement that a frail woman could be the death of so many strong men. Verily, the star of Azrael hovers over the birth of a beautiful woman, the King of the Dead laughs aloud, and ravens whet their black beaks.

She was brave enough. She ceased her whimpering and made shift to cleanse and rebandage my wounded leg, for which I thanked her. And while so occupied there was a thunder of hoofs, and Muhammad Khan was upon us. The riders numbered at least five hundred men, perhaps more, and their horses reeled with weariness. They drew rein at the beginning of the broken ground and gazed curiously at the silent band in the defile. I saw Muhammad Khan, slender, tall, with the heron feathers in his gilded helmet. And I saw Kai Kedra, Mirza Khan, Yar Akbar, Ahmed el Ghor

the Arab, and Kojar Khan, the great emir of the Kurds, he
who had led the riders who harried the Arabs.

Now Muhammad stood up in his golden stirrups and,
shading his eyes with his hand, turned and spoke to his
emirs, and I knew he had recognized Sir Eric beside King
Harold. Kai Kedra reined forward his steed through the
broken gullies as far as it could go, and, making a trumpet
of his hands, called aloud in the tongue of the Crusaders:
"Harken, Franks, Muhammad Khan, sultan of Kizilshehr,
has no quarrel with you; but there stands one who has stolen a woman from the sultan; therefore, give her up to us
and ye may depart peacefully."

"Tell Muhammad," answered Sir Eric, "that while one
Frank lives, he shall not have Ettaire de Brose."

So Kai Kedra rode back to Muhammad, who sat his
horse like a carven image, and the Persians conferred
among themselves. And I wondered again. But yesterday
Muhammad Khan had fought a fierce battle and destroyed
his foes; now he should be riding in triumph down the
broad streets of Kizilshehr, with crimson standards flying
and golden trumpets blaring, and white-armed women
flinging roses before his horse's hoofs; yet here he was, far
from his city, and far from the field of battle, with the dust
and weariness of hard riding on him, and all for a slender
girl-child.

Aye—Muhammad's lust and Sir Eric's love were whirl-
pools that drew in all about them. Muhammad's warriors
followed him because it was his will; King Harold opposed
him because of the strangeness in his brain and the mad
humor Franks call chivalry; Hrothgar, who hated Sir Eric,
fought beside him because he loved Harold, as did Skel
Thorwald's son and his Vikings. And I, because Sir Eric
was my brother-at-arms.

Now we saw the Persians dismounting, for they saw
there was no charging on their weary horses over that
ground. They came clambering over the gullies and boulders in their gilded armor and feathered helmets, with their
silver-chased blades in their hands. Fighting on foot they
hated, yet they came on, and the emirs and Muhammad
himself with them. Aye, as I saw the sultan striding forward with his men, my heart warmed to him again and I
wished that Sir Eric and I were fighting for him, and not
against him.

I thought the Franks would assail the Persians as they

clambered across the ravines but the Vikings did not move out of their tracks. They made their foes come to them, and the Moslems came with a swift rush across the level space and a shouting of *"Allaho akbar!"*

That charge broke on the shield-wall as a river breaks on a shoal. Through the howling of the Persians thundered the deep rhythmic shouts of the Vikings and the crashing of the axes drowned the singing and whistling of the scimitars.

The Norsemen were immovable as a rock. After that first rush the Persians fell back, baffled, leaving a crescent of hacked corpses before the feet of the blond giants. Many strung bows and drove their arrows at short range but the Vikings merely bent their heads, and the shafts glanced from their horned helmets or shivered on the great shields.

And the Kizilshehrians came on again. Watching above, with the trembling girl beside me, I burned and froze with the desperate splendor of that battle. I gripped my scimitar hilt until blood oozed from beneath my fingernails. Again and again Muhammad's warriors flung themselves with mad valor against that solid iron wall. And again and again they fell back broken. Dead men were heaped high and over their mangled bodies the living climbed to hack and smite.

Franks fell too, but their comrades trampled them under and closed the ranks again. There was no respite; ever Muhammad urged on his warriors, and ever he fought on foot with them, his emirs at his side. *Allaho akbar!* There fought a man and a king who was more than a king!

I had thought the Crusaders mighty fighters, but never had I seen such warriors as these, who never tired, whose light eyes blazed with strange madness, and who chanted wild songs as they smote. Aye, they dealt great blows! I saw Skel Thorwald's son hew a Kurd through the hips so the legs fell one way and the torso another. I saw King Harold deal a Turk such a blow that the head flew ten paces from the body. I saw Hrothgar hew off a Persian's leg at the thigh, though the limb was encased in heavy mail.

Yet there were no more terrible in battle than my brother-at-arms, Sir Eric. I swear, his sword was a wind of death and no man could stand before it. His face was lighted strangely and mystically; his arm was thrilled with superhuman strength, and though I sensed a certain kinship between himself and the wild barbarians who chanted and smote beside him, yet a mystic, soul-something set him apart from and beyond them. Aye, the forge of hardship and suffering had burned from soul and brain and body all dross, and left only the white-hot fire of his inner soul that lifted him to heights unattainable by common men.

On and on the battle raged. Many Moslems had fallen, but many Vikings had died, too. The remnant had been slowly hurled back by repeated charges until they were battling on the beach, almost beneath the ledge whereon I stood with the girl. There the formation was broken among the boulders and the conflict changed to a straggling series of single conflicts. The Norsemen had taken fearful toll—by Allah, no more than a hundred Persians remained able to lift the sword! And of Franks there were less than a score.

Skel Thorwald's son and Yar Akbar met face to face just as the Viking's notched sword broke in a Moslem's skull. Yar Akbar shouted and swung up his scimitar, but ere he could strike the Viking roared and leaped like a great lion. His iron arms locked about the huge Afghan's body and I swear I heard above the battle the splintering of Yar Akbar's bones. Then Skel Thorwald's son dashed him down, broken and dead, and, catching up an axe from a dying hand, made at Muhammad Khan. Kai Kedra was before him. Even as the Viking struck, the Seljuk drove his scimitar through mail links and ribs and the two fell together.

I saw Sir Eric hard beset and bleeding, and I rose and spoke to the girl.

"Allah defend you," said I, "but my brother-at-arms dies alone and I must go and fall beside him."

She had watched the fight white and still as a marble statue.

"Go, in God's name," she said, "and His power nerve your sword-arm—but leave me your dagger."

So I broke my trust for once, and, dropping from the ledge, came across the battle-tramped beach, my scimitar in my right hand. As I came I saw Kojar Khan and King Harold at sword strokes, while Hrothgar, beard abristle, dealt mighty blows on all sides with his dripping axe. And the Arab, Ahmed el Ghor, ran in from the side and hacked through Harold's mail so the blood flowed over his girdle. Hrothgar cried out like a wild beast, and lunged at Ahmed, who faltered an instant before the Saxon's terrible eyes. And Hrothgar smote him a blow that sheared through mail like cloth, severed the shoulder, and split the breastbone, and splintered the haft in the Saxon's hand. At almost the same instant King Harold caught Kojar Khan's blade on his left forearm. The edge sheared through a heavy golden armlet and bit to the bone, but the ancient king split the Kurd's skull with a single blow.

Sir Eric and Mirza Khan fought while the Persians surged about, seeking to strike a blow that would drop the Frank and yet not touch the emir. And I strode untouched through the battle, stepping over dead and dying men, and so came suddenly face to face with Muhammad Khan.

His lean face was haggard, his fine eyes shadowed, his scimitar red to the hilt. He had no buckler and his mail had been hacked to open rents in many places. He recognized me and slashed at me, and I locked his blade hilt to hilt; leaning my weight upon my weapon, I said to him, "Muhammad Khan, why be a fool? What is a Frankish girl to you, who might be emperor of half the world? Without you Kizilshehr will fall, will crumble to dust. Go your way and leave the girl to my brother-at-arms."

But he only laughed as a madman laughs, and tore his scimitar free. He leaped in, striking, and I braced my legs and parried his stroke, and, driving my blade beneath his, found a rent in his mail and transfixed him beneath the heart. A moment he stood stiffly, mouth open, then as I freed my point, he slid to the blood-soaked earth and died.

"And thus fade the hopes of Islam and the glory of Kizilshehr," I said bitterly.

A great shout went up from the weary, bloodstained Persians who yet remained, and they stood frozen. I looked for Sir Eric; he stood swaying above the still form of Mirza Khan, and as I looked he lifted his sword and pointed waveringly out to sea. And all the living looked. A long, strange craft was sweeping inshore, low in the waist, high of stern and bows, with a prow carved like a dragon's head. Long oars hurtled her through the calm water and the rowers were blond giants who roared and shouted. And as we saw this, Sir Eric crumpled and fell beside Mirza Khan.

But the Persians had had enough of war. They fled, those who were left to flee, taking with them the senseless Kai Kedra. I went to Sir Eric and loosened his mail, but even as I did so, I was pushed away, and the girl Ettaire was sobbing on her lover. I helped her get off his mail and, by Allah, it but hung in bloodstained shreds. He had a deep stab in his thigh, another in his shoulder, and most of the mail had been hacked clean away from his arms, which bore many flesh wounds; and a blade had cut through steel cap and coif links, making a wide scalp wound.

But none of the hurts was mortal. He was insensible from weakness—loss of blood and the terrific grind of the previous days. King Harold had been slashed deeply in the arm and across the ribs, and Hrothgar bled from gashes in the face and across chest muscles, and limped from a stroke in the leg. Of the half-dozen warriors that still lived, not one but was cut, bruised, and gashed. Aye, a strange and grisly crew they made, with rent, crimson mail and notched and bloodstained weapons.

Now as King Harold sought to aid the girl and me in stanching Sir Eric's blood-flow, and Hrothgar cursed because the king would not allow his own wounds to be seen to first, the galley grounded and the warriors thronged the shore. Their chief, a tall, mighty man, with long black locks, gazed at the corpse of Skel Thorwald's son and shrugged his shoulders. "Thor's love on a valiant warrior," was all he said. "He will revel in Valhalla this night."

Then the Franks took up Sir Eric and others of the wounded and took them aboard the ship, the girl clinging to his bloodstained hand and having no eyes or thought for any but her love, which is the way of womenkind, and as it should be. King Harold sat on a boulder while they bandaged his wounds, and again deep awe came over me to see him so, with his sword across his knees and his white elflocks flying in the rising wind, and his strange aspect, like a grey and ancient king of some immemorial legend.

"Good sir," he said to me, "you cannot abide in this naked land. Come with us."

But I shook my head. "Nay, my lord, it may not be. But one thing I ask; let one of your warriors bring to me here the steeds that we left down on the beach. I can walk no more on this wounded leg."

It was done, and the horses had so revived that I believed that by slow riding and changing mounts often I could win back out of the wilderness. King Harold hesitated as the rest went aboard. "Come with us, warrior! The sea-road is good for wanderers and landless men. There is quenching of thirst on the grey paths of the winds, and the flying clouds to still the sting of lost dreams. Come!"

"Nay," said I, "the trail of Azrael ends here. I have

fought beside kings and seen sultans fall, and my mind is dizzy with wonder. Take Sir Eric and the girl, and when they tell their sons the tale in that far land beyond the plains of Frankistan, let them sometimes remember Kosru Malik. But I may not come with you. Kizilshehr has fallen on this shore, but there be other lords of Islam who have need of my sword. Salaam!"

And so, sitting my steed, I saw the ship fade southward, and my eyes made out the ancient king standing like a grey statue on the poop, sword lifted high in salute, until the galley vanished in the blue haze of the distance, and solitude brooded over the quiet waves of the sea.

The Way of the Swords

THE WAY OF THE SWORDS
I

Though the cannon had ceased, their thunder seemed still to echo hauntingly among the hills that overhung the blue water. A league from the shore, the loser of that sea-fight wallowed in the crimson wash; just out of cannon-shot the winner limped slowly away. It was a scene common enough on the Black Sea in the year of our Lord 1595.

The galley heeling drunkenly in the blue waste was a high-beaked Barbary corsair. Death had reaped a plentiful harvest there. Dead men sprawled on the high poop; they hung loosely over the scarred rail; they slumped along the runway that bridged the waist, where the mangled oarsmen lay among their broken benches. Even in death these had not the appearance of men born to slavery; they were tall men, with dark hawk-like countenances. In pens about the base of the mast, fear-maddened horses fought and screamed.

Clustered on the poop stood the survivors, twenty men, many of them dripping blood from raw wounds. They were tall and lean, most of them, as men become who spend their lives in the saddle. They were burnt dark by the sun; beardless, their mustaches drooped below their chins; their heads were shaven except for a scalplock. They were clad in boots and baggy breeches; some wore *kalpaks,* some steel caps; others had no headwear. Some wore shirts of chain mail, others were naked to their sash-girt waists, their muscular arms and broad shoulders burnt almost black. Naked sabers were in their hands. Their dark eyes were restless; there was something of the eagle about them all—something wild and untamable.

They were standing about a man who lay dying on the poop. This man's drooping mustache was shot with gray, his face twisted with old scars. His *svitka* was thrown back, his shirt dyed by the blood that welled from a sword-cut in his side.

"Where is Ivan—Ivan Sablianka?" he muttered.

"Here he is, *asavul*," came the chorus, as a big warrior strode forward.

"Yes, here I am, uncle." The big man twisted his mustache uncertainly. He was the tallest man there, and heavily built. Clad like the others, he differed subtly from them. His wide eyes were blue as the waters of a deep sea, his scalplock and flowing mustache the color of spun gold.

He bent lower to hear the words of the dying *asavul*.

"He has escaped us, sir brothers," whispered this one. "Does any of the *sotniks* live?"

"Nay, little uncle," answered a lean, dark warrior who was binding a rude bandage about a gashed forearm. "Tashko swallowed a bullet the wrong way, and—"

"Nay, I saw the others die," murmured the older man. "I am the only officer among you, and I am dying. Ivan—*kunaks*—your task is not done. When we stood about the body of Skol Ostap, our Hetman, on the banks of Father Dnieper, we swore by our Cossack honor not to rest until we brought back the head of the devil that killed him. Now, after we've followed him clear across the Black Sea in one of his own galleys, he's beaten us off and staggers away; nay, he'll not ride far on a nag we foundered with cannon balls. He'll run in to shore. You have horses—follow! To Stamboul or to hell if you must! Ivan, you are *essaul* now. Follow! Die or take the head of Osman Pasha—who—killed—Skol—Ostap—"

The shaven head dropped on the scarred breast. The Cossacks doffed their *kalpaks* and crossed themselves awkwardly. They looked expectantly at Ivan Sablianka. He gnawed his mustache reflectively, glanced at the lateen sail drooping in the windless air, and stared at the shoreline. No harbor or town was visible on that wild and lonely coast. Low, tree-covered hills rose from the waterline, climbing swiftly to blue mountains in the distance, on whose snow-tipped peaks the sinking sun shone red. There was a reason why Ivan should know more about seas and ships than his comrades, but he had no exact idea as to where they were. They had crossed the Black Sea; therefore they were now in Moslem territory. These hills were doubtless full of Turks—he lumped all Muhammadan races under one contemptuous term.

He glared at the slowly receding galley. Its crew had been glad enough to break away from the death-grapple. The crippled corsair was making for a creek which wound out of the hills between high cliffs. She moved slowly, heeling to port. On the poop he could still make out a tall figure on whose helmet the sun sparkled. Ivan remembered the features under that helmet, glimpsed in the frenzy of battle: hawk-nosed, gray-eyed, black-bearded, stirring in the Cossack an elusive sensation of semi-recollection. That was Osman Pasha, until recently the scourge of the Levant.

Ivan went to one of the steering sweeps. He could not follow the corsair to the creek mouth, but he believed he could run the galley ashore on a sloping headland that ran out from the hills nearer at hand.

"Togrukh and Yermak, take the other sweep," he directed. "Dmetri and Konstantine, quiet the horses. The rest of you dog-souls tie up your cuts and then go down into the waist and bend your backs on the oars. If any of those Algerian pigs are still alive, knock them on the head."

There were not. Those whom the cannon balls of their former comrades had spared had been cut down by the Cossacks as they broke their chains and strove to swarm up out of the waist.

Laboriously, they worked the galley inshore. The sun was setting; a haze like soft blue smoke hovered over the dusky water. The corsair galley had limped into the creek, vanishing between the cliffs. Ivan and his comrades toiled stolidly. The starboard rail was almost awash, and the Cossacks abandoned the oars and came up on the poop. The horses were screaming again, mad with fear of the rising water.

The Cossacks looked at the shore, teeming, for all they knew, with hostile tribes, but they said nothing. They followed Ivan's directions as implicitly as if he had been elected *ataman* by regular conclave in the *Sjetsch*, that stronghold of free men on the lower reaches of the Dnieper.

To that brotherhood, where men took new names and new lives, Ivan had come five years before, speaking brokenly the speech of the Muscovites. He had aroused some suspicion, at first, by his reluctance to cross himself, though he swore he believed in God. After argument he had compromised by cutting a cross in the air with his sword. But he soon proved his honesty in battles against the Moslems, and, whatever his former life and tongue, he was all Cossack now.

His sword was one departure from form among men

where curved blades were the rule. It was straight, four and a half feet in length, broad and double-edged. Not half a dozen men on the frontier could wield it. It was in Ivan's fingers now as he leaned on the useless sweep and stared at the headland, which loomed nearer and nearer with each heave and roll of the floundering galley.

2

In the fertile valley of Ekrem happenings were coming to pass. The river that wound through the small patches of meadow and farmland was tinged red, and the mountains that rose on either hand looked down on a scene only less old than they. Horror had come upon the peaceful valley-dwellers, in the shape of wolfish riders from the outlands. They did not turn their gaze toward the castle that hung as if poised on the sheer slope high up the mountains; there, too, lurked oppressors.

The clan of Ilbars Khan, the Turkoman, driven westward out of Persia by tribal feud, was taking toll among the Armenian villages in the valley of Ekrem. It was but a raid for cattle, slaves, and plunder. He was ambitious; his dreams embraced more than the leadership of a wandering tribe. Kingdoms had been carved out of these hills before.

But just now, like his warriors, he was drunk with slaughter. The huts of the Armenians lay in smoking ruins. The barns had been spared, because they contained fodder for horses, as well as the ricks. Up and down the valley the lean riders raced, stabbing and loosing their barbed arrows. Men howled as the steel drove home; women screamed as they were jerked naked across the raiders' saddle-bows.

The horsemen in their sheepskins and high fur *kalpaks* were swarming in the straggling streets of the largest village—a squalid cluster of huts, half mud, half stone. Routed out of their pitiful hiding places, the villagers knelt, vainly imploring mercy, or as vainly fled, to be ridden down as they ran.

In this sport Ilbars Khan lost the chance of a kingdom. He spurred between the huts, out into the meadow, chasing a ragged wretch whose heels were winged by the fear of death. Ilbars Khan's lance point caught him between the shoulder blades. The shaft snapped and the drumming hoofs spurned the writhing body as the chief swept by.

"Allah il allah!" Beards were whitened with foam at the blood-mad yelp.

The *yataghans* whistled, ending in the zhukk! of cloven flesh and bone. A fugitive turned, crying out wildly, as Ilbars Khan swooped down on him, his wide kaftan spreading out in the wind like the wings of a hawk. In that instant the dilated eyes of the Armenian saw, as in a dream, the bearded face with its thin down-curving nose, the wide sleeve falling away from the lean arm that lifted, ending in a broad curving glitter of steel. In that instant, too, the Turkoman saw the gaunt stooped figure tensed beneath the rags, the wild eyes glaring from under the lank tangled hair, the long glimmer of light along the barrel of a musket. A wild cry rang from the lips of the hunted, drowned in the bursting roar of the firelock. A swirling cloud of smoke enveloped the figures, in which a flashing ray of steel cut the murk like a flicker of lightning. Out of the cloud raced a riderless steed, reins flowing free. A breath of wind blew the smoke away.

One of the figures on the ground drew itself up on one elbow. It was the Armenian, life welling fast from a ghastly cut across the neck and shoulder. Gasping for life, he looked down with wild glaring eyes on the other form. The Turkoman's *kalpak* lay yards away, blown there by the close-range shot; most of his brains were in it. Ilbars Khan's beard jutted upward as if in ghastly comic surprise. The Armenian's arm gave way and his face crashed into the dirt, filling his mouth with dust. He spat it out, dyed red. A ghastly laugh slobbered from his frothy lips. He fell back thrashing the sand with his hands. When the horrified Turkomans reached the spot, he was dead, with a ghastly smile frozen on his lips. He had recognized his victim.

The Turkomans squatted like evil vultures about a dead sheep, and conversed over the body of their khan. Their speech was evil as their countenances, and when they rose from that buzzards' conclave, the doom had been sealed of every Armenian in the valley of Ekrem.

Granaries, ricks, and stables, spared by Ilbars Khan, went up in flames. All prisoners were slain; infants tossed living into the flames, young girls ripped up and flung into the bloodstained streets. Beside the khan's corpse grew a heap of severed heads; the riders galloped up, swinging the ghastly relics by the hair, to toss on the grim pyramid. Every place that might conceivably lend concealment to a shuddering wretch was ripped apart.

It was while engaged in this that one of the tribesmen, prodding into a stack of hay, discerned a movement in the straw. With a wolfish yell he pounced upon it and dragged his victim to light, giving tongue in lustful exultation as he saw his prisoner. It was a girl, and no stodgy Armenian woman, either. Tearing off the cloak which she sought to huddle about her slender form, he feasted his vulture eyes on her beauty, scantily covered by the garb of a Persian dancing girl. Over her filmy *yasmaq* (veil) her dark eyes, shadowed by long kohl-tinted lashes, were eloquent with fear.

She said nothing, struggling desperately, her lithe limbs writhing in his cruel grip. He dragged her toward his horse; then quick and deadly as a cobra she snatched a curved dagger from his girdle and sank it under his heart. With a groan he crumpled, his sheepskins dyed red, and she sprang like a she-panther to his horse, seeming to soar to the high-peaked saddle, so lithe were her movements. The tall steed neighed and reared, and she wrenched it about and raced up the valley. Behind her the pack gave tongue and streamed out in hot pursuit. Arrows whistled about her head, and she flinched as they sang by, urging the steed to more frenzied efforts.

She reined him straight at the mountain wall on the south, where a narrow canyon opened into the valley. Here the going was perilous and the Turkomans reined to a less headlong pace among the rolling stones and broken boulders. But the girl rode like a leaf blown before a storm, and so it was that she was leading them by several hundred yards when she came upon a cluster of tamarisk-grown boulders that rose island-like above the level of the canyon floor. There was a spring among those boulders, and men were there.

She saw them among the rocks, and they shouted at her to halt. At first she thought them Turkomans; then she saw otherwise. They were tall and strongly built, chain mail glinting under their cloaks. Their white turban cloths were wrapped about spired steel caps. If the Turkomans were jackals, these were hawks. This she realized, her quick perception whetted by desperation. She saw the muzzles of matchlocks among the rocks, and caught the flicker of burning fuses. And she made up her mind instantly.

Throwing herself from the steed, she ran up the rocks, falling on her knees.

"Aid, in the name of Allah, the Merciful, the Compassionate!"

A man emerged from a clump of bushes and at the sight of him she cried out again, incredulously.

"Osman Pasha!" Then recollecting her urgent need, she clasped his knees, crying, "*Yah khawand,* protect me! Save me from those wolves which follow!"

"Why should I risk my life for you?" he asked indifferently.

"I knew you of old in the court of the Padishah!" she cried desperately, tearing off her veil. "I danced before you. I am Ayesha, the Persian."

"Many women have danced before me," he answered.

"Then I will give you a *talisman,*" said she in final desperation. "Listen!"

As she whispered a name in his ear, he started as if stung. Jerking up his head, he stared at her as if to plumb the depths of her inmost mind. For an instant he stood like a statue, his gray eyes turned inward; then, clambering upon a great boulder, he faced the oncoming riders with lifted hand.

"Go your way in peace, in the name of Allah!"

His answer was a whistle of arrows about his ears. He sprang down, waving his hands. Matchlocks began to crash from the rocks, the smoke billowing about the thicket-clad knoll. A dozen wild riders rolled from their saddles. The rest fell back, yelling in dismay. They wheeled and raced back up the gorge toward the main valley.

Osman Pasha turned to Ayesha, who had modestly resumed her veil. He was a tall man, with eyes like frosted steel. There was in his manner a certain ruthless directness rare in an Oriental. His cloak was of crimson silk, his chain mail corselet threaded with gold. His green turban was held in place about the silver-chased helmet with a jeweled brooch. Salt water, powder, and blood had stained his apparel, yet its richness was notable, even in that age of peacock splendor.

His men were gathered about him, forty stalwart Algerian pirates, bristling with weapons. In a depression behind the knoll were picketed horses of a rather inferior breed.

"My daughter," said Osman Pasha in a benign manner that was belied by his cruel eyes, "I have made enemies in this strange land on your behalf, because of a name whispered in my ear. I believed you—"

"If I lied may my skin be stripped from me," she swore.

"It will be," he promised gently. "I will see to it personally. You spoke the name of Prince Orkhan. What do you know of him?"

"For three years I have shared his exile."

"Where is he?"

She pointed up toward the mountains that overhung the distant valley, where the turrets of the castle were just visible among the crags.

"Across the valley, in yonder castle of el Afdal Shirkuh, the Kurd."

"It would be hard to take," he mused.

"Send for the rest of your seahawks!" she cried. "I know a way to bring you to the very heart of that keep!"

He shook his head.

"These you see are all my band."

Then, seeing her incredulity, he said, "I am not surprised that you wonder. I will tell you. . . ."

With the disconcerting frankness which his fellow Moslems found so inexplicable, Osman Pasha briefly sketched his fall. He did not tell her of his triumphs; they were too well known to need repeating. Five years before he had appeared suddenly on the Mediterranean as the *reis* of the famed corsair, Seyf ed-din Ghazi. He soon outstripped his master and gathered a fleet of his own, which owed allegiance to no ruler, not even the Barbary beys. At first an ally of the Grand Turk and a welcome guest at the Sublime Porte, he had later enraged the Sultan Murad by his raids on Turkish shipping.

Pillaging along the Dardanelles, the corsair had been trapped by an Ottoman fleet and all but two of his ships destroyed. The Sultan had spared his life, giving him a task that virtually amounted to a death sentence. He was commanded to sail up the Black Sea to the Dnieper mouth and there destroy another foe of the Turks—Skol Ostap, the Hetman of the Zaporogian Cossacks, whose raids into Moslem dominions had driven the Sultan well-nigh to madness.

The Cossacks at intervals shifted their *Sjetsch*—their armed camp—secretly from island to island to avoid surprise attacks. But a Greek traitor had led the corsair to the Dnieper island then occupied by the free warriors, at a time when many of them were away fighting the Tatars

across the river. The flying raid had failed in capturing
Skol Ostap, lying helpless of an old wound, because of the
ferocious resistance of the Cossacks with him. In the midst
of the battle the riders had returned from pounding the
Tatars, and Osman fled, leaving one of his ships in their
hands. He knew the penalty for failure, and instead of
fleeing toward the Turkish fleet which waited down the
coast, he struck straight out across the Black Sea, soon pursued by the Cossacks in his captured ship, using its crew
for oarsmen. He did not understand their persistence, not
knowing that a bursting shell from his cannon had slain the
wounded Skol Ostap and maddened his *kunaks*.

With the eastern shore in sight, they had drawn up
within cannonshot, and in the ensuing battle only the rising
of the oarsmen on their craft had won the day for the corsair.

"So we ran the galley ashore in the creek. We might
have repaired it, but the Sultan's fleets hold the gateway
out of the Black Sea, and he will have a bowstring ready
for me when he knows I've failed. We found a village up
along the creek; Moslems of a sort who toiled among vin-
yards and the fishing-nets. There we procured horses and
struck through the mountains, seeking we know not
what—a way out of Ottoman dominions or a new kingdom
to rule."

They had pushed on through the mountains for days,
fearing to fall afoul of Turkish outposts. Osman Pasha believed that swift couriers had already carried the word
throughout the empire that he was doomed. Whatever else
they were, the Turkish sultans were thorough in their
vengeance. He had been wandering without a plan, trusting
to luck.

Ayesha listened, and without comment began her tale.
As Osman well knew, it was the custom of the sultans,
upon coming to the throne, to butcher their brothers and
their brothers' children. Whatever its moral aspects, it can
not be denied that the custom saved the empire from many
disastrous civil wars, each Ottoman prince considering the
throne his prerogative. Sometimes a prison took the place
of the bowstring.

And so with Prince Orkhan, son of Selim the Drunkard
and brother of Murad III. When Selim passed out of his
besotted life, Murad had won in the race for the capital.
Another custom among the Turks was that of granting the

crown to whichever heir first reached Stamboul after the death of the sultan. The viziers and beys, dreading civil war, generally supported the first comer, who in turn bought the janizaries with rich gifts and set about eliminating his brothers. Even with this advantage the weak Murad could never have conquered his aggressive brother, had it not been for his *harim* favorite, Safia, a Venetian woman of the Baffo family. She was the real ruler of Turkey, and by her wiles, whereby the Venetians were drawn in to Murad's aid, Orkhan was driven into exile.

He sought refuge in the Persian court, but discovered that the Shah was corresponding with Safia in regard to poisoning him. In an attempt to reach India, he was taken captive by the nomadic Bashkirs, who recognized him and sold him into the hands of the Ottomans. Orkhan considered his fate sealed, but Murad dared not have him strangled, for he was still popular with the masses, especially the subject but ever turbulent Mamelukes of Egypt, and the *Sipahis*, the independent landholders of Anatolia. He was confined in a castle near Erzeroum, and furnished with all luxuries and forms of dissipation calculated to soften his fiber.

This was gradually being accomplished, Ayesha said. She was one of the dancing girls sent to entertain him. She had fallen violently in love with the handsome prince, and, instead of seeking to ruin him with her passion, had striven to lift him back to manhood. She had succeeded so well— though without being suspected—that the prince had been hurriedly and secretly taken from Erzeroum and carried up into the wild mountains above Ekrem, there to be put in charge of el Afdal Shirkuh, a fierce semi-bandit chief, whose family had reigned as feudal lords over the valley for a generation or so, preying on the inhabitants, though not protecting them.

"There we have been for more than a year," concluded Ayesha. "Prince Orkhan has sunk into apathy. One would not recognize him for the young eagle who led his Egyptian horsemen into the teeth of the janizaries. Imprisonment and wine and *bhang* have drugged his senses. He sits on his cushions in *kaif*, rousing only when I sing or dance for him. But he has the blood of conquerors in him. In him his grandfather, Suleyman the Magnificent, is reborn. He is a lion who but sleeps. . . .

"When the Turkomans rode into the valley, I slipped out

of the castle and came looking for Ilbars Khan, for I had heard of his ambitions. I wished to find a man bold enough to aid Orkhan. Let the young eagle's wings feel the wind again, and he will rise and shake the dust from his brain. Again he will be Orkhan the Splendid. But I saw Ilbars Khan slain before I could reach him, and then the Turkomans were like mad dogs. I was afraid and hid, but they dragged me out.

"Oh, my lord, aid us! What if you have no ship and only a handful at your back? Kingdoms have been built on less! When it is known that the prince is free—and thou art with him—men will flock to us! The feudal lords, the *Timariotes,* supported him before. Nay, had they known the place of his confinement, they had torn yon keep stone from stone! The Sultan is besotted. The people hate Safia and her mongrel son Muhammad.

"The nearest Turkish post is three days' ride from this place. Ekrem is isolated, unknown to most except wandering Kurds and the wretched Armenians. Here an empire can be plotted unmolested. You, too, are an outlaw. Let us band together to free Orkhan! To place him on his rightful throne! If he were Padishah, all wealth and honor were yours; Murad offers you naught but a bowstring!"

She was on her knees before him, her white fingers convulsively gripping his cloak, her dark eyes ablaze with the passion of her entreaty. Osman was silent, but cold lights glimmered in his steely eyes. He knew that what the girl said of Orkhan's popularity was true; nor did he underrate his own power. Kingmaker! It was a role such as he had dreamed of. And this desperate adventure, with death or a throne for prize, was just such as to stir his wild soul. Suddenly he laughed, and whatever crimes stained his soul, his laugh was as ringing and zestful as a gust of sea wind.

"We'll need the Turkomans in this venture," he said, and the girl clapped her hands with a brief passionate cry of joy.

3

"Hold up, *kunaks!*" Ivan Sablianka pulled up his steed and glanced about, craning his thick neck. Behind him his comrades shifted in their saddles. They were in a narrow canyon, flanked on either hand by steep slopes, grown with stunted firs. Before them a small spring welled up among straggling trees and trickled away down a moss-green channel.

"Water here, at least," grunted Ivan. "Light."

The Cossacks dismounted, drew off the saddles, and allowed the weary horses to drink their fill, before they satisfied their own thirst. For days they had followed the trail of the wandering Algerians. Since leaving the coast they had seen only one sign of life: a huddle of huts among the crags, housing nondescript skin-clad creatures who fled howling into ravines at their approach. They had been throughly looted by the Algerians, so that the Cossacks had been hard put to it to scrape together feed for the horses. For the men there was no food.

Their saddlebags, which they had filled in the village on the creek, were empty. The Algerians had taken heavy toll of its storehouses, and the Cossacks, coming after, had stripped them. There was little grass for grazing in these mountains. Now the Cossacks were without food for man or beast, and they had lost the trail of the pirates.

The previous nightfall had found them rapidly overhauling their prey, as shown by the freshness of the spoor, and they had pushed recklessly on, thinking to come upon the Algerian camp in the night. But with the setting of the young moon they had lost the trail in a maze of gullies, and had wandered blindly and at random. Now at dawn they had found water, but their horses were worn out, and they themselves completely lost. But they had no word of blame for Ivan, whose recklessness had gotten them into their present situation.

"Get some sleep," he growled. "Togrukh, you and Stefan and Vladimir take the first watch. When the sun's over that fir tree, wake three others. I'm going to scout up this gorge."

He strode away up the canyon and was soon lost among the straggling growth. The slopes on either hand changed to towering cliffs that rose sheer from the rock-littered floor which tilted upward. And with heartstopping suddenness, from a tangle of bushes and broken boulders, a wild shaggy figure sprang up and confronted the Cossack. Ivan's breath hissed through his teeth as his sword glittered high in the air; then he checked the stroke, seeing the apparition was weaponless. It was a lean gnome-like man in sheepskins, whose eyes, glaring wildly, took in every detail of the

giant Cossack, from his scalplock to his silver-heeled boots;
the mail shirt thrust into the wide breeches, the pistol-butts
jutting from the broad silk girdle.

"God of my fathers!" exclaimed the vagabond in the
speech of the Cossacks. "What does one of the free brotherhood in this Turk-haunted land?"

"Who are you?" grunted Ivan warily.

"I was the son of a *kral* of the Armenians," answered the
other with a strange wild laugh. "Call me Kral. One name
is as good as another to an outcast. What do you here?"

"What lies beyond this canyon?" Ivan countered.

"Over yonder ridge, which closes the lower end of this
defile, lies a tangle of gulches and crags. If you thread your
way among them, you will come out overlooking the broad
valley of Ekrem, which until yesterday was the home of my
tribe, and which today holds their charred bones."

"Is there food there?"

"Aye—and death. A horde of Turkomans hold the valley."

As Ivan ruminated this, a quick step brought him about,
to see Togrukh approaching.

"*Hai!*" Ivan scowled. "You had an order to watch while
the *kunaks* slept!"

"The *kunaks* are too cursed hungry to sleep," retorted
the saturnine Cossack, eyeing the Armenian suspiciously.

"Devil bite you, Togrukh," growled the big warrior. "I
can't conjure them mutton out of the air. They must gnaw
their thumbs until we find a village to loot—"

"I can lead you to enough food to feed a regiment," in-
terrupted Kral.

"Don't mock me, *Ermenie*," scowled Ivan. "You just said
the Turkomans—"

"Nay!" cried Kral, "there is a place not far from here,
unknown to the Moslems, where my people stored food
secretly. Thither I was going when I saw you coming up
the gorge."

Togrukh looked at Ivan, who drew and cocked a pistol.
"Then lead on, Kral," said the Zaporogian, "but at the
first false move—bang! goes a ball through your head."

The Armenian laughed, a wild scornful laugh, and motioned for them to follow. He made straight toward the
nearer cliff, and, groping among a cluster of brittle bushes,
disclosed what looked like a shallow crack in the wall.
Beckoning them after him, he bent and crawled inside.

"Into that wolf's den?" Togrukh glared suspiciously, but Ivan followed the Armenian, and the other came after him. They found themselves not in a cave but a narrow cleft of the cliff, in breathless twilight gloom. Forty paces farther they came out into a wide circular space, surrounded by towering walls that resembled monstrous honeycombs.

"These were the tombs of an ancient, unknown people," said Kral. "Their bones have long turned to dust. My people stored food in the caves against times of famine. Take your fill; there are no Armenians to need it."

Ivan looked curiously about him. It was like being at the bottom of a giant well. The floor was solid rock, worn smooth as if by the feet of ten thousand generations. The walls, honeycombed with regular tiers of tombs for fifty feet on all sides, rose stupendously, ending in a small circle of blue sky, where a vulture hung like a black dot.

"Your people should have dwelt in these caves," said Togrukh. "One man could hold that outer cleft against a horde."

The Armenian shrugged his shoulders. "Here there is no water. When the Turkomans swooped down there was no time to run and hide. My people were not warlike. They only wished to till the soil."

Togrukh shook his head, unable to understand such natures. Kral was pulling food for horses and men out of the lower caves: leather bags of grain, rice, moldy cheese, and dried meat, skins of sour wine.

"Go bring some of the lads to help carry the stuff, *kunak*," directed Ivan, staring up at the higher caves. "I'll stay here with Kral."

Togrukh swaggered off, his silver heels rapping on the stone, and Kral tugged at Ivan's steel-clad arm.

"Now do you believe I'm honest, *effendi*?"

"Aye, by God," Ivan answered, gnawing a handful of dried figs. "Any man that leads me to food must be a friend. But where were the villages of these ancients? They couldn't raise grain in that rocky gorge outside."

"They dwelt in the valley of Ekrem."

"But why didn't they lay away their dead closer by then? It must be a long, steep road from here to Ekrem."

Kral's eyes gleamed like a hungry wolf's. "That is the secret locked in the heart of these hills, known only to my people. But I will show you—if you will trust me."

"Well, Kral," said Ivan, munching away with relish, "w

Zaporogians have no need to lie and hide. We're following that black devil Osman Pasha the corsair, who is somewhere in these mountains—"

"Osman Pasha is no more than three hours' ride from this spot."

"Ha!" Ivan dashed down the figs and caught at his sword, his blue eyes ablaze.

"*Kubadar*— take care!" cried Kral. "There are forty corsairs, armed with matchlocks, and entrenched in Diva gorge. They have been joined by Arap Ali and a hundred and fifty Turkomans. How many warriors have you, *effendi*?"

Ivan twisted his mustache without reply, scowling heavily. He scratched his head, wondering what an *ataman* would have done under the circumstances. Deep thinking always made him drowsy, and he detested the effort. His head swam and his heavy arms ached with the desire to draw his great sword and forget the weariness of meditation in the dealing of gigantic strokes. Though he was the foremost swordsman of the *Sjetsch,* he had never before been given the leadership of his comrades. He swore now at the necessity. He was wiser than his *kunaks,* but he knew that was no great evidence of wisdom. Like him, they were reckless and improvident. Well led, they were invincible; without wise leadership they would throw their lives away on a whim. He had made a mistake in pushing on after dark, last night, but it was doubtful if that fact had occurred to them. Kral watched him keenly, reading the big Cossack's mental workings from the expressions of his broad bluff face.

"Osman Pasha is your enemy?"

"Enemy!" Ivan repeated aggrievedly. "I'll line my saddle with his hide."

"*Pekki!* Then come with me, *Kazak,* and I will show you what no man save an Armenian has seen for a thousand years!"

"What's that?" demanded Ivan suspiciously.

"A road of death for our enemies!"

Ivan took a step, then halted. "Wait. Here come the sir brothers. Listen to them swear, the dogs!"

"Send them back with the food," whispered Kral, as half a dozen scalplocked warriors swaggered out of the cleft and gaped about. Ivan faced them portentously, boot legs widestretched, belly thrust out, thumbs hooked into his girdle.

"Take up this stuff and lug it back to the spring, *kunaks*," he said with a grand gesture. "I told you I'd find food."

"And what of you?" demanded Togrukh, who was bitten by the devil of curiosity, as he gnawed a strip of *pasderma* [sun-dried mutton].

"Don't fret about me!" roared Ivan. "Am I not *essaul*? I have words with Kral. Go back to camp and eat beans, devil bite you!"

As the clatter of their boot-heels faded down the cleft, Kral led the way up a series of steps carved in the rock wall. High above the last tier of tombs, the dim ladder ended at the mouth of a cavern much larger than the others. In it Ivan could stand upright, and he saw that it ran back and disappeared in darkness.

"Up this shaft from the valley of Ekrem came the ancients bearing their dead," said Kral. "If you follow it you will come out behind the castle of the Kurd, el Afdal Shirkuh, that overlooks Ekrem."

"How shall it profit us?" grunted Ivan.

"Listen!" Kral squatted in the semi-darkness, his back against the cave wall. "Yesterday when the slaying began, I strove for awhile against the Turki dogs; then, when my comrades had been cut down. I fled the valley, running down the gorge of Diva. In the midst of this gorge there is a great heap of boulders, masked by thickets. This was held by strange warriors. I was among them before I was aware of them, and they beat me down with their pistol-barrels, and bound me, asking me questions to learn what went on in the valley; for as they rode down the gorge they had heard the shots and shouting, and had halted and entrenched themselves, and were about to send scouts forward. They were Algerian pirates, and they called their emir Osman Pasha.

"While they questioned me, a girl came riding like mad, with the Turkomans at her heels. When she sprang from her horse and begged aid of Osman Pasha I recognized her as the Persian dancing girl who dwells in the castle. A volley from the matchlocks scattered the Turkomans, and then he talked with the girl, Ayesha. They had forgotten me, and I lay near and heard all they said.

"For more than a year, Shirkuh has held a captive in his castle. I know, because I have taken grain and sheep to the castle, to be paid for after the Kurdish fashion, with curses and blows, *Kazak*, the prisoner is Orkhan, brother of Murad *Padishah!*"

The Cossack grunted in surprise.

"Ayesha disclosed this to Osman, and he swore to aid her in freeing the prince. As they talked, the Turkomans returned and reined in at a distance, vengeful, yet fearing the matchlocks. Osman hailed them, and they had speech, he and their chief Arap Ali, who commands since their khan was slain; and at last the Turkoman came among the rocks and squatted at Osman's fire and shared bread and salt. And the three plotted to rescue Prince Orkhan and put him on the throne.

"Ayesha had discovered the secret way from the castle. This day, just before sunset, the Turkomans are to attack the castle openly, and while they thus attract the attention of the Kurds, Osman and his pirates are to come to the castle by the secret way. Ayesha will have returned to Orkhan, and will open the secret door for them. They will take away the prince, and ride into the hills, recruiting warriors. As they talked night fell, and I gnawed through my cords and slipped away.

"You wish vengeance—here is a chance for vengeance and profit! I will show you how to trap Osman. Slay him—slay the girl—and their followers; take Orkhan and wring a mighty price from Safia. She will pay you richly to keep him out of the way, or to slay him."

"Show me," grunted the Cossack incredulously. Groping into a heap of goods in a corner, Kral produced a torch, which he lighted with flint and steel. As he set off down the cavern, the Zaporogian followed, drawing his broadsword. "No tricks, Kral, " he cautioned, "or your head leaves your shoulders."

The Armenian's laugh rang savagely bitter in the gloom. "Would I betray Christians to the butchers of my people?"

The cave had opened into a tunnel where three horses might have been ridden abreast. The smooth floor slanted downward, and from time to time short flights of steps cut into the stone gave onto lower levels. Ivan had no idea how far they had travelled when he heard the ripple of falling water, and the tunnel ended abruptly against a huge symmetrical block of stone, with a thin gray light stealing about the edges. Kral extinguished the torch, and Ivan heard him strain and grunt in the darkness. The block, hung on a stone pivot, swung aside and a sheet of silver shimmered before the Cossack's eyes.

They stood in the narrow mouth of the tunnel, which was masked by a sheet of water rushing over the cliff high above. From the pool which foamed at the foot of the falls a narrow stream raced away down the gorge. Kral pointed out a ledge that ran from the cavern mouth, skirting the pool, and Ivan followed him, first wrapping his powder-flasks and pistol-locks carefully in his silken sash. Plunging through the thin edge of the falls, Ivan found himself in a gorge that was like a knife-cut through the hills. Nowhere was it more than fifty paces wide, with sheer cliffs higher on the left than on the right. No vegetation grew anywhere, except for a fringe along the course of the stream. This stream meandered across the canyon floor to plunge into a narrow crack in the opposite cliff, eventually to find its way into the river that traversed Ekrem. The falling water completely masked the tunnel mouth, hiding all signs of the secret opening.

Ivan followed Kral up the gorge, which twisted like a tortured snake,. Within three hundred paces they lost sight of the waterfall, and only a confused murmur came to their ears. The gorge floor slanted upward at a steep pitch, and shortly Kral drew back, clutching his companion's arm. A stunted tree stood at a sharp angle of the rock wall, and behind this the Armenian crouched, pointing.

The Zaporogian grunted. Beyond the angle the gorge ran on for perhaps eighty paces, then ended in a blank impasse. On his right hand the cliff seemed curiously altered, and he stared for an instant before he realized that he was looking at a manmade wall. They were almost behind a castle built in a notch of the cliffs. Its wall rose sheer from the edge of a deep crevice; no bridge spanned this chasm, and the only apparent entrance in the wall was a heavy iron-braced door.

"By this path the girl Ayesha escaped," said Kral. "This gorge runs almost parallel to Ekrem; it narrows to the west and finally comes into the valley beyond where the village stood. The Kurds blocked the entrance there with stones so that it can not be discovered from the outer valley, unless one knows of it. They seldom use this road, and even they know nothing of the tunnel behind the waterfall, or the Caves of the Dead. But yonder door Ayesha will open to Osman."

Ivan gnawed his mustache. He yearned to loot the castle himself, but he saw no way to come to it. The chasm was too wide for a man to leap, and anyway, there was no ledge to cling to on the other side.

"By Allah, Kral," said he, "I'd like to look on this noted valley."

The Armenian glanced at his bulk and shook his head.

"There is a way we call the Eagle's Road, but it is not for such as you."

"By God!" roared the giant Cossack, bristling instantly, "is a skin-clad heathen a better man than a Zaporogian? I'll go anywhere you dare!"

Kral shrugged his shoulders and led the way back down the gorge until, within sight of the waterfall, he stopped at what looked like a shallow groove corroded in the higher cliff wall. Looking closely, Ivan saw a series of shallow handholds notched into the solid rock.

"Dogs bite you, Kral," he grumbled, "an ape could hardly scale these pockmarks."

Kral grinned mirthlessly. "Unsling your girdle and I'll aid you."

Ivan's pride struggled with his curiosity in his broad face; then he kicked off his silver-heeled boots and unwound his girdle—a strong length of silk, yards long. One end he bound to his sword-belt, the other to the Armenian's girdle. Thus equipped, they began the dizzy journey. The Cossack clung to the shallow pits with toes and fingernails, and time and again his blood turned to ice as he slipped on the sheer of the cliff. Half a dozen times only Kral's support saved him. But at last they gained the pinnacle, and Ivan sat down, his feet dangling over the edge, and tried to regain his breath. The gorge twisted like a snake track beneath him, and he looked over the southern wall into the valley of Ekrem, with its river flowing serpentine through it.

Smoke still floated lazily up from the blackened masses that had been villages. Down the valley, on the right bank of the river, were pitched a number of hide tents. Ivan made out men swarming about these tents, like milling ants in the distance. These were the Turkomans, Kral said, and pointed out the mouth of a narrow canyon up the valley, on the southern side, up which the Algerians were encamped. But it was the castle which drew Ivan's interest.

It was set solidly on a promontory of rock that jutted out

from the cliffs and sloped down into the valley. The castle faced the valley, entirely surrounded by a massive wall twenty feet high. A ponderous gate, flanked on either hand by a tower pierced with slanting slits for arrows, commanded the outer slope.

This slope was not too steep to be climbed with ease, but the ascent offered no cover. Men charging up it would be naked to a raking fire from the towers. Ivan swore.

"The devil himself couldn't take that castle by storm. How are we to come at the Soldan's brother in that pile of rock? Lead us to Osman Pasha. I want to take his head back to the *Sjetscha.*"

"Be wary if you wish to wear your own, *Kazak*," answered Kral grimly. "Look down into the gorge. What do you see?"

"A vastness of bare stone, and a fringe of green along the stream," grunted Ivan, craning his thick neck.

Kral grinned like a wolf. "*Taib!* And do you notice the fringe is much denser on the right bank, which is likewise higher than the other? Listen! Hidden behind the waterfall, we can watch until the Algerians come up the gorge. Then we will hide among the bushes along the stream and waylay them as they return. We'll kill them all except Orkhan, whom we will take captive. Then we'll go back through the tunnel, to the horses, and return to your land."

"That's easy," responded Ivan, twisting his long mustache. "We'll take a galley from the Turks. We'll swim out by night with our sabers in our teeth, and climb up the chains. Slash, stab! That's the way it'll be. We'll cut the heads off the *begs* and make the rest row us back across the sea. But what's this?"

Kral stiffened. Men were galloping out of the distant Turkoman camp, lashing their horses across the shallow river. The sunlight struck glints from lance-points. On the castle walls helmets began to sparkle.

"The attack!" cried Kral, glaring. "*Janam!* They've changed their plans! They were not to attack until nigh sunset! *Chabuk*—quick! We must get down the gorge before the Algerians come up it and catch us like rats in a trap!"

He glared down the defile, vanishing to the west like a saber-cut among the cliffs, straining his eyes for glint of shield or helmet. As far as he could see, the gorge lay bare of life. He urged Ivan over the cliff, and the big warrior cautiously levered his bulk into the shallow groove, cursing bitterly as he bumped his elbows.

Descending seemed even more perilous than ascending, but at last they stood in the gorge, and Kral hastened toward the waterfall, a furtive, hurried figure, grotesque in his sheepskins. He sighed as they reached the pool, crossed the ledge and plunged through the fall. But as they came into the ghostly twilight beyond, he halted, gripping Ivan's iron-sheathed arm. Above the rush of the water, his keen ears had caught the clink of steel on rock. They looked out through the silver shimmering screen that made all things look ghostly and unreal, and hid themselves effectually from the eyes of any outsider. A shudder shook Kral. They had not gained their refuge an instant too soon.

A band of men was coming along the gorge—tall men in mail hauberks and turban-bound helmets. At their head stood one taller than the rest, whose features, black-bearded and hawk-like as theirs, yet differed subtly from them. His gray eyes seemed to look full into the smoldering blue eyes of the giant Cossack, as the corsair glanced at the waterfall. A deep sigh rose from the depths of Ivan's capacious belly, and his iron hand locked convulsively about his hilt. Impulsively he took a quick step forward, but Kral threw his knotted arms about him and hung on desperately.

"In God's name, *Kazak!*" he cried in a frenzied whisper. "Don't throw away our lives! We have them in a trap. If you rush out now, they'll shoot you down like a rat; then who'll take Osman's head back to the *Sjetsch?*"

Like many of his race, Kral had wandered among the Cossacks as a trader, and he knew their utterly reckless spirit.

"I could send a ball through his skull from here," muttered Ivan.

"Nay, it would betray us, and even if you brought him down, you could not take his head. Patience, oh, patience! I tell you, not a dog of them shall escape. Hate? Look at that lean vulture in sheepskins and *kalpak* beside Osman. That is Arap Ali, the Turkoman chief who slew my young sister and her husband. Do you hate Osman? By the God of my fathers, my very brain reels with madness to leap out upon Arap Ali and rend his throat with my teeth! But patience! Patience!"

The Algerians were crossing the narrow stream, their

khalats girt high, holding their matchlocks above their heads to keep the charges dry. On the farther bank they halted, in an attitude of listening. Presently, above the rush of the waters, the men in the cave mouth heard a faint booming sound that came from up the gorge.

"The Kurds are firing from the towers!" whispered Kral.

As if it were a signal for which they were waiting, the Algerians shouldered their pieces and started swiftly up the gorge. Kral touched the Cossack's arm.

"Bide ye here and watch. I'll hasten back and bring the sir brothers. It will be touch and go if I can get them here before the pirates return."

"Haste, then," grunted the giant, and Kral slipped away like a shadow.

4

In broad chamber luxuriant with gold-worked tapestries, silken divans and embroidered velvet cushions, the prince Orkhan reclined. He seemed the picture of voluptuous idleness as he lounged there in a green satin vest, silk *khalat* and velvet slippers, a crystal jar of wine at his elbow. His dark eyes, brooding and introspective, were those of a dreamer, whose dreams are tinted with hashish and opium. But the strong lines in his keen face were not yet erased by dissipation, and under the rich robe his limbs were cleancut and hard. His gaze rested on Ayesha, who tensely gripped the bars of a casement, peering eagerly out, but there was a faraway look in his eyes. He seemed not aware of the shots, yells, and clamor that raged without. Absently he murmured the lines written by a more famous exile of his house:

"*Jam-i-Jem nush eyle, ey Jem, bu Firankistan dir—*"

Ayesha moved restlessly, glancing at him quickly over her slim shoulder. Somewhere in this daughter of Iran burned the blood of ancient Aryan conquerors who knew not Kismet. A thousand overlying generations of Oriental fatalism had not washed it out. Outwardly Ayesha was a devout Moslem. Inwardly she was an untamed pagan. She had fought like a tigress to keep Orkhan from falling into the gulf of degeneracy and resignation his captors had prepared. "Allah wills it"—the phrase embraces a whole Turanian philosophy, is at once excuse and consolation for failure. But hot in Ayesha's veins ran the blood of yellow-haired kings who trod down Nineveh and Babylon and knew no god but their own desires. She was the scourge that kept Orkhan stung into life and ambition.

"It is time," she breathed, turning from the casement. "The sun hangs at the zenith. The Turkomans ride up the slope, lashing their steeds and loosing their arrows vainly against the walls. The Kurds shoot down on them—hark to the roar of the firelocks. The bodies of the tribesmen strew the slopes and the survivors give back—now they come on again like madmen. They are dying for thee, *yah khawand!* I must hasten; thou shalt yet sit on the throne on the Golden Horn, my lover!"

Casting her lithe body prostrate before him, she kissed his slippered feet in an ecstasy of passion, then, rising, hurried out of the chamber, through another where ten giant black mutes kept guard night and day, and, traversing a corridor, found herself in the outer court that lay between the castle and the postern wall. No one had tried to halt her. She was free to come and go within the walls as much as she liked, though Orkhan was not allowed outside his chamber unguarded. Few questions had been asked her when she returned to the castle, feigning great fear of the Turkomans. She had carefully hidden her infatuation for the prince from the eagle eyes of the Kurdish chief, who thought her no more than a tool of Safia.

Crossing the court, she approached the door that let into the gorge. One warrior leaned there, disgruntled because he could not take part in the fighting that was going on. Shirkuh was a cautious man. The rear of his castle seemed invulnerable, but he never took unnecessary chances. It was not his fault that he was unaware of a traitress in his midst. Wiser men than he have been duped by women like Ayesha.

The man on guard was an Uzbek, his small turban knotted over his left ear, his wide girdle loaded with knives and pistols. He leaned on a matchlock, scowling, as Ayesha approached him, her dark eyes eloquent above the filmy veil.

He spat and glowered. "What do you here, woman?"

She drew her light mantle closer about her slender shoulders, trembling. "I am afraid. The cries and shots frighten me, *bahadur*. The prince is drugged with opium, and there is none to soothe my fears."

She would have fired the frozen heart of a dead man as

she stood there, in her attitude of trembling fear and supplication. The Uzbek plucked his thick beard.

"Fear not, little gazelle," he said finally. "I'll soothe thee, by Allah!" He laid a black-nailed hand on her shoulder and drew her close to him. "None shall lay a finger on a lock of thy hair," he muttered. "I—*ahhhh!*"

Snuggling in his arms, she had slipped a dagger from her sash and thrust it through his bull throat. One hand lurched from her shoulder to claw at the hilts in his girdle, while the other clutched at his beard, blood spurting between his fingers. He reeled and fell heavily. Ayesha snatched a bunch of keys from his girdle and, without a second glance at her victim, ran to the door. Her heart was in her mouth as she swung it open; then she gave a low cry of joy. On the opposite edge of the chasm stood Osman Pasha with his pirates.

A heavy plank, used for a bridge, lay inside the gate, but it was far too heavy for her to handle. Chance had enabled her to use it for her previous escape, when rare carelessness had left it in place across the chasm and unguarded for a few minutes. Osman tossed her the end of a rope, and this she made fast to the hinges of the door. The other end was gripped fast by half a dozen strong men, and three Algerians crossed the crevice, swinging hand over hand as agilely as apes. They lifted the plank and spanned the chasm for the rest to cross. There was no sight of a defender. The firing from the front of the castle continued without a break.

"Twenty men guard the bridge," snapped Osman. "The rest follow me."

Leaving their matchlocks, twenty desperate sea-wolves drew their steel and followed their chief. Osman grinned as he led them swiftly after the light-footed girl. Such a touch-and-go venture, in the heart of the lion's lair, fired his wild blood like wine. As they entered the castle, a servitor sprang up and gaped at them, wild-eyed. Before he could cry out Arap Ali's razor-edged yataghan sliced through his throat, and the band rushed recklessly into the chamber where the ten mutes sprang up, gripping their scimitars. There was a flurry of fierce, silent battling, noiseless except for the hiss and rasp of steel and the croaking gasp of the wounded. Three Algerians died, and over the mangled bodies of the blacks, Osman Pasha strode into the inner chamber.

Orkhan rose up and his quiet eyes gleamed with an old fire as Osman, with an instinct for dramatics, knelt before him and lifted the hilt of his bloodstained scimitar.

"These are the warriors who shall set you on your throne!" cried Ayesha, clenching her white hands in passionate joy. "*Yah Allah*! Oh, my lord, what an hour is this!"

"Let us go quickly, before the Kurdish dogs are aware of us," said Osman, drawing his warriors up about Orkhan in a solid clump of steel.

Swiftly they traversed the chambers, crossed the court and approached the gate. But the clang of steel had been heard. Even as the raiders were crossing the bridge, a medley of savage yells rose behind them. Across the courtyard rushed a tall figure in silk and steel, followed by fifty helmeted swordsmen.

"Shirkuh!" screamed Ayesha, paling. "*La Allah—*"

"Cast down the plank!" roared Osman, springing to the bridgehead.

On each side of the chasm matchlocks flashed and roared. Half a dozen Kurds crumpled, but the four Algerians who had stooped to lift the plank went down in a writhing heap before a raking volley, and across the bridge rushed Shirkuh, his hawk face convulsed, his scimitar flashing about his steel-clad head. Osman Pasha met him breast to breast, and in a glittering whirl of steel the corsair's scimitar grated around Shirkuh's blade, and the keen edge cut through the camail and the thick muscles of the Kurd's neck. Shirkuh staggered and with a wild cry pitched back and over, headlong down the chasm.

In an instant the Algerians had cast the bridge after him, and the Kurds halted, yelling with baffled fury, on the far side of the crevice. What had been their strength was now their weakness. They could not reach their foes, but sheltered by the wall they opened up a vengeful fire, and three more Algerians were struck before the band could get out of range around the angle of the cliff. Osman cursed. Ten men was more than he had expected to lose on that flying raid.

"All but six of you go forward and see that the way is clear," he ordered. "I will follow more slowly with the prince. *Mirza*, I could not bring a horse up the defile, but I will have my dogs carry you on a litter of cloaks slung between spears—"

"Allah forbid that I should ride on the shoulders of my deliverers!" cried the young Turk in a ringing voice. "I will not forget this day! Again I am a man! I am Orkhan, son of Selim! I will not forget that either, *Inshallah!*"

"*Mashallah*—God be praised!" whispered the Persian girl. "Oh, my lord, I am blind and dizzy with joy to hear you speak thus! In good truth you are a man again, and shall be *Padishah* of all the Osmanli!"

They were within sight of the waterfall. The first detachment had almost reached the stream, when suddenly and unexpectedly as the strike of a hidden cobra, a pistol cracked in the bushes on the other side, and a pirate fell, his brains oozing from a hole in his skull. Instantly, as if the shot were a signal, there crashed a volley from the bushes. The foremost corsairs went down like ripe corn, and the rest gave back, shouting in rage and terror. They could see no sign of their attackers, save the smoke billowing across the stream and the dead men at their feet.

"Dog!" foamed Osman Pasha, turning on Arap Ali. "This is your work!"

"Have I matchlocks?" squalled the Turkoman, his dark face ashen. "*Ya Ali, alahu!* It is the work of devils!"

Osman ran down the gorge toward his demoralized men, cursing like a fiend. He knew the Kurds would rig up some sort of a bridge across the chasm and pursue him, then he would be caught between two fires. Who his assailants were he had no idea. Up the gorge toward the castle he still heard the cracking of matchlocks, and suddenly a great burst of firing seemed to come from the outer valley; but pent in that narrow gorge which muffled and distorted all sounds, he could not be sure.

The smoke had blown away from the stream, but the Moslems could see nothing except a sinister stirring of the bushes on the opposite bank. There was no shelter, except back up the gorge, into the fangs of the maddened Kurds. They were trapped. They began to loose their matchlocks blindly into the bushes, evoking only mocking laughter from the hidden assailants. Osman started violently as he heard that laughter, and beat down the muzzles of the firelocks.

"Fools! Will you waste powder on shadows? Draw your steel and follow me!"

And with the fury of desperation, the Algerians charged headlong at the ambush, their cloaks streaming, their eyes blazing, naked steel glittering in their hands. A raking volley thinned their ranks, but they plunged on, leaped into the water and began wading across. And now from among the thick bushes on the farther bank rose wild figures, mail-clad or half-naked, curved swords in their hands. "Up and at them, sir brothers!" bellowed a great voice. "Cut, slash!—ho, Cossacks, fight!"

A yell of incredulous amazement rose from the Moslems at sight of the lean eager figures from whose headpieces and sabers the sun struck fire. Then with a deepthroated, thunderous roar of savagery they closed, and the rasp and clangor of steel rose and re-echoed from the cliffs. The first Algerians to spring up the higher bank fell back into the stream, their heads split, and then the berserk Cossacks leaped down the bank and met their foes hand to hand, thigh-deep in water that swiftly swirled crimson. No quarter was asked or given; Cossack and Algerian, they slashed and slew in blind frenzy, froth whitening their mustaches, sweat and blood running into their eyes.

Arap Ali ran into the thick of the mêlée, his eyes glaring like those of a rabid dog. His curved blade split a shaven head to the teeth; then Kral faced him, barehanded and screaming.

The Turkoman recoiled, daunted by the wild beast ferocity in the Armenian's writhing features; then with an awful cry Kral sprang, and his fingers locked like steel hooks in the chief's throat. Heedless of the dagger that Arap Ali drove again and again into his side, Kral hung on, blood starting from under his fingernails to mingle with the crimson that gushed from the Turkoman's torn throat, until, losing their footings, both pitched into the stream. Still tearing and rending, they were washed down the current; now one snarling face showed above the crimsoned waters, now another, until both vanished for ever.

The Algerians were driven back up the left bank, where they made a brief, bloody stand; then they fell back, dazed and ferocious, toward where Prince Orkhan stared trance-like in the shadow of the cliff, with the small knot of warriors Osman had detailed to guard him. Ayesha knelt, gripping his knees. The prince's eyes were stunned; thrice he moved as though to seize a sword and cast himself into the fray, but Ayesha's arms were like slender steel bands about his knees. Osman Pasha, breaking away from the battle, hastened to help him. The corsair's scimitar was red to the

hilt, his mail hacked, blood dripping from beneath his helmet. All about raged and eddied single combats and struggling groups, as the fighting scattered out over the gorge,
which was become a blood-splashed shambles. Not many
were left on either side to fight, but there were more Cossacks on their feet than Muhammadans.

Through the wash of the mêlée Ivan Sablianka strode,
brandishing his great sword in his sledge-like fist. Those
who opposed him were beaten down with strokes that shattered leather-covered bucklers, caved in steel caps and
clove alike through chain mail, flesh, and bone.

"Hey, you rascals!" he roared in his barbarous Turki. "I
want your head, Osman, and the fellow beside you there—
Orkhan. Don't be afraid, prince; I won't harm you. You'll
bring us Cossacks a pretty penny, may I eat pap if you
won't!"

Osman's keen eyes flickered about, desperately seeking
an avenue of escape. He saw the dim groove leading up the
cliff, and his keen brain instantly divined its use.

"*Chabuk, yah khawand!* Quick, my lord!" he whispered.
"Up the cliff! I'll hold off this barbarian while you climb!"

"Aye!" Ayesha urged eagerly. "Oh, haste! I can climb
like a cat! I will come behind you and aid you! It is desperate, but oh, my prince, it is a chance, and this is but to fall
back into chains again!"

She was tense and quivering with eagerness to strive and
fight like a wild thing for the man she loved. But the mask
of fatalism had descended again on Prince Orkhan. He did
not lack courage even for such a climb. But the paralyzing
philosophy of futility had him in its grip. He looked about
where the victorious Cossacks were cutting down the last
of his new-found allies. And he bowed his handsome head.

"Nay, this is Kismet. Allah does not will that I should
press the throne of my fathers. What man can escape his
fate?"

Ayesha blenched, her eyes flaring in a sort of horror, her
hands catching at her locks. Osman, realizing the prince's
mood, whirled, sprang for the shaft himself, and went up it
as only a sailor could climb. With a roar Ivan charged after
him, forgetting all about the prince. Cossacks were approaching, shaking red drops from their sabers. Orkhan
spread his hands resignedly, and Ayesha watched him, her
lips parted in dumb agony.

"Take me if you will," he said simply, facing his new captors. "I am Orkhan."

Ayesha swayed, her hands clasped over her closed eyes, as if about to faint. Then, springing like a flash of light, she thrust her dagger straight through Prince Orkhan's heart, and he died on his feet, so quickly that he scarcely felt the sting of the stab. And as he fell, she turned the point and drove it home in her own breast, and sank down beside her lover. Moaning softly, she cradled his princely head in her weakening arms, while the rough Cossacks stood about, awed and not understanding.

A sound up the gorge made them lift their heads and stare at one another. There was but a handful, weary and dazed with battle, their garments soaked with water and blood, their sabers nicked and clotted. Ivan was gone, and they were at a loss as to what to do.

"Get back into the tunnel, brothers," grunted Togrukh. "I hear men coming down the gorge. Get back through the tunnel to the place where we left the horses. Saddle and make ready to ride. I'm going after Ivan."

They obeyed, and he started up the cliff, swearing at the shallow handholds. They had scarcely vanished behind the silvery sheet, and he had not reached the crest of the cliff, when a number of men came into sight, marching hurriedly. The gorge was thronged with warlike figures. Togrukh, peering down with the curiosity of the Cossack, saw the turbans and *khalats* of the Kurds of the castle, and with them the peaked white caps of Turkish janizaries. One wore half a dozen bird-of-paradise plumes in his cap, and Togrukh gaped to recognize the Agha of the janizaries, the third man of power in the Ottoman empire. He and his followers were dusty, as if from long, hard riding. Glancing toward the valley, the lean Cossack saw the Agha's standard of three white horsetails flying from the castle gate, and along the river the sheepskin-clad Turkomans were riding hard for the hills, pursued by horsemen in glittering mail—the Turkish spahis. Togrukh shook his head in wonder. What brought the Agha of the janizaries in such array to the lonely valley of Ekrem?

Down in the gorge rose a chorus of horrified voices, as the newcomers halted dumfounded among the corpses. The Agha knelt beside the dead man and the dying girl.

"Allah! It is Prince Orkhan!"

"He is beyond your power," murmured Ayesha. "You can not hurt him any more. I would have made him king. But you had robbed him of his manhood—so I killed him—better an honorable death, than—"

"But I bring him the crown of Turkey!" cried the Agha desperately. "Murad is dead, and the people have risen against Safia's half-caste son—"

"Too late!" whispered Ayesha. "Too—too—late!" Her dark head sank on her white round arm like a child when it falls asleep.

5

As Ivan Sablianka went up the shaft ladder, Kral was not there to aid him, because Kral lay dead beside dead Arap Ali under the bloodstained stream. But this time hate spurred him on, and he swarmed up the precarious path as recklessly as if he clambered a ship's ratlines. Bits of crumbling stone gave way beneath his grasp and rattled down the cliff in tiny avalanches, but somehow he cheated death each time, and heaved relentlessly upward. He was not far behind Osman Pasha when the corsair came out on the cliff and set off through the stunted firs. Ivan came after him, his long legs carrying his giant frame across the ground at a surprising rate, and presently Osman, turning and seeing he had but one foe to deal with, faced round with a curse.

A fierce grin bristled the corsair's curly black beard. Here was a huge frame on which he could carve his savage disgust at the muddling of his plans. Only a few months before he had been the most feared sealord in the world with the broad blue Mediterranean at his feet. Now he was shorn of all following and power, except that gripped in his strong right hand, and locked in his skull. He was too much of the true adventurer to waste time in bemoaning his fall, but he was filled with a grim satisfaction at the chance of hewing down this pestiferous Cossack.

Easier thought than done. For all his slow wits and his bulk, Ivan was quick as a huge cat on his feet. Steel clanged on steel, the long straight blade of the Zaporogian beat down on the Algerian scimitar. The corsair was almost as tall as the Cossack, though not so heavily built. His scimitar was straighter and heavier than most Moslem blades, and he showed an unusual aptitude for the point a

well as the edge. Thrice, only Ivan's tattered mail saved
him from the corsair's vicious thrust. These he alternated
with whistling cuts which nicked bits of metal from Ivan's
harness and soon had him bleeding from half a dozen flesh
wounds. It was Osman's purpose to keep the giant on the
defensive, where his superior strength would not aid him as
it would in attack. His shaven, sunburnt head bobbed before the corsair's eyes, the tawny scalplock flowing in the
wind, and Osman hacked and hewed at it until the sweat
ran into his eyes and his breath came short. But somehow
Ivan always managed to parry or avoid his most dangerous
strokes. Osman's scimitar slithered off the straight blade, or
clashed on the flaring handguard.

There was no sound except the clangor of steel, the gasp
of harddriven breath, and the thud and shuffle of the fighters' feet. The sheer power of the Cossack began to tell.
From a whirlwind offensive, Osman found himself gradually forced back on the defense, using all his strength and
skill to parry the Cossack's terrible, sweeping blows. With a
gasping cry he staked all on a desperate onslaught and
leaped like a tiger, scimitar glittering above his head. He
was aware of an icy pain under his heart, and, convulsively
clutching with his naked hand the blade that had impaled
him, he slashed with his last ounce of strength at his slayer's head. Ivan caught the stroke on his upflung left arm;
the keen edge bit through mail links and flesh to the bone.
The scimitar dropped from Osman's nerveless hand, and he
slid off the impaling blade to the blood-soaked earth. And
from his pallid lips burst words in a strange tongue. "God
ha' mercy on me—I'll see Devon no more!"

Ivan started violently, blenching, and then with a cry
dropped to his knees beside him, forgetful of his own
blood-spurting wound. Gripping his foe he shook him
fiercely, crying in the same tongue, "What did ye say?
What did ye say?"

The glazing eyes rolled up at him, and Ivan tore the
helmet from the dying man's head. And he cried out as if
Osman had stabbed him.

"God's mercy! *Roger!* Black Roger Bellamy! Don't ye
know me, lad? 'Tis John Hawksby—old Jack Hawksby that
fought wi' ye and for ye when we were lads together in
Devon! Ah, God forgive us, that we should meet like this!
And in a naked land, unknowing. How come ye in such
pagan guise, Roger?"

"A long yarn and scant time to spin it," muttered the renegade. "Nay, John," as the big man began tearing strips from his garments to stanch the blood he had just let so willingly. "Nay. I'm done for. Let me bide. I was with Drake when he struck for Lisbon and lost so many good ships and stout lads. I was one the Dons took. They bound me to a galley's oar. Something broke in me as I toiled there beneath the lash. I forgot England—aye, and God, too.

"A Barbary rover took the galley and the *kapudan-pasha*—Seyf-ed-din it was—offered us slaves our lives if we became Moslems. The galleys make a man forget much; even that he was a Christian. 'Tis maybe no great step from buccaneer to corsair. I only wanted to hammer Spain, at first. Then as I rose in power I forgot more and more the blood in me. I swept the seas o' Christian and Muhammadan and Papist alike. Aye, now the tang o' paynim fame and red glory is dust in my mouth. How come you in the manner o' a Cossack, John?"

"Drink and the women, lad," answered Ivan Sablianka, who had been John Hawksby of Devon. "I couldn't bide in Devon because o' feuds and fights wi' divers people. I wandered eastward until I lost the memory and feelings o' England. Sink my bones, I've been as great a heathen as you, Roger. But do ye mind the great old days when we pounded the Dons on the Main?"

"Remember?" the dying man's eyes blazed and he lurched up on his elbow, blood gushing from his mouth. "God, to sail again with Drake and Grenville! To laugh with them as we laughed when we ripped Philip's Armada to shreds! Let go the weather braces!—that's Sidonia's flagship!—man the pumps, bullies, I'll not strike while there's a plank beneath my feet!—give 'em a broadside—the sta'board guns—pikes and cutlasses, there—"

He sank back, the babble of delirium dying on his lips. Ivan, kneeling beside the dead man, was lost in memory until a clink of steel on stone brought him round instinctively, sword ready. Togrukh stood near him in the gathering twilight.

"I see you've run down the dog. The lads have gone back into the tunnel. There's only nine of 'em left to run, besides ourselves. The gorge is full of Turks. We'll have to make our way across the cliffs to where we left the horses. What are you about?"

Ivan had spread the corsair's mantle over the dead pirate.

"I'm going to lay stones over him, so the vultures can't pick his bones," he answered stolidly.

"But his head!" expostulated the other. "His head to show the sir brothers!"

The giant faced about in the dusk so grimly that To-grukh involuntarily stepped back.

"He's dead, isn't he?"

"Aye, right enough!"

"And you'll bear witness to the sir brothers that I killed him, won't you?"

"Yes, but—"

"Then let it rest there," grunted Ivan, bending his powerful back as he began to lift the stones and heap them in place.

ABOUT THE AUTHOR

ROBERT ERVIN HOWARD was born in the small town of Cross Plains, Texas, in 1906. His first story, "Spear and Fang" was published when he was eighteen, in *Weird Tales*. Over the next twelve years, Howard wrote over a million words of fantasy, westerns, pirate yarns, detective and adventure stories for the pulp magazines. He is best known for his larger-than-life heroes: King Kull, Solomon Kane, Bran Mak Morn, and the greatest hero of them all, Conan, who swaggers through exotic and far-off lands and times having fabulous adventures, conquering kingdoms and beautiful women with equal ease.

FANTASY AND SCIENCE FICTION FAVORITES

antam brings you the recognized classics as well as
ne current favorites in fantasy and science fiction.
ere you will find the beloved Conan books along
ith recent titles by the most respected authors in
ne genre.

]	01166	URSHURAK	
		Bros. Hildebrandt & Nichols	$8.95
]	13610	NOVA Samuel R. Delany	$2.25
	13534	TRITON Samuel R. Delany	$2.50
	13612	DHALGREN Samuel R. Delany	$2.95
	11662	SONG OF THE PEARL Ruth Nichols	$1.75
	12018	CONAN THE SWORDSMAN #1	
		DeCamp & Carter	$1.95
	12706	CONAN THE LIBERATOR #2	
		DeCamp & Carfer	$1.95
	12970	THE SWORD OF SKELOS #3	
		Andrew Offutt	$1.95
	14321	THE ROAD OF KINGS #4	$2.25
		Karl E. Wagner	
	11276	THE GOLDEN SWORD Janet Morris	$1.95
	14127	DRAGONSINGER Anne McCaffrey	$2.50
	14204	DRAGONSONG Anne McCaffrey	$2.50
	12019	KULL Robert E. Howard	$1.95
	10779	MAN PLUS Frederik Pohl	$1.95
	13680	TIME STORM Gordon R. Dickson	$2.50
	13400	SPACE ON MY HANDS Frederic Brown	$1.95

them at your local bookstore or use this handy coupon for ordering:

Bantam Books, Inc., Dept. SF2, 414 East Golf Road, Des Plaines, Ill. 60016
Please send me the books I have checked above. I am enclosing $_____
(please add $1.00 to cover postage and handling). Send check or money order
—no cash or C.O.D.'s please.

Mr/Mrs/Miss _____

Address _____

City_____ State/Zip_____

SF2—7/80

Please allow four to six weeks for delivery. This offer expires 1/81.

OUT OF THIS WORLD!

That's the only way to describe Bantam's great series
science fiction classics. These space-age thrillers are fil
with terror, fancy and adventure and written by Americ
most renowned writers of science fiction. Welcome to ou
space and have a good trip!